ALSO BY JAMES MACMANUS

On the Broken Shore

Ocean Devil: The Life and Legend of George Hogg

Black Venus

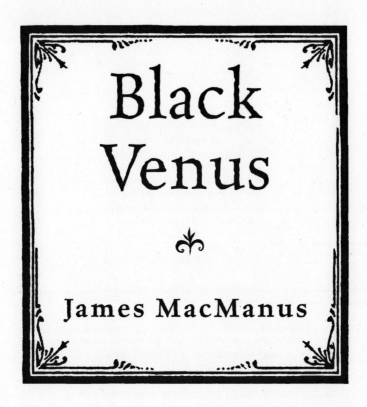

❧

James MacManus

DUCKWORTH OVERLOOK

First published in the UK in 2014 by
Duckworth Overlook
30 Calvin Street, London E1 6NW
T: 020 7490 7300
E: info@duckworth-publishers.co.uk
www.ducknet.co.uk
For bulk and special sales please contact
sales@duckworth-publishers.co.uk,
or write to us at the above address.

First published in the USA in 2013 by
Thomas Dunne Books, an imprint of St Martin's Press.

This is a work of fiction. All of the characters, organisations and
events portrayed in this novel are either products of the
author's imagination or are used fictitiously.

A catalogue record for this book is available
from the British Library

ISBNs
Hardback 978-0-7156-4742-4
Paperback: 978-0-7156-4847-6

Printed and bound in Great Britain by
TJ International Ltd, Padstow, Cornwall

To Geoffrey Shepherd,
a great teacher of French language and literature
to generations of boys at
Westminster School in London

Acknowledgments

I wish to thank Karyn Marcus, to whom I pitched the story of *Black Venus* over a few glasses of white wine in a New York bar. She liked it and took the idea to Thomas Dunne, for whom she then worked. It is to Tom Dunne and his colleagues at his own imprint within St. Martin's Press in New York that I owe a debt of gratitude that I hope one day to repay.

Tim Waller made a major contribution to this book both by fine editing of the text and helpful suggestions that strengthened the narrative. I am also indebted to Peter Joseph, my editor at Thomas Dunne, for the forensic skill with which he improved the final draft. I would like to thank Barbara Wild for her fine copyediting. My thanks also to production editor Edward Allen, who exceeded even his usual high standard with this book.

The UK publication of this book would not have happened without the generous support of Peter Mayer, who runs Duckworth in London and its sister publishing house, the Overlook Press in New York. His Assistant Editor in New York, Kelsey Osgood, fell in love with the story of Charles Baudelaire and his dangerous mistress, and persuaded her boss to take the book on. So thank you Kelsey – and likewise my thanks to Jamie-Lee Nardone, Publicity Manager, and Matt Nieman Sims, Head of Marketing, at Duckworth in London who made sure it happened. Between them they produced a jacket that for once justifies that overworked and devalued word *stunning*.

Dr. Martin Scurr in London helped with providing the medical backgrounds of both Charles Baudelaire and Jeanne Duval. To the staff of the London Library I owe, as usual, my thanks for their unstinting help in tracing the many books I required for research.

Finally, to Sophie Hicks, my agent and friend, and to her boss, Ed Victor, I owe more than I can say. Sophie provides the support and encouragement that every writer and friend needs in dark moments. Ed is a magisterial and inspiring presence in any author's life.

Black Venus

Prologue

Jeanne Duval was already seated at a table by the window when the publisher arrived. She was wearing a peach-colored silk dress with a light-blue sash at the waist and ruffles around the neck. Her hair, tied back in a bun, was concealed by a blue hat with a small brim that matched the sash. She wore black hooped earrings and a rhinestone ring on her forefinger.

He was surprised. He had seen her once before at the trial, and she had looked nothing like the elegantly dressed lady at his table. He was immediately struck by her eyes, which were large and round, with ink-black irises. There was not a hint of color in those eyes, and long lashes accentuated their hypnotic effect. They were cold and implacable, like those of a lion he had once seen in a painting, gazing over a plain in Africa.

The lunch had not been easy to arrange. At first Duval had refused to meet him. She had many creditors and suspected that the invitation was a trap. It was only when

Poulet-Malassis reassured her and offered lunch at the Café Anglais on the boulevard des Italiens that she relented. Reservations at the restaurant were the most sought after in Paris. The menu stretched to thirty-six pages and the cellar was said to have two hundred thousand bottles of wine, many from great pre-Revolutionary vintages.

Auguste Poulet-Malassis did not intend this to be a long or extravagant lunch. They would have a single course and a small carafe of wine. He had no doubt she would accept his offer. She needed the money. The restaurant was full and he had already seen several people he knew—lawyers, publishers like himself, and a sprinkling of government officials. They would all notice his lunchtime companion with interest. The trial had made Jeanne Duval famous, but few knew what she looked like.

They were handed the thick, leather-bound menus. He thanked her for coming, made sure she was comfortable, and got to the point.

"Our mutual friend is a great artist. I wonder if you realize just how important you are to him."

"Shall we have a glass of wine?" she said, without looking up from the menu.

"Of course," he said, beckoning a waiter.

"The Montrachet '22 is very good," she said. "But not too chilled."

The waiter looked inquiringly at Poulet-Malassis. The publisher did not often lunch at the restaurant, but he knew the château's wine to be one of the more expensive on the list. He nodded to the waiter. Duval turned to Poulet-Malassis.

"You know he threw my clothes into the street—my best dresses?" she said.

"He is very high-strung."

"So am I."

She put the menu down.

"I'll have the salmon mayonnaise. It's the *specialité de la maison*. The recipe is a secret, but they serve it warm and use the whites of duck eggs. And I'll have the turtle soup to start."

This wasn't what Poulet-Malassis had expected. Nothing he had heard about Jeanne Duval suggested she would be familiar with the menu at the Café Anglais. If you listened to Baudelaire and his friends, she was a gold digger who had somehow wormed her way into his soul and would happily do anything for money.

"You've been here before?"

"Manet used to take me—after he had sold that painting of the absinthe drinker."

"Of course."

Poulet-Malassis ordered the wine. He knew Manet planned to paint her portrait, but he didn't realize they were having an affair. Why else would he bring her here? The lunch was going to be more difficult than he thought—and more expensive. He ordered salmon mayonnaise for both of them, with a tomato salad. She reminded him about the turtle soup. He frowned and nodded agreement.

"What do you think of his work, the poems?" he said.

"They're pathetic, so depressing."

"But you gave evidence on his behalf at the trial."

"Yes, but I offered no judgment on the poems."

"But you stood by him."

"Then, yes."

"And now?"

"Never again."

"What if I told you that I would be prepared to pay off your debts and cover some of your living costs, say the rent of an apartment?"

The waiter arrived and uncorked the wine with a flourish. He poured a little into a glass. Poulet-Malassis swilled it around, tasted it, and nodded.

The waiter was pouring her wine when Duval leaned forward and said, "Is this a proposal? You want to sleep with me?"

The publisher sighed and looked at the waiter, who smiled and left.

"No, no, not at all," he said. "I just wonder whether you would be prepared to meet him again, maybe see if there was a way of renewing . . . ?"

The sentence trailed into her giggles. Then she threw her head back with a wild, pealing laugh that turned heads at neighboring tables. The waiter, anxious to move back into earshot of a conversation that promised more than most that lunchtime, returned and poured more wine. Poulet-Malassis waved him away.

"You find that amusing?" Poulet-Malassis said with irritation.

Duval dabbed tears of laughter from her eyes. "No, not really . . . I mean yes," she said. She dipped into her purse and produced a letter. "It's just that suddenly everyone seems to want to give me money. This arrived yesterday. The offer of a substantial sum on the promise that I will never see the famous author of *Les Fleurs du Mal* ever again—from his mother. And you are offering to pay me to do exactly the opposite. You can see why I laugh. It's rather funny, isn't it?"

Poulet-Malassis did not find it amusing at all. Baudelaire's mother was always interfering. And this lunch was turning into a disaster.

"The fact is he needs you," he said.

"No he doesn't. And I'm not going back to him."

"What are you going to do?"

"I have plans."

"Really? You have no job. You're in debt. You are living, I understand, with a friend. At least with him you would have a life—and you would have no debts."

"How so?"

"As I said, we would pay off your debts."

The soup arrived. Duval wondered if the publisher had any idea what she owed her dressmakers and landlords, not to mention the proprietors of several cafés and restaurants. He was a good man but naïve. He was never going to make any money out of Charles Baudelaire. The loyalty he showed his author was admirable but misplaced.

She finished her soup quickly and watched him spoon the last of the broth into his heavily bearded face. His mouth was almost invisible beneath a thick mat of facial hair. Globules of soup clung to his beard and mustache. Was it vanity or laziness that made men refuse to shave? she wondered. They sat back, allowing the waiter to remove the plates.

"Why do you do this for him?" she asked. "He's not making you any money. He's just trouble; you know that."

The publisher looked across the restaurant. At every other table people were talking about things that really mattered: money, infidelity, politics, and the latest production at the Opéra. And here he was, being asked to justify his author's talent to his mulatto mistress.

"There is always a price to pay for genius," he said. "But I truly believe that he will come to be seen as one of the great poets of this century."

" 'Come to be seen'? I have heard that for years. When exactly is France going to wake up and recognize the creative prodigy in its midst? I'll tell you when. Never. It's always *going* to happen with that man, but it never does."

The waiter arrived with the salmon mayonnaise. The fish was indeed warm and the mayonnaise had been carefully spooned in a circle around it. Asparagus spears with hot butter and thinly sliced cucumber completed the dish. Duval began to eat enthusiastically. Poulet-Malassis watched her fork pieces of moist pink salmon into her mouth. She probably hadn't eaten properly for days.

"You know he wrote many of those poems for you," he said.

Duval picked up an asparagus spear and pushed it into the remnants of the mayonnaise.

"So they say," she said.

She ate the spear with two bites and picked up another.

"He can't work without you—you know that."

Jeanne Duval finished her wine and dabbed at her mouth with the linen napkin. She rose from the table and he struggled to his feet, upsetting his chair.

"Thank you for lunch," she said. "I'm afraid I won't stay, but I will say this: poetry never made a penny for anybody."

He watched her leave. Her dress was a little too tight and the swing of her hips a little too obvious for lunchtime at the

Café Anglais. At the reception desk a woman gave her a black silver-lined cloak. The doorman was one big smile as she reached the door. She turned and gave him a little wave.

Poulet-Malassis drained his glass and watched her walk into the street. So, Jeanne Duval was not going back to him. He consoled himself with the thought that they might all be well rid of her. She had a feline charm, it was true. But she was trouble. The way she had walked through the restaurant told him that.

For a few brief seconds she had held the attention of the whole room: the curve of a well-cut dress over a full bosom, the contours of a shapely rear evident beneath the shimmer of silk—the obvious and age-old promissory notes of sexual attraction. But that was not the explanation. It was her eyes, he decided. They were dark, deep, and unfathomable. Baudelaire had called them black chimneys that vented smoke from her soul. That was the attraction. She was dangerous. Men found that irresistible. But she had left for good. Baudelaire had lost her. His Black Venus had gone. Of that he was sure.

I

"Out, Mama! Out! Out! Out!"

The young man turned from the window and smiled at his mother. "That is where I am going: out! And you are going to say, 'What, again?' And I shall say, 'Why not?' and you will say, 'This is the fifth time this week.' Let's not repeat ourselves."

Caroline Aupick looked at her son. He wore a velvet burgundy-colored jacket over a cream waistcoat edged in red velvet to match the jacket. A pleated cream shirt rose to a red cravat held in place by a pearl tiepin. He had shaved carefully around a well-cut mustache and beard that made him look older than his twenty years.

If she was not mistaken, he had applied a little of her face powder around his eyes. His trousers were tight, emphasizing shapely calves, as fashion demanded, and he wore buttoned-up spats. He looked the caricature of a dandy, which was exactly his intention.

"Come here," she said.

Charles Baudelaire paused at the window, gazing down at the street. It was a foggy night, and a phantom had emerged from the yellow vapor, weaving its way unsteadily over the cobbles. Looking more closely, he saw that it was a woman, a skeletal figure hunched against the cold and wearing little more than rags. He opened the window and reached into his pocket. The coin fell into the foggy darkness and he heard a metallic clink as it landed. He saw the figure scurry toward the sound. He closed the window and crossed the room.

He embraced his mother and then held her tighter, burying his face in long, curled locks of black hair. She was dressed for dinner and wore a blue satin off-the-shoulder dress with a fashionably revealing décolletage. The dress fell to her satin slippers. Teardrop earrings brushed his cheeks as he held her, breathing in the intense perfume of sandalwood that he had known since childhood.

The scent awoke memories of days in the nursery in the little house with a garden in Neuilly. Mama had never let the maid put him to bed. She was always there after his bath, to tuck him between the sheets. She would bend over to kiss him good night and he would cling to her, his arms around her neck, refusing to let go, breathing in the scent of her perfume. Every night she wore different jewelry—diamonds, rubies, emeralds, set as pendants, brooches, earrings, and rings.

She always had to take his arms gently from around her neck and tuck them under the blankets in return for a final kiss. He would not let her go. Many nights she would come to his room dressed for a night at the opera with friends. He loved those nights best because she wore satin or silk, each with its own feel and fragrance.

She would brush his damp hair, leaning over him in the

soft light, allowing him to toy with her earrings and pendants. He would hold them against the candlelight so that they flashed and sparkled. And as she rose to go, he would bury his face in her chest, breathing in the scent of powder and perfume.

There were goldfish in the garden pond at Neuilly, big lazy creatures that hung motionless just below the surface, their mouths opening in little Os. He would spend hours staring at them, rippling the water with his fingers to make them move. On one occasion he had fallen in, trying to catch them. After that, his mother had turned the pond into a rockery. He always wondered what had happened to the fish. Mama said Mariette had cooked them for her supper. He had refused to eat fish ever since.

Baudelaire stepped back and lifted the heart-shaped ruby set in a silver clasp that hung low from her neck. The jewel shone in the gaslight, casting a roseate glow onto her pale skin.

"Beautiful—have I seen it before?"

"No. The general gave it to me. You like it?"

Baudelaire let the jewel drop back. Of course the general had given it to her. Who else? His mother, unlike many women of her station, did not take lovers. She was a lady of honor, a good woman. She had cherished him when his father had died. How old was he then—five, six? For two years they had been together, just the two of them, with no one else but Mariette the maid. When he opened his eyes in the morning, there his mother would be, with a hot towel to wipe the sleep from his eyes. They would take breakfast together, out in the garden if it was warm, always with fresh coffee, and pastries baked in the oven that morning.

They hardly left each other's company in those years after his father died. At night he refused to go to sleep without the good-night kiss and the longed-for embrace. She would tell him stories about two swallows flying to Africa when winter came to Europe. The stories were always about the same two swallows, although the adventures were different. The swallows were lucky, she told him. They could fly so far on their tiny wings that they never knew winter but lived in summer all year long.

She told him about the father he had hardly known. He was an old man, generous, kind, and an amateur painter of some note. He had spent little time with his son, except for morning walks in the Luxembourg Gardens. That's how Baudelaire remembered him: a white-haired old man of seventy, using his stick to point out the beauty of the statues and sculptures around them.

François Baudelaire had died after one of those morning walks—a hot day in June—taking his pension with him. Mama was forced to sell the big apartment in rue Hautefeuille, with all its fine furniture and paintings, and move to a new and much smaller home in the place Saint-André des Arts. But she kept the little house in Neuilly. It was their special place, she said, and one day it would be his.

The move did not unsettle the young boy. In fact, he rejoiced in his new home, because it now meant that his mother would take him for long walks. Better still, those walks were not in the manicured beauty of the Luxembourg Gardens, but through one of the oldest and most unfashionable parts of Paris—the Left Bank, where little had changed since the fifteenth century.

They wandered hand in hand along the river, then crossed

the pont Saint-Michel to explore the narrow streets around Notre-Dame. They always entered the cathedral itself and lit a candle for François Baudelaire. Home before dark was the rule, but often his mother had to plead with him to hurry as they walked through the gloaming, casting fearful eyes at the sinister shadows around them. But he was not afraid. He knew he could protect her from whatever lurked in the darkness.

Then she had met Jacques Aupick, a handsome cavalry officer with a prospering career that promised Caroline the comfort and security she craved. He had had to watch his mother fall in love with a man who embraced her with a passion she had never experienced in her marriage.

Baudelaire sighed. He walked to a mantelpiece and stared intently at his favorite possession—apart from his clothes. A traditional round-faced mantel clock with Roman numerals set in a mahogany case. The hands had been removed and across the face was written: *It is later than you think*. He opened the clock, took out a silk kerchief, and carefully wiped the enamel face.

"We must talk about money," she said.

He turned and smiled. He loved his mother deeply, but she was never less than single-minded about his perceived failings. He did not have one friend who had not run up debts. And very few of them were going to inherit the substantial sum that was due to him on his twenty-first birthday in two weeks' time. The year was 1842 and with luck, and money, he would see the century out. He would receive ten thousand francs, he had been told, together with the little house in Neuilly. That would more than satisfy his creditors. Thank you, dear, departed father. May your weary body rest in peace.

"Of course. But perhaps not tonight," he said.

Caroline Aupick frowned and shrugged. "As you wish. But I would like you to join us for dinner tomorrow night."

Baudelaire skipped across the room, took her hand, and bowed low to kiss it.

"Of course, my darling mama. I should be delighted."

"Take care. It's late and the streets are not safe," she said.

"Don't worry."

Baudelaire held up a silver-knobbed cane and twirled it in one hand like a child's toy windmill, a skill she supposed he had acquired from a barman in some nightclub, which was where he seemed to spend all his time. Then, taking a silk top hat and a cape, he was gone, closing the door noisily behind him.

She sighed as he clattered down the wooden staircase. The room suddenly seemed empty. Caroline Aupick crossed to the window and peered into the clearing fog. She turned at the sound of footsteps coming back up the staircase. The door opened and his head appeared.

"I hear Le Chat Noir has a new chef," he said.

Baudelaire saw the woman the moment he stepped into the street. She was lying a few feet from the front door, one arm at her side, the other stretched out in front of her. He knelt down and looked at the death-white face and sightless eyes. He saw the coin he had thrown her, tightly clasped in her outstretched hand.

He stood up, made the sign of the cross, and walked off into the fog. Another hand would soon reach for that coin and within an hour the few rags she wore would have been stripped from her corpse. The night-soil carrier would find the body on his rounds and take it to the new mortuary on the île de la Cité, where he would be paid a small fee.

In death, the woman, just another of the anonymous poor in Paris, would achieve the attention she had never found in life. Her body would be stripped and laid out on one of the twelve ramped marble slabs in the viewing room. A small cloth would be placed over her loins to provide some modesty. What was left of her clothes would be hung beside her as a means of identification for the relatives she did not possess. For a fee, mourners and the curious public would inspect the daily display of the Paris dead.

The mortuary had been specially built with high windows to throw light on the scene, and all day long visitors filed through to look on the corpses through a large glass screen. This had been erected to shield the public from the odor of decomposition, but some bodies had been in the river for more than a week. Visitors were advised to use heavily perfumed handkerchiefs. After two days the corpses were moved and the marble slabs hosed down, ready for a fresh intake. The city made good money from this ghoulish display and defied repeated demands from the Church authorities to end the practice.

Baudelaire headed toward the river. He was almost twenty-one years old and had known the city since childhood. He felt Paris itself was his real home, more than any house in which he had lived. This was his city. He knew how it awoke at daybreak yet never slept at night—the paradox of a restless metropolis. He had roamed the streets of Paris for years in all weathers and all seasons. The city opened itself to him like a book, revealing its present, remarking on its past, and foretelling its future.

That night the fog rolled up the Seine, sliding beneath bridges, pushing cold, wet fingers into slums that tumbled to the very edge of the river's muddy foreshore. Wharves and jetties jutted through reed beds into deeper water, allowing hundreds of barges and sailing vessels to tie up.

Baudelaire crossed the pont Royal and made his way around the Tuileries Palace. Here King Louis Philippe held court, an unlikely monarch empowered by the mob that had deposed two earlier Bourbon rulers. Baudelaire knew they would overthrow him too in a few years. Everyone in Paris knew that. There was always unfinished business for the Paris mob.

The young man gripped his cane more tightly and walked into the dark underbelly of the city. Huddled between the great public buildings and large private houses were the dwellings of the poor: wattle-and-daub wooden houses separated by narrow lanes running with filth.

Even on a foggy night, the stench was unbearable to a stranger. Wealthier neighborhoods were served by night-soil carriers, who took their reeking cargo of human waste in open wagons to the forest of Bondy in the northeast or, more often, to be unloaded into the Seine. For most of the nine-hundred-thousand-strong population the street or the river provided the only sanitation. The Seine, like so many of the lanes and alleyways in the city, was an open sewer.

Baudelaire left the slums and turned left on the rue de Rivoli. Larger and busier streets such as this now had gas lighting, which had recently begun to replace the whale-oil lamps that had lit the city for centuries. Here city authorities had covered the cobbles with bitumen to prevent them being dug up during outbreaks of mob violence—a fruitless gesture, as it turned out, but it had made the evening promenade easier on the feet.

On nights such as this, Le Tout Paris shrugged off the fog and walked the grander streets seeking pleasure and profit in the flaring gaslight. Sparks flew as iron-rimmed wheels clashed on the boulevard. Horse-drawn carriages jostled for road space with wagons bringing farm produce to the city for the next day's markets. Gentlemen and their ladies dressed in the fashions of the day—top hats and brass-knobbed canes for the men; bonnets, shawls, and crinoline dresses for their women—walked slowly up one side of the boulevard and then back down the other. Dancing dogs, tame rats on long leads, conjurors, fire-eaters, snake charmers, costumed monkeys—all competed with lavishly stocked shop windows for the attention and money of the passing public.

Young prostitutes, some still children, scampered between the wheels of the carriages, offering thin, undernourished bodies to the occupants comfortably seated in the plush interiors. No one paid any attention as a carriage stopped, a door swung open, and a beckoning hand pointed to a young girl—or boy. A flick of the whip and the carriage rolled on. A couple of streets away, the child would be set down, richer by a few francs.

The politics and poverty of Paris did not concern the patrons of Café Momus, not far from the Louvre, or those in the Café Procope, south of the river. These were his favorite places in Paris, but Baudelaire was going elsewhere that night. For once he would forgo the company of writers, poets, and painters—the famous, the would-be famous, and the hopeless dreamers who gathered at night to drink coffee with a dash of cognac or sip tall glasses of green, anise-flavored absinthe. Their drugs of choice, hashish and opium, were taken openly and liberally. The first was smoked in long cheroots, while opium was added to drinks in the form of liquid laudanum.

He could imagine the scene. The young painter Gustave Courbet sitting in awed silence in the Momus as Honoré de Balzac and his friend Alexandre Dumas discussed matters of the day: the recent arrival of the railroad in Paris, the sudden rise in the price of wine, and the latest cholera epidemic in the slums. Balzac had just finished his masterwork, *La Comédie humaine,* and presided over the patrons of the café with casual ease, a literary lion with flowing beard, long, graying hair, and a favorite six-button moleskin waistcoat liberally flecked with ash and stained with wine and food.

Dumas was busy planning his own masterpiece, *Les Trois Mousquetaires,* a romantic tale of swordsmanship and honor in the seventeenth century that would eclipse Balzac's social realism and become the most successful and widely translated French novel of all time. Courbet, although only twenty-three, listened and dreamed of his own success.

The patrons of the Momus and the Procope styled themselves as the bohemians, a group of artists, journalists, and hangers-on who were deliberately careless of contemporary manners and morals and intent only on the pursuit of their chosen art form—and, rather more discreetly, on the fame and wealth that went with it.

They despised the grasping bourgeoisie of Paris who had been galvanized by the clarion call of a reactionary prime minister, François Guizot: "Enrichissez-vous!" he famously told France. On that foggy evening in Paris everyone— beggars, prostitutes, merchants, and the titled aristocracy in their town houses—was heeding his advice.

The patrons of the Momus and the Procope would not admit it, but they were the same. Balzac had already made a fortune and Dumas was well on the way to doing likewise. New and faster printing presses and the rise of literacy were helping writers become rich. Those artists might enjoy the bohemian pleasures of Paris and affect indifference to everything except their art, but to many of the true bohemians they seemed as greedy as the bankers they chose to despise.

Eugène Delacroix would be there that night, as usual taking wine and a little hashish with Balzac and Dumas. Baudelaire felt a frisson of regret. He enjoyed teasing the artist. Delacroix had given France a painting that remained one of the nation's enduring political symbols: a bare-breasted woman holding aloft the Revolutionary tricolor flag with one hand and a bayoneted musket with the other, leading the mob forward over bodies of the fallen—*Liberty Guiding the People*. Thus had a single work of art immortalized the Revolutionary ethos in France.

Baudelaire knew that was a lie. Liberty had guided the people to nothing but a new dictatorship. The barricades would rise again. Delacroix did not enjoy being reminded of the fact.

Old Paris was made for revolution. Baudelaire loved the seedy tangle of streets, the cobweb of alleys, the fat-trunked plane trees rooted in little squares. This was a Paris that Voltaire would find little different from the city in which he grew up 150 years earlier. But Baudelaire recognized the contradiction within himself. He relished the change that was coming. The royal household in the Tuileries, the poor in their festering slums, and the great artists in their cafés all knew it. Delacroix's painting, hanging in splendor in the Louvre, was there to remind them that the barricades would rise again and old Paris would fall.

Baudelaire pulled out his pocket watch. It was almost ten o'clock. He was going to be late. It was March 1842 and the year of his twenty-first birthday, the year of his majority, the year when he would receive the money his father had left him. It was the year when he would be free.

2

The fog was clearing when Jeanne Duval set out to walk the two miles from her lodging house to the Latin Quarter. She was due onstage at ten o'clock and needed at least thirty minutes to prepare—or less if that idiot maid Céleste was not around. She hurried, keeping to the better-lit streets and taking care to avoid the horse dung and sewage thrown up by passing carriages.

Her long-caped coat covered a simple black dress. A bonnet was pulled tightly around her head. There were holes in her leather boots, but a stuffing of trussed straw would keep her feet dry until she reached the theater. She smiled to herself: "theater" was a generous description of a cabaret club for poorly paid government pen pushers and other riffraff with a little money to spend. But it was a job, and she knew how to make those men forget the miseries of their working day. A low-cut dress, a few songs, and as much cheap wine as they could afford was all they wanted. Their lack of ambition surprised her. But she needed a better job, a club where

the men would be well dressed, well behaved, and generous.
She had turned thirty-two in the spring. She had little to
show for her three years in Paris. It was time to make some
money.

She still regarded the city with the same wide-eyed wonder as when the wagon piled high with potatoes from Bordeaux had set her down at a coaching inn near Les Invalides.
She had had no money and the wagoner had demanded the
usual payment in kind.

"I'm a fair woman," she said, "and you will get your pay,
but you look—you don't touch. That's the deal."

He had grunted and taken her to the stables at the back
of the inn. There, between two horses, he had tried to push
her down onto the foul straw bedding. She surprised him
with her strength, pushing him back and kicking him hard
on the shins. She spat out her terms again. The horses were
whinnying, stamping, and tossing their heads in fear as she
pulled down the front of her dress, wriggled out of the chemise, and raised her arms above her head. She was a full-
figured woman and knew the value of those shapely breasts.

He lunged at her. She ducked under the horse's head and
faced him over the animal's heaving back. He was a big-
boned farmer's boy, angry now, with rivulets of sweat on a
red face coarsened by years of field work. She stared at him,
but he wouldn't meet her eye. He was going to come at her
under the horse and get them both trampled to death.

God, you're all the same, she thought. A rush of blood
quickens your heart, stiffens the cock, and swamps the brain.
She had seen the pitchfork in the hayrack and, keeping her
eyes on the wagoner, she reached behind her and drew it out.
He stepped back as she slid the fork over the horse's back.

"I am not a whore. You've been paid. Now get back to your potatoes."

She walked through darker streets now, tightening her grip on the bag. The city authorities had promised gas lighting in every street leading from the grand boulevards, but it had not happened. Not that she minded. Even in a dark alleyway reeking of sewage and slippery with horse dung, Paris was the center of her universe. She loved the city. It had given her freedom, the right to make her own life, to live on her wits and her charm. This was the city that had inspired her own people in Haiti to rise up against the French plantation owners. The slave revolt had followed the heroic example of the mob that had stormed the Bastille.

She laughed out loud, a rippling noise that startled those who heard it in the surrounding hovels. They weren't her people. Haiti was not her country. She had been born there but never belonged. She was Creole, a half-caste, mulatto, mixed-race, half-breed. Whatever word you chose, it meant only thing: she was not wanted in the land of her birth by either black or white.

Her French father had remained on his coffee plantation after the uprising and Haiti's independence in 1804. He finally fled to New Orleans eight years later as the country sank into anarchy. She had been born six months before he left, to a woman who was a slave in all but name: his housekeeper and mistress, plucked from the fields when he had seen her as a young girl bent over the coffee bushes with a wicker basket on her back.

That's how the plantation worked. The black girls picked the coffee beans, and the white plantation owners picked the best girls, used them, and threw them back into the fields.

Her mother had been lucky. She was promoted to work in the kitchen and shielded by the house staff when the slave workers rose in revolt against the government in Port-au-Prince.

As for Jeanne's father, there had been one letter from New Orleans. He planned to import cattle from France and drive them to the new ranches being carved out of the wildness in the West. He asked after the daughter he had hardly seen and promised to send money. He never did, and her mother never heard from him again.

The alley was dark and silent. Hearing footsteps behind her, Duval lengthened her stride. She would not turn until those footsteps were louder, closer. She was not afraid. She had lived like an animal after bandits had burned the plantation and forced her mother to flee into the hills with her infant daughter. She could hold her own against any man in a street fight.

The alley gave way suddenly to the clamor and flaring gaslight of the rue Jacob. The footsteps behind her turned back. From a dark and silent medieval world she stepped into a street crowded with people jostling along the newly laid paving stones and taking care to avoid the crush of horse-drawn traffic on the rutted street itself. Duval paused, allowing the window-shoppers and hurrying pedestrians to flow past her in an endless stream. This was her Paris, a chaotic city hungry for profit and pleasure.

A man with a monkey on his shoulder held up an oyster shell on which had been painted a miniature scene of ships in a harbor. She bargained briefly, bought it, tucked the shell into her bag, and skipped across the road, dodging between carriages. She was due onstage in fifteen minutes: the same old songs, same music, and same old Céleste. And, as she reminded herself when Céleste opened the door, the same filthy dressing room. There was a bunch of faded flowers in one corner, lighting from a gas lamp, and a large mottled mirror. An open closet contained a long red dress.

"You have ten minutes," said Céleste.

"Get me some water and clean that awful mirror," snapped Duval. She changed rapidly, looked into the mirror, and took a brush to her long, thick, black hair. The dress was cut low, but no more than the fashion of the day demanded. The men liked it. No woman would dare be seen at Le Rêve.

The fog was clearing as Baudelaire walked down rue Danton, turned left, and, taking care to keep to the main streets, soon found himself approaching the Latin Quarter. He stopped beneath one of the new gas lamps and pulled out his pocket watch. It was just past ten o'clock. He was on time. He had not learned much at that academy in Lyon, apart from one lesson that his favorite teacher had repeated endlessly. "There is no greater treasure on earth than time," he had said. "Treat it like gold; hoard it."

He turned off the street and tightened his grip on his cane as he entered a narrow street lit only by the occasional lamp. After a few hundred yards the lane turned sharply and suddenly lamplight, music, and laughter rippled from a row of taverns on both sides of a street still shrouded in yellow fog.

Through small misted windows, drinkers, diners, and dancers could be seen, a press of humanity seeking the fleeting pleasures of wine, food, and lust. This was just one small part of the Latin Quarter, and Baudelaire carried on, side-stepping the occasional drunk who had been projected into the street to end an evening of licentious gaiety facedown on the cobbles.

The street split into two. At the junction stood a large door set back into the curved façade of a building. In gilt lettering above the door were the words "LE RÊVE." Baudelaire crossed the street and at a single knock from his cane the door silently swung open. He stepped into a small hall with sawdust on the floor, lit by several candles set on a table at which sat a small, shriveled man, his face bearing the scars of long-ago battles fought for French imperial glory. The man inspected his guest and nodded. Baudelaire refused offers to take his top hat, cane, and cape and walked through a second door.

Le Rêve had once been a school and the room that Baudelaire now entered had been the assembly hall. On a platform at one end, where the headmaster and his staff used to address their pupils, three musicians were tuning their instruments: cello, piano, and double bass. Men lounged against a long bar that stretched along one side of the room. Wooden pillars held up a small gallery. A haze of tobacco smoke almost as thick as the fog outside hung over the throng of people.

The floor was packed with tables, allowing little room for the waitresses to move. They were the only women in the room and they wore knee-length black dresses and white bonnets. At the tables men were smoking pipes, drinking from thick glass tumblers, rolling dice, shuffling cards, and occasionally falling backwards in their chairs as they leaned over to talk to a neighboring table.

Baudelaire saw his friends at the far end of the bar and raised his cane to attract their attention. He was lucky. He had known them all since childhood. They had grown up together, shared regular beatings at various schools, endured parental rage at poor exam results, and, as they grew older, enjoyed endless adventures as they roamed the Latin Quarter looking for life, love, laughter—anything to break the boredom of life at home, with its repetitive routine of servants, parents, mealtimes, and, supposedly, study.

There was Le Vavasseur, a blond giant of a man whose ungainly bulk belied a mind in thrall to the delicate rhythms of modern poetry; then Michel Prarond, who was trying to become a painter; and Jules Buisson, with a mop of blond hair framing a choirboy face, still a virgin at twenty and with a stutter that glued every word to the back of his throat. The friends joked that if someone could cure Buisson's stutter he would talk without pause for a year. Like Baudelaire, they all had short-cut beards. Only Baudelaire chose a silk top hat, unusual headgear in a club such as Le Rêve. His friends wore velvet caps and smoked pipes.

The friends shook hands with easy familiarity and moved to a table already set with glasses and two bottles of wine. Le Vavasseur poured generously into each glass while Prarond produced a deck of cards. Baudelaire handed his cape and hat to a waitress and rested his cane carefully against the table.

"What are we doing here?" he said. "I liked the other place."

There was a general muttering around the table about the need for a change, better wine, and cheaper food.

Prarond shuffled and passed the deck to Buisson, who

dealt. Onstage the musicians had begun playing, but with little effect in the general hubbub. A voice shouted for quiet, but no one paid any attention.

Baudelaire lit a small cheroot and studied his hand. "What are we playing for?" he asked.

"Love," said Le Vavasseur.

"Twenty centimes a hundred," said Prarond.

"Heeerrrrrrrrr," said Buisson, pointing to the stage as the word exploded from his mouth with the velocity of a champagne cork.

The men turned, as did most of those at other tables. Conversation fell to a murmur. Without any introduction, a woman wearing a long dress had walked to the center of the stage carrying a small bouquet. She was not young, maybe early thirties, and wore a diamanté pendant that sparkled in her deep décolletage. The musicians opened with a few bars and then she sang, pointing in turn to men at each of the tables.

"What would you give
For a girl like me?
How far would you go
For a girl like me?

"Spare me your answer.
I read your mind.
You like what you see,"

She leaned forward, giving the audience a good view of her décolletage.

"Both front . . ."

She turned and wiggled her rear.

". . . and behind.

"I know they'll tell you
To leave me alone.
They say I'll crush you
With my heart of stone.

"But love knows no limits;
There are no frontiers to cross.
You're just a lone traveler,
Mapless and lost.

"So look up at the stars
And ask yourself this:
How far would you go
For a girl like me?"

Jeanne Duval bowed low to the audience as the pianist rounded off with a long crescendo of chords.

Men rose at their tables to applaud. Roses were thrown onto the stage. Baudelaire found himself almost the only man left seated. His friends were all on their feet clapping. He leaned forward and pulled Le Vavasseur down to his chair by his jacket.

"I thought we'd come to play cards," he said.

"Come on, Charles—she's worth more than a card game, isn't she?"

"Oh, I see! That's why we came here. I should have known. Now, are we playing or not?"

Reluctantly the three friends took their seats. Baudelaire reshuffled the cards and dealt.

"Anyone mind telling me what we're playing for?" said Prarond.

Baudelaire leaned forward and placed a white note on the table.

"That's too high," said Prarond.

"You'll be rich if you win."

"And if I lose . . . ?"

"Simple. You go to your bank—"

"Not my bank; they won't talk to me," said Prarond.

"Not that bank, you fool. The only bank that matters, the bank that always lends without interest, the bank that is open twenty-four hours a day, the bank that loved you from the day it squirted milk into that rosebud mouth of yours."

There was a silence at the table. The three men looked at their friend.

"My mother died two years ago," said Prarond. "Now, take that off the table and let's get on with the game."

There was a cheer from across the room as a drunk clambered onto the stage and staggered toward the singer with the remnants of a glass of wine in an outstretched hand. Most of the contents had been spilled by the time she graciously took the gift, handing it to the pianist as the drunk lunged at her. She sidestepped and watched as the man tottered past and fell off the side of the stage amid loud cheers.

With helping hands from members of the audience, she stepped off the stage onto the floor of the room and immediately allowed herself to be helped onto a chair and then up onto a table. She pulled up her skirts above the glasses and bottles, nodded to the pianist, and then reprised the last verses.

> *"But love knows no limits;*
> *There are no frontiers to cross.*
> *You're just a lone traveler,*
> *Mapless and lost.*

> *"So look up at the stars*
> *And ask yourself this:*
> *How far would you go*
> *For a girl like me?"*

The card game stopped as the group turned to watch Duval. She allowed herself to fall forward into outstretched arms. A chair was pulled up and a glass of wine poured. Duval sat down. The men at the table raised their glasses to her. She put her fingers to her lips, kissed them lightly, and waved her arm in an arc, scattering blown kisses over the table. The men cheered, drank deeply, refilled their glasses, and raised them to her again. The whole room was watching her now.

Baudelaire looked at his hand, picked out one of the playing cards, and flipped it through the air toward Duval's table. For a second the card was lost in the fog of smoke and then it fluttered onto the table close to her, facedown. She was too busy talking to the men around her to notice. One of the men picked up the card and turned it over: the ace of hearts. He looked around and, seeing no sign of the sender, dropped it onto the floor.

Le Vavasseur reached across, taking Baudelaire by the arm as he was about to pluck another card from his hand.

"What are you doing? We've got a game to play."

Baudelaire smiled. "That's what I'm doing." He flicked the card across the room.

This time it landed faceup in front of Duval: the king of spades. She picked it up and looked at the men around her. Most had their heads down now, intent on their drink, dice, and gossip. On the far side of the room she noticed a table of younger men, better dressed than most, looking in her direction. Students maybe, she thought, or rich youngsters slumming it in a workingman's club. There was one thin-faced man, with aquiline features, bearded like the others but somehow different. He was smiling at her. She stared back briefly, flipped the card over her shoulder, and returned to the chatter at her table.

"Thanks, Charles," said Le Vavasseur. "I had a great hand."

Baudelaire took the note off the table and leaned back to give it to a passing waitress. He whispered something to her. He turned back to the table and looked at Prarond.

"I'm sorry about your mother," he said.

The waitress returned with a bottle and four small glasses. Buisson picked up the bottle and looked at the label. Cognac: La Grande Ferme 1822.

"G— G— G," tried Buisson.

Prarond put a finger to his lips, motioning his friend to stay silent. Baudelaire placed a hand on Buisson's shoulder and said, "Don't talk, my friend. Just drink." Buisson was the baby of the group. His speech impediment was such that

he could hardly converse with anyone, although it was said
he could manage whole sentences with his mother.

Baudelaire looked across the crowded room. There was
no sign of the singer. The stage was empty.

3

Baudelaire and his friends gathered every week on a Thursday morning, weather permitting, at La Florentine, a sidewalk café opposite the main entrance to the Luxembourg Gardens, for a meeting of the Lost and Doomed Souls Club. They had chosen the name to signal to the literary establishment and society in general their disillusionment with the politics of avarice and poverty and their rejection of the cloying sentimentality of the Romantic movement. Several literary magazines in Paris responded with the unkind observation that the Pompous and Pretentious Club would be a more suitable name for a group of idlers who would be better off back at college studying something that might, just might, be of use to their country one day.

Baudelaire wore a long velvet cloak against the fall chill and stood with one leg on a chair and an open book in his hand. His friends were slumped around a circular table. Steam rose from small cups of coffee, the musky aroma mingling with tobacco smoke as the first pipes were lit. A waitress fussed round them, pouring cognac into small glasses. A sharp wind gusted leaves across the cobbles and swayed the bare-branched trees across the road. With their velvet and leather jackets, colorful waistcoats, peaked caps, tight trousers, and gaitered footwear, the group made a striking sight, causing passersby to pause, thinking some form of street theater was about to begin.

"Come on, Charles!" shouted Le Vavasseur.

"Get on with it!" shouted someone else.

Baudelaire looked up from his book and raised his hand.

"All of us have a choice," he said. "There exists in everyone, at every moment of their life, two conflicting impulses. One toward God and the other toward the Devil."

An old woman dressed in sacking, her face muddied, her breath one long tubercular wheeze, shuffled up and stopped to listen. Baudelaire beckoned her to him. She sidled over and allowed him to put an arm around her. He turned his head as the dank odor of the gutter hit him.

"Good morning, my dear. Welcome. Take a seat. We are discussing the existential nature of good and evil. Give her a coffee and a cognac, someone."

An empty chair was kicked toward her and the group eased their own chairs away as the warm aroma of coffee gave way to the smell of a long-unwashed body and street sewage. Someone handed her a glass of cognac and a coffee. She sniffed at the cognac suspiciously, threw it back, and then doubled up with a hacking cough.

Ignoring his guest, Baudelaire took up his book again.

"We wish to believe in God, do we not? Why? Because belief in the divine allows us to believe we are immortal. But the Devil makes a better offer, doesn't he? He leads us to his underworld, to enjoy those pleasures we so desire, our lust for women, for instance. The trouble, my friends, is that the Devil does not offer you an afterlife. There is no redemption in Hell, just damnation. So what? He gives you a good time here on earth. So here's to the Devil in this life, and to hell with Heaven in the next!"

Baudelaire raised his glass of cognac and held it high. There was a general mumble of approval and everyone raised their glasses.

The woman noisily slurped down her coffee, rose to her feet, and, after pocketing two rolls, shuffled off, muttering to herself. She suddenly turned and shouted, "Never heard such rubbish! Blasphemy, that's what it is."

Le Vavasseur stood up and bowed low. "Well said, madame! Charles, give us a poem. Stop being so bloody miserable."

Baudelaire pointed to the departing beggar. "There's my poetry. She came from the gutter, she stinks of the gutter, and she'll die in the gutter. And in the gutters of Paris you will find my poetry; that's where real life is, and . . ."

He paused, looking across to the Luxembourg Gardens and the two women who had just walked arm in arm through the arched entrance. Something about the taller of the two was familiar: a bright piece of costume jewelry, the black hair tied in a bun beneath a bonnet. The women disappeared into the crowd around a statue just inside the gates.

Baudelaire drained his glass and without a word walked across the road.

"You haven't paid the bill!" Le Vavasseur shouted.

"As bloody usual!" said Prarond.

• • •

Jeanne Duval and her friend Simone walked quickly along the flagged pathway and skirted the Medici Fountain, which threw a curved curtain of water far beyond the ornate pond in which it stood. The women vanished as if they had stepped through a waterfall and emerged wet and laughing on the far side.

"I still don't understand. You've never been up this early in your life," said Simone.

"Nonsense. Anyway, concentrate. That fountain is famous."

"What for?"

"I'm not sure. Soaking people stupid enough to try to walk through it?"

"Do you mind my asking where we are going?"

"Just keep walking."

Baudelaire had lost sight of the women and quickened his pace, striding past puppet shows, children on pony rides, and ladies wheeling baby carriages. He arrived breathless at the Medici Fountain. He paused, remembering childhood afternoons spent there with his father.

François Baudelaire had been a good man but too old for Charles's mother. She had married because he offered security, an income, a home with servants, and, well, that was enough, wasn't it? Many women with her breeding had to settle for a lot less. There was no passion in the marriage, but she had found happiness when Charles was born. "You are my happiness," she had told him—every night. She always said they would be together forever. And what happened? She fell into the arms of a cavalry officer young enough to give her the physical love she craved and rich enough to provide the lifestyle that went with it. At least that's what he supposed. He couldn't blame her—could he?

He walked slowly around the fountain, taking care not to get wet. Almost four hundred yards beyond lay the boating lake. The two women were paying a boatman and getting into a rowing skiff. Baudelaire turned, made a short bow to the exact spot where his father always sat—a bench crudely hewn from rock—and walked toward the lake.

Simone pulled on the oars while Duval faced her, holding two cords attached to the rudder.

"He's talking to the boatman. He's definitely following us," said Simone. "Oh! He's turned back; no, he's starting to walk around the lake."

"Ignore him. Shall I row?"

Baudelaire had begun to run around the lake when he stopped. Pursuit was hopeless. The two women were pulling away strongly. He turned to rejoin his friends, wondering what had possessed him. He was never going to drink cognac so early in the day again.

4

The cardboard-thin walls of her dressing room meant that Duval could hear the audience as she changed for the night's show. They were warming up now, banging tables, shouting for more wine, trying to run their hands up the waitresses' skirts and pinch their bottoms.

By the time she appeared, the audience would be drunk and the manager would begin to worry about the inevitable fights. That's really what she was there for—a calming influence to steady the crowd and allow the bar to sell even more wine. Keep them drinking with a few songs, that was her job. They always wanted the same songs. Every time she tried to sing something different they booed and yelled for "How Far Would You Go for a Girl like Me?" Some nights she reprised that four times. It drove the musicians mad.

She looked around the dressing room: squashed flies, faded flowers, and just enough space for a dressing table, chair, and stool. There wasn't room for a rat and his tail in the place. When Céleste came in, the two of them could hardly move.

Sometimes she wondered why she hadn't escaped from Haiti earlier. She had grown up quickly and by the age of twelve looked more like a woman than a girl. She could surely have got to New Orleans on a boat. She would have found him easily, and he would not have turned her away. So she was a half-caste, a bastard, but she was his daughter. What would he have done—thrown her out onto the street? No, he was a Frenchman, a man of honor; her mother always said that deep down, hidden away behind his arrogance and occasional cruelty, the plantation manager was a kind man. She could have made a life with him in America. He would have sent her to school in a town where there would have been nothing unusual about her color. She would have looked after him, cooked for him, washed his clothes. And together they would have traveled to the new territories in the West and reared cattle.

As it was, she had stayed with her mother. She tried hard not to remember the years that followed, the years of pain and punishment; years in which she saw her home—the plantation—burned to the ground; years in which she and her mother lived in the wooded hills. They thought they were safe there, until the bandits surprised them by the fast-flowing river in a deep gorge where they went to wash and draw water. Her mother had told her to run for the trees before she turned and faced them. They threw her to the ground, six of them. The last she saw of her mother was her face turned toward her, twisted with pain and shouting for her to run, run, run. And she had.

She went to Port-au-Prince and lived like an animal on the streets of a ruined city. She never found out what had happened to her mother and she didn't like to think. She once asked a priest to help look for her, but he shook his head and told her there was no hope. "God will receive her in his mercy and send you deliverance," he said. They were sitting in his private room in the church after a Sunday service. He told her to close her eyes and pray for deliverance from all sins—and then she felt his hands and fled.

She found her deliverance soon after in the Port-au-Prince harbor. The *Hirondelle* was a four-hundred-ton, three-masted French brig riding high in the water, having unloaded a cargo of wine and spirits. When she saw the ship's tricolor fluttering amid the masts of a score of other vessels, she knew that this was her moment.

She had tried to stow away a couple of times and had been thrown back ashore before a sail had been unfurled. This time would be different. She knew where the sailors drank and she soon found out the date and time of sailing. The *Hirondelle* was bound for Bordeaux with a cargo of coffee beans and sugar. It would be a three-week voyage. The rest was easy.

She never gave herself to any of the sailors. "You can look, but you don't touch," she had told them. That was enough to get her on board, but three days out at sea Jeanne Duval found herself in front of a gray-haired, bushy-bearded captain and two of his senior officers. She didn't know who had betrayed her and it didn't really matter. She had been dragged from her hiding place in the anchor room and marched onto the foredeck. The captain seemed bored and

did not even ask her name. He demanded the names of the
crew who had smuggled her on board.

"In truth, I do not know," she said. "I am here because I
wish to find freedom in France and escape the tyranny in my
homeland."

The captain looked at her with interest but said nothing:
a young, light-skinned mulatto, shoeless and wearing a thin
cotton dress. She was thin but with a big bosom. He was
struck by her thick black hair, which fell below her shoulders and had not seen a comb or brush these last few days.

Male stowaways could be made to work and then handed
over to the police in the home port. Women were more difficult. They unsettled the crew. He knew of some captains
who would have them thrown overboard during the quiet
night watch.

"Can you cook?" he asked.

Duval shook her head.

"Sew, mend clothes?"

She gazed at the wooden decking and shook her head
again.

The captain sighed, turned, and nodded to the two sailors. They closed in on her and grasped her roughly by the
arms.

"I can sing," she said suddenly.

The captain turned, eyebrows arched.

"Sing? What can you sing?"

There and then she sang an old song her mother had
sung to her almost every night from her cradle years, a la-
ment sung by the slaves in the fields for the land they had
never seen and would never know, Africa. She could speak

French well enough, but the song was in the Creole patois and she doubted the captain understood a word.

After the first verse she hesitated and looked around nervously. Seeing the rapt expressions on the faces of her audience, she continued, her soprano voice rising above the creaking timber of the vessel and the whisper of the waves beyond.

She finished and lowered her head. "Never look a white man in the eye," her mother had said. "Always look down, show deference and respect, and you will survive."

The captain turned to his officer. "M. Monterre plays the fiddle, doesn't he? Bring him up after dinner tonight and we will have some music."

And that was how Jeanne Duval paid for her passage across the Atlantic: singing every night after supper to the captain and his officers. When they reached Bordeaux she was put onto the quayside along with the sacks of coffee beans and sugar. The captain wished her good luck and gave her some money to buy clothes, the first act of kindness she had experienced from a stranger. Every time she smelled coffee she remembered that handshake, the fumbled gift of a few coins, and the gruff words bidding her good fortune.

Duval took a cigarette holder from a pot of makeup brushes and inserted a cigarette. She was wearing a chemise and lace-up boots that reached almost to the knee. In a minute Céleste would appear and help her into the dress. She brushed a film of sweat from her face with the back of her arm. It was a cold night outside, but somehow the temperature in the dressing room was always tropical. With the heat came the flies. Céleste lumbered in, banging the door behind her so that the whole room shook. Without a word she swatted a fly against the mirror with a rolled-up magazine.

Duval twisted around in her chair, seized the magazine, and flung it into the corner with the flowers. "How many times have I told you to stop doing that? Now get a cloth, clean the mirror, and put up some flypaper."

Céleste looked at her, sniffed, and wiped her nose with the back of her hand.

"There is no flypaper."

"Well, clean the mirror. How can I make up in that thing?"

Céleste was a big ox of a girl from Bordeaux, and Duval always thought she might be the sister of the wagoner she had dealt with so satisfactorily in the stables all those years ago. She was certainly the type, big and stupid.

There was a polite knock at the door, just audible over the noise from the hall.

"I'm busy. Tell them to go away," said Duval.

Céleste took the two steps required to reach the door and said, "Come back later."

There was the muffled sound of someone speaking outside.

Céleste bent her ear to the door and looked back at Duval. "Says it's the manager."

"We buried him last week."

Céleste shrugged and went to retrieve her magazine. There was another knock at the door, louder this time, and the indistinct sound of a voice. Duval got up, inhaled deeply on the cigarette, went to the door, pulled it open, and exhaled a long plume of smoke.

Baudelaire stood in the doorway, waved the smoke away,

and began coughing. He pulled a handkerchief from the top pocket of his jacket and flapped it at the fumes. Duval stepped back, looking surprised.

"May I come in?" he said.

"Another time. I'm on in ten minutes," she replied.

She closed the door. Men were always coming backstage, but usually after the show and not as well dressed as this one. Hearing a thud behind her, she turned to see Céleste trying to swat another fly against the mirror. Duval crossed the room, seized the woman by the nape of the neck, and bundled her to the door.

"How many times do I have to tell you?" she shouted, opening the door and pushing the maid out.

Céleste sprawled across a pair of expensive spats and looked up to see a face with a prominent nose and bushy eyebrows smiling down at her.

Baudelaire stepped over the woman and pushed open the door.

Duval was peering at the mirror, powdering her face with one hand while her cigarette smoldered in the other. She did not turn to look at the stranger.

"I thought I told you to come back later," she said.

"I came to congratulate you. That was a great show last night."

Duval turned and breathed another plume of smoke toward him. "What are you doing here?"

"I told you, I—"

"I mean, what are you doing in this club? We don't normally get your sort here."

"What sort is that?"

Duval got up and walked around her uninvited guest,

eyeing his clothes. She came full circle and put the point of her cigarette holder under his cravat, then flipped it out of his shirt. Baudelaire remained motionless.

"The idle, decadent rich—that's your sort. Why are you slumming it with those sweaty peasants out there?" she said.

"I like your act. You're a good singer."

"You would know, of course."

"I know you're worth more than this."

"I know what I'm worth, Monsieur . . . ?"

"The name doesn't matter. What does matter is that you could make real money in one of the bigger clubs."

"Maybe I like it here."

"Maybe you don't."

"Maybe you're right. What does it have to do with you?"

They eyed each other silently. Several flies continued to drone in lazy circles around them. Baudelaire picked up the magazine and swatted one against the mirror.

Duval sighed, sat down, pulled her petticoat well up her thighs, raised one booted leg, and rested it on the stool.

"Nice. Since you're here, make yourself useful. Unlace this," she said.

Baudelaire looked down at the boot, knelt without a word, and began to fiddle with the lace. It had been tied with a knot rather than a bow and he struggled to undo it. Finally, he unthreaded the lace and pulled the boot open. Her petticoat rode higher up her thighs, but after a glance he kept his eye on the boot and pulled it off. She swung the other leg onto the stool. Still kneeling, Baudelaire looked up at her. Keeping her eyes on him, she nodded to her booted leg. He began fiddling with the knot. She pulled her foot away.

"I'll be here all night at this rate. Céleste!"

She walked to the door and opened it. Baudelaire got up, adjusted his cravat in the fly-smeared mirror, and left, passing a weeping Céleste in the corridor.

"Come in here, Céleste!" Duval said.

The maid entered and Duval turned on her chair and stared into the mirror. She began to put on makeup.

"What happened to the gentleman?"

Duval put down her makeup brush, reached into a tin, and fished out another cigarette.

"He'll be back," she said. "Here, lace this up."

She swung her leg onto the stool, lit the cigarette, and leaned back. Céleste started putting on the boot that Baudelaire had just taken off.

5

Caroline Aupick sat at a writing desk in the bay window that looked onto the bare branches of the plane trees that lined the street. She held a quill pen in one hand, dipping it occasionally into a silver inkwell. She was reading slowly through a pile of documents at her side, making notes and holding each one up to the light from the window, as if trying to ensure that it was hiding no secrets.

At the next window Baudelaire stood holding a book in his hand, which he was pretending to read. Not wishing to give his mother any further cause to accuse him of extravagance, he had taken care that morning to dress in his oldest clothes: a brown wool jacket, plain white shirt, patched twill trousers. He wore no jewelry and had left his hair uncombed.

He slid the occasional glance at his mother, trying to gauge her mood. This was not difficult. Every document she looked at drew a louder sigh and a deeper frown. Knowing full well what was coming, he had been tempted to walk out but reflected that such an act of disobedience would have merely delayed the maternal storm that was about to break. He might as well get it over with now. He closed his book. His mother looked up from her papers.

"Two thousand francs so far and I haven't even got to your tailors yet."

She spoke in a loud whisper, always the case when she was angry. She picked up the papers and waved them at her son.

"You'll bankrupt us all at this rate!"

Baudelaire stared out the window. Down there beside the plane tree the beggar woman had lain dead only last night. Now she would be in the city mortuary, a near-naked, skeletal figure providing little to satisfy the voyeurs who filed through.

"It's my money, Mama. I'll spend it how I wish," he said.

Caroline Aupick threw the papers down on her desk, reached for the inkwell, and hurled it at her son.

"You cannot and you will not!" she shouted.

Baudelaire stepped back, looking with astonishment at the ink spattered over his shirtfront and jacket. His first thought was relief that he had worn such old clothes. He dabbed at his face and inspected his inky fingers. Never mind the clothes, how do I wash ink off my face? How am I going to go out looking like a chimney sweep? Damn her! Why does she get so worked up about a few bills?

"The moneylenders have their claws into you, haven't they?" she said. "Never mind the tradesmen's bills—what about those bloodsuckers? What security do you give them? My name and your stepfather's name! You think we don't know? You think we're going to let you beggar us with your endless extravagance?"

Baudelaire gazed at his mother with fury but said nothing. He began to rip off his jacket.

"Don't dare undress here!" she said. "Go to your room!"

Baudelaire flung his jacket to one side and tore off his shirt. The buttons flew across the room. He threw the stained shirt at his mother's feet and went to the door.

"I'm leaving. I'm going to get my own apartment. And I shall pay for it myself."

He banged the door behind him.

From high windows shafts of light pierced the gloom of a large room in which a dozen clerks were working at desks. They were writing in ledgers with thick metal-nibbed pens that moved scratchily over the pages, creating the sibilant murmur of a distant sea. At a larger desk sat two men. The older peered myopically at a pile of documents through thick-lensed glasses, while the younger counted out banknotes, placing them in a neat pile under a paperweight. Two brass carriage clocks were placed at either end of the desk.

A clerk led Baudelaire through the office and motioned to a chair in front of the larger desk.

"M. Baudelaire," he said.

The younger man looked up briefly and returned to counting out the money. Baudelaire sat down, pulling out the tails of his cloak. There was no sound but the ticking of the clocks and the murmur of pens on paper. He noticed that one clock was ten minutes ahead of the other. He leaned over the desk, opened the glass front of the clock, and moved the minute hand back. He looked up to see the old man staring at him.

"Five thousand francs for six months at nine percent," said the old man.

"That is the arrangement, yes," Baudelaire said.

"That's not the arrangement—yet. You have collateral?"

"I have a legacy worth five times that."

"It is entailed. You must know that. Your stepfather has just appointed a lawyer, has he not? You will get three hundred a month from your legacy. Every lender in Paris knows that."

He held up a document.

"So—where is the collateral?"

"I am an artist. I have my work."

"Your work?"

"I am a published writer, and an art critic. I have a reputation; anyone will tell you."

"You certainly have a reputation, M. Baudelaire: for extravagance; for being a connoisseur of the finer things in life—the cognac of Napoléon, the ladies in the fine salons, and, how shall I put this, the ladies in the somewhat less fashionable salons, not to mention the clothes from those fancy shops in the rue de Rivoli. That's what your reputation is worth to me."

He clicked his fingers.

Baudelaire rose to his feet, pale with anger. "I shall go elsewhere," he said.

The old man bent over the desk, opened the front of the carriage clock, and pushed the minute hand forward ten minutes. "As you wish," he replied.

Baudelaire turned and walked rapidly toward the door. The clerks raised their heads from their work to watch as he swept past, his open cape brushing documents from tables so they fluttered to the floor behind him. He reached the door and turned the handle.

"Three thousand for three months at fifteen percent," said the old man loudly.

The clerks sat up, pens motionless in their hands. They looked from one man to the other. The room was silent.

Baudelaire sighed and shrugged. "My mother was right. Very well."

He retraced his steps along the trail of paper. The old man pushed a prepared document across the table.

"Sign here."

Baudelaire signed the document. The old man took a stick of sealing wax and held one end into the flame of the candle on the table. He waited a second, then held the dripping wax over the paper until a large blob had formed below the signature. Baudelaire took off his ring, pushed it into the wax, held it for a second, then put the ring back in his waistcoat pocket, taking care to wipe it first on the corner of a document lying on the desk. He turned and began to walk away.

"M. Baudelaire!" said the old man.

Baudelaire wheeled around.

The old man lifted the paperweight off the pile of banknotes that had been counted out on the desk.

"Your money," he said.

6

Le Rêve was crowded, noisy, and smoky, and as the musicians climbed back onto the stage they peered into the haze looking for their singer. In a sea of cheap shiny suits, shabby shirts, and greasy bow ties she stood out in her red dress, scalloped revealingly at the front, with a heart-shaped pendant hanging low from her neck. They waved her toward them. She looked up, nodded, and turned back to the three men at her table.

They watched as she took a small dark glass bottle from her purse and pulled the cork out with her teeth. She shook several drops into the wineglasses in front of them, then stirred each with a silver spoon. The men stared suspiciously at the treatment of their wine.

"All right, what is it?" said one.

"Try it," said Duval, holding a glass out to him.

The man sipped cautiously and shrugged. "It tastes different, but not bad."

"The poppy and the grape make a fine wine together," said Duval, pouring a generous slug into her own glass. She drank deeply and the men followed suit. They nodded approvingly to one another. One picked up the bottle.

"What do you call this stuff?" he said.

"Call it what you like. It's heaven to me. And it's one franc a bottle to you. You can pay me later."

She got up and walked to the stage, where the musicians were tuning up. The hubbub in the hall died as she turned to face her audience.

"I have written a new song for you tonight," she said. "It's about a little girl I once knew—but it could just as well be about you."

And she sang, the same soprano voice that had paid her passage across the Atlantic and got her the job at Le Rêve:

"In the silver mirrors of my mind,
I see the girl I left behind.
I shed tears for her childish dreams,
Because life is never what it seems.

"Oh, to step back and take her hand
And try to make her understand.
I didn't want to betray those dreams;
I didn't mean to lose my way.

"But the hopes we shared and held so high
Were passing clouds in an empty sky.
Now I turn from the truth I find
In the silver mirrors of my mind."

The conversation resumed after sparse applause. The pianist shook his head at her and said, "You're wasting your time."

"Encore!" came a cry from the back of the room.

Duval peered into the smoke and saw Baudelaire wearing a long cloak and a top hat and holding what looked like a cane. Another man with him, tall, fair-haired, and good-looking, was equally well dressed. They looked as if they had wandered out of a gala evening at the royal palace across the river.

The two men lifted their glasses to her from the back of the hall. She raised her hand to stop the music and quiet the crowd.

"I see some *gentlemen* have joined us," she said.

Heads turned to look at the well-dressed strangers.

"Look at those fine clothes, those well-fed faces. I'll bet they have a carriage outside with a driver waiting until they've had their fun here. And you know what their fun is? Looking down those long noses at you, the hardworking people of Paris. You thought we'd got rid of that lot, didn't you? Well, you were wrong."

There was a buzz of anger from the crowd. People craned their necks to look at the intruders. Baudelaire acknowledged them by raising his hat to the room. Le Vavasseur had taken a step back and was looking over his shoulder at the door.

"Time to go, Charles," he said.

"She's playing a game—don't worry. Give me the cards," said Baudelaire.

Le Vavasseur dug in his pockets and handed Baudelaire a deck of cards.

"I'm not afraid of any mob; you know that," Le Vavasseur said. "But she's not worth a pitched battle with this lot."

Baudelaire threw his arms around his friend. "You're

right. You're always right," he said. "You go home. Safe journey."

Le Vavasseur embraced his friend and turned to leave. "Want some advice?"

"No, thanks."

"She's trouble."

By the time Le Vavasseur headed to the door, the crowd seemed to have forgotten the provocative presence of two well-dressed strangers. They had turned their attention instead to the stage, pressing forward to get closer.

Duval was leaning over the front of the crowd now, her hands on her hips, allowing the diamond pendant to swing from side to side. She brushed away the hands that reached up to grab it, then unhooked the jewel from her neck and walked the length of the stage, swinging it out over the outstretched arms of the front row.

The pianist began playing, pounding the keys to create maximum effect, as she swung the pendant around her head and then launched it into the crowd. There was a scramble as half the room scrabbled on the floor while the remainder clambered onto their chairs and looked on, laughing.

Duval left the stage, skirted the heaving mass of bodies, and accepted a seat at a table littered with bottles and glasses. A shout of triumph came from the center of the room as a man emerged from the ruckus holding aloft the pendant. Duval blew him a kiss and nodded to the offer of a glass of wine from her table.

She dipped into her purse, produced the dark bottle, and raised a questioning eyebrow at her four new companions. They nodded, holding out their glasses. She gave each several drops and put the bottle away. The men toasted her just as a playing card landed faceup on the table: the ace of hearts. One of the men reached out for it, but Duval got there first and leaned back on her chair, holding it away from him. The man was drunker than she realized and got to his feet.

"I saw it first," he said.

She looked around but saw no one who could have thrown the card.

"Sit down," she said to the drunk.

"Give it to me," he said, sweeping aside glasses and bottles and lunging over the table.

Duval rose and stepped back as two other men grabbed the drunk and tried to drag him to his chair. The man lashed out and the three men fell backwards onto the floor in a flurry of fists and elbows.

This is how it always begins, she thought. Every other night, two drunks argue over a bet that was never made, a waitress they can never have, a job they will never get, or a bill they will never agree on. There's a push, then a punch or a slap; they fall to the floor, kicking and gouging, and the whole room joins in. It's what they come for: to get drunk and fight. Outside this room they have nothing but a grinding job and a hungry family. Here at least they can find some release in what they enjoy most—drinking and fighting.

A general brawl now engulfed the club. The waitresses had fled. Tables were being turned over, chairs raised as weapons, and bottles thrown. Duval was buffeted by three men who were holding one another by the throat and hair. They crashed into her and she felt hands pulling at her dress, groping her. She disengaged from the mêlée and grabbed a bottle of wine. The fight was worse than usual tonight, she thought; it must be the end of the month, payday. She noticed that the shoulder strap had been ripped off her dress. Holding it up with one hand, she stepped behind a pillar as groups of fighting men eddied around her. Another hand grabbed her arm and she turned, raising the bottle of wine.

"It's time you went home," said Baudelaire.

He had his cane half-raised in one hand, but she noticed that the top hat had gone and his cloak had been tied back behind his waist. He let go of her arm and picked up a chair to ward off a knot of men who clung to one another in a murderous embrace. A glass crashed into the pillar above their heads. There was a laugh from the man who had thrown it and who now advanced on them with a broken bottle.

"What did you call him?" said the man. "Decadent rich, was it?"

"No," said Duval, "that was—"

"Shut up," said Baudelaire. He raised his cane and pressed a button below the silver knob. The knob popped up, revealing a short length of shiny steel blade. The man looked at him for a second, hurled the bottle, and ran. The bottle shattered on the wall close to Baudelaire. He flinched, feeling a stab of pain. He reached back to undo his cloak and drew it around him.

"What is that thing?" she said.

Baudelaire took the silver top of the cane and drew out a thin sword.

"It's what the decadent rich use to fend off the poor—only they never give me a chance to use it," he said, and replaced the blade.

"Thank you," said Duval.

She turned to leave, but Baudelaire grabbed her by the arm. She shook him off. He grabbed her arm again.

"Don't be silly. You can't stay here," he said.

The apartment was lit with candles. There was a small table in one corner holding bottles and glasses and two armchairs. An intricately patterned Oriental rug lay on the floor. There was no other furniture. A carriage clock was placed in the center of the mantelpiece, over which hung the portrait of a beautiful young woman. A log fire burned low in the grate. Duval walked cautiously over the carpet to the mantelpiece and looked at the clock. She frowned and peered at the clock face. She was still holding up her torn dress and carried a purse.

"It's later than you think," she said.

She turned at the soft plop of a cork being removed from a bottle. Baudelaire was pouring wine into two glasses. He was still wearing his cloak.

"That's right; it's always later than you think," he said, and waved the wine bottle at the room. "You like it?" he said.

"Who is that?" she said, nodding to the painting.

"My mother, when she was young. So what do you think?"

"She's beautiful."

"No, I mean the apartment."

"It's a little empty. You live here?" she said.

"Look at this," he said, ignoring the question. He opened the door of a bedroom off the main drawing room. The only furniture was a large brass bed, a bedside table, a washbasin on a stand, and a closet. They walked in. Duval opened the closet. It was empty.

"No furniture and no clothes—you don't live here, then?" she said.

"It's not my apartment."

"Whose is it?"

"Have a glass of wine and I'll tell you."

He poured the wine and Duval sat on the bed. Her torn dress almost slipped off her shoulder. She drank most of the wine in one gulp.

"So tell me."

"*You* live here," he said.

Duval laughed and dipped into her bag, bringing out a pendant.

"I don't think so. I know where I live. Here, help me on with this, would you?"

Baudelaire took the necklace and fastened it behind her neck.

"More wine?" he said.

"Thank you. Then I must go. I'm very tired."

Baudelaire poured them both a glass.

"You seemed to enjoy yourself tonight," she said.

"I found it amusing."

"Exactly. Playing the white knight with that sword thing of yours. You loved it: a gentleman rescuing a lady from a drunken mob."

"So we're a lady now, are we?"

Duval flashed a glance at him. "I'm a lady when I want to be."

"And when you don't?"

"That's my business."

Baudelaire took the pendant in his hands. He raised it against the light of the gas lamps.

"Beautiful," he said.

"It's cheap paste and you know it. I throw one to the audience every night."

Baudelaire suddenly sat down on the bed clutching his side. He groaned and his face turned gray. He threw off his cloak and opened his jacket. His shirt was bloodstained. He ripped it open. His stomach was smeared with blood.

"It must be splinters from that bottle," she said. "Lie down."

He fell back on the bed while she dipped a towel into the basin. She washed away the blood, picked a sliver of glass from the wound, and pressed the towel against his stomach.

"Hold this," she said. "It's only a shallow cut and the bleeding should stop in a minute; you should have said something earlier."

"I didn't think the bastard had got me. Bring me some wine, can you?"

"It's not wine you need . . . ," she said.

In the half-light the pendant swung back and forth, glistening with liquid that fell in drops over his face. His head moved from side to side as he kept his eyes on the cut-glass heart hanging from the chain around her neck.

"Taste it," she said, kneeling over him and lowering the pendant so that it swung slowly just above his mouth. He put his tongue out and licked the white salty liquid that clung viscously to the glass.

She turned away from him, quite naked, and dipped the

heart into a glass of milky liquid by the bed. He noticed thin white scars running down her lower back and buttocks. He ran his fingers down them, feeling the dead scar tissue. She shivered and brushed his hand away.

"Open your mouth," she said, kneeling on all fours over him again.

He opened his mouth and took the glass heart, sucking it as he had done those large boiled sweets his father had given him as a child on their morning walks in the Luxembourg Gardens. Her breasts brushed his face. She turned to drink from the glass and then kissed him, allowing the drink to flow between them.

She broke off the embrace. "The taste of heaven?" she asked.

"I'll tell you when I get there," he said.

Duval woke alone in the bed. The room was in semidark-ness. She looked around drowsily, then sat up. There was no sign of Baudelaire. A robe lay across the bed. She slipped into it and walked through the drawing room, then looked into the bathroom and small kitchen. In all the rooms the shutters were drawn.

Puzzled, she walked back to the bedroom, then saw an envelope on the drinks table. "JEANNE" was scrawled on the front. She opened it and a key fell to the floor. She picked it up, looked at it, then opened the front door and tried the key in the lock. The lock turned.

She threw back the shutters with a crash, flooding the room with light. She went from room to room, opening shut-ters and letting in the daylight. She stopped to look out of a window. The roofs and chimneys of Paris stretched away in waves of thatch, slate, and brick, from which the towers of Notre-Dame and, more distantly, the ornate limestone of the Arc de Triomphe rose like ships at sea. She turned back. She looked at the portrait, moved around the room, and looked again. The eyes of Mme Aupick followed her.

7

Baudelaire's mother spent most of the summer months from the end of May to the middle of September at a small villa in the fishing village of Honfleur on the Normandy coast. Every morning between eleven and noon she would walk along the beach from the harbor wall to the lighthouse and back before taking coffee at the Hôtel Normandie.

She enjoyed these walks both because her doctor had said the sea air was good for her and because she liked the ever-changing weather along the Channel coast. One moment slate-gray clouds, fat with rain, would drift in from the west, darkening the sky and scattering showers; the next they parted like curtains, allowing the sun to sparkle on the creamy crests of the waves. On this morning's walk there was a strong and strengthening wind from the west. The tide was high, leaving only soft sand to walk on, but her son was beside her and she was happy.

It was Caroline Aupick's good fortune to have inherited the house at Honfleur and then to find a second husband who allowed her the time to enjoy it. She regarded herself as a lucky woman and thus a happy one. Her father, an officer in Louis XVI's army, had fled to England during the Revolution. She had been born in a suburb of London called Saint Pancras, which, her friends told her, had now become the site of one of the capital's first railroad stations.

Orphaned at an early age, she had returned to France to live with an old friend of her father. Having passed her twenty-fifth birthday without marrying, she seemed doomed to live as a spinster, until an elderly friend of her guardian proposed. François Baudelaire was fifty-nine and she was twenty-six. He had a child by a previous marriage, a son called Alphonse, and a substantial pension. She had no money and no home of her own.

François was a courtly, white-haired gentleman of the old school with a taste for fine furniture and paintings. She was pretty and ambitious. She knew she would find neither love nor passion in the marriage but accepted him as the only escape from the solitary and impoverished future that lay before her. The couple began married life in a comfortable apartment in an old house in rue Hautefeuille on the Left Bank, and it was there that Charles Baudelaire was born in April 1821. And that was the greatest good fortune of all.

She looked at him as he walked beside her on the beach, the boy who had given her the love she lacked in a loveless marriage, who had clung to her at bedtime every night as her husband never did. Now the tousle-haired little boy had become a grumpy twenty-one-year-old, who was walking into the wind and occasional burst of rain with his head down, shoulders hunched, and one hand in his pocket while the other held a small umbrella. This attempt to shield them both from the elements proved fruitless, as the wind frequently changed direction. Each time he cursed silently and turned to reshape the inverted spokes.

After a while she took the umbrella and put her arm through his. He allowed her to draw him close so that they walked in step. But for his mother, he would have hated the idea of a seaside walk on a gray day at the end of summer. In fact, he hated the idea of traveling anywhere outside Paris. Why leave a city that gave him everything he wanted in life: friends, a literary world waiting to embrace him, entertainment, women, drink? Besides, what did the countryside have to offer? It was always wet, the people never washed, and there was never anything to do. The coast was the same, although more beautiful. Paris was where he felt alive, where he found the vital need, stronger than hunger or desire, to write.

He had been writing poetry for years. Now he felt his work was good enough to show to his friends. He could trust Le Vavasseur, Prarond, and Buisson to tell him the truth. And they did. They honestly liked what he had written. They said his verse was modern, striking, and dangerous. Those were their words. They had encouraged him to take the poems to established writers such as de Vigny and Victor Hugo, but he didn't want to do that. He wasn't like them; he was different and so was his poetry.

He despised the Romantic nonsense about nature, the absurd view that man could find his destiny in the beauty of mountains, lakes, forests, or the raging sea. He was going to write about the struggle between good and evil, between sobriety and drunkenness, between chastity and lust, love and loneliness. It was on those battle lines that the fate and

future of mankind would be decided, and he, Charles Baudelaire, would define the nature of that conflict in his poetry.

He felt completely confident in his work, but he needed
to find a publisher, someone who would take a risk on new
work that defied conventional and commercial reality. His
friends had told him of a man who might be so inclined. He
would show him a few verses when he was back in Paris.

Right now, however, he knew he had to be in Honfleur
with his mother. She had not been bluffing. His legacy had
been entailed and placed with a lawyer. He was twenty-one
years old and he had been denied his father's legacy. Worse
still, his mother could control what remained of his legacy
for the rest of his life. Even if he lived to be an old man,
which was both unlikely and unwished for in his view, he
would not be granted his rightful estate. Only his mother
could reverse the court decision. And clearly she was not
minded to do so. That was an outrageous injustice. He would
challenge the decision. Three hundred francs a month was
not enough.

He imagined his plea to the family lawyer. He would say
he had decided to follow his stepfather into the diplomatic
service. That was credible because General Aupick had indeed suggested such a career. To become a diplomat, he would
need further education, especially training in languages. His
English was good, but he would need Arabic. That would
cost money. Then there was the question of clothes. To repre-
sent France abroad, he would require a new wardrobe. Therefore, his allowance would need to increase—hugely.

She turned to him at the end of the beach. "You're miles
away," she said. "Who are you talking to?"

He laughed. She knew him so well.

"You will always love me, won't you, Mama?" he said.

"Of course. Don't be silly," she said.

"You remember when I was little—after Father died? When we were together—just the two of us?"

"How could I ever forget those years? We had each other."

"Exactly," he said. "We needed nobody else."

In those days it was true. At breakfast his mother would sit at the dining table, sipping coffee and taking tiny bites of pastry while reading the newspaper. He would always finish first and would wriggle onto her lap, pretending to take great interest in the day's news. She would sigh and complain but never put him down.

Sometimes she would take him to the opera, when he would wear a velvet suit and black shoes with silver buckles. She would never let Mariette dress him but would always come to his bedroom and help him with his clothes herself. Looking back, he realized his mother had been a little jealous of Mariette. She was a sweet girl and he liked spending time with her in the kitchen or garden, but his mother did not approve. She wanted him all to herself.

He loved the nights at the opera. The music bored him and he didn't understand what was happening onstage, but he would snuggle up to her while she fanned herself against the heat. It was always too hot, but she gave him iced sherbet and allowed him to play with the charms hanging from her bracelet. Long before the end, he would fall asleep with his head nestling into her chest and her arm around him.

He would never forget the day he ran in from the garden to tell her that Mariette had killed a large rat in the woodshed.

He looked everywhere and finally burst into her bathroom. His mother was naked, bending forward with one foot on the tub, drying her leg with a towel. She turned in surprise. He stopped, shocked. She straightened up and wound a towel around herself. He wanted to tell her about the rat but found no words. He had never seen her, or even thought of her, without clothes. She smiled, gesturing for him to come to her. He turned and ran from the room.

Then she met General Aupick, a dashing cavalry officer from a good regiment. He had dark curly hair and deep blue eyes. He was well mannered and respectful, but passionate in his pursuit of her. An orphan like her, he had joined the army as the only career open to him. His bravery on the battlefields of Europe during the Napoleonic era had brought him swift promotion. He was thirty-nine when they met and she was thirty-five. She fell in love for the first time in her life. They married soon after meeting. Baudelaire was seven years old. He never stopped loving his mother. But he never forgave her.

The night of the wedding, Baudelaire locked himself in his room and put a chair against the door. He smashed the window with a table lamp and hurled everything he could lift out of the window. Sheets, toys, clothes, even his rocking horse, went through the jagged glass and fell to the street below.

His mother finally forced her way into the room and found him crying beneath the bed. He refused to come out until she lay down, still in her wedding dress, and pleaded with him. She spent an hour soothing him, whispering stories about swallows, before he finally fell asleep in her arms.

When she went downstairs to apologize, her new hus-

band, resplendent in his uniform, was sitting in front of the
fire with a glass of champagne in his hand, an empty bottle
in the grate. He smiled a warm, lopsided smile and said that
he understood and that he loved her very much. But soon he
too was asleep.

The wind had strengthened and shifted to the north,
whipping up the dry sand above the tidemark and flinging it
in their faces.

"We must go back," she said.

They turned and he held her tightly.

"You loved your boy when he was little, didn't you?"

"I love him just as much now."

"I don't think so, Mama. You think he wastes his time
and money on frivolous luxuries. You think his poetry is
worthless—and let me assure you, you are not alone. Above
all, you think he keeps the wrong company."

"If you mean that girl, yes."

"She's not a girl. She's a woman. And I like her."

"So I hear. I also hear she's a cabaret singer, putting it
politely."

"Mama!"

"It's your life, Charles. You have every right to throw it
away if you want. I will always love you. But at least know
this: The general can get you a good position in the diplomatic service. You will have time for your writing."

Baudelaire shook his head. "You don't understand. I am
going to be famous. I am going to be rich. One day people
will see me for what I really am."

"Which is?"

"A poet. A famous man of letters. You know why? I see
things that other people don't see. I—"

"You spend money that other people don't see—because you don't have it."

"Money, money, money! Why is it always money?"

"Because you throw it away like sand in the wind, Charles. You have huge debts, and you are just twenty-one. That's why we have put your money into a trust."

"That's really what I want to talk to you about, Mama. Please give me my money. Father left it to me. It's mine."

"No, Charles. Your stepfather and I have decided. You are going to get your monthly allowance—and no more."

Baudelaire stopped, took his arm from her waist, and stepped back. The wind had kicked up a small sandstorm around them and both had lowered their heads, shielding their faces with their hands.

"Damn him, damn the bastard," Baudelaire said, and walked away along the beach, waving his arms like a mad conductor trying to turn the sound of waves and wind into a symphony.

He strode swiftly into the port of Honfleur along streets now covered in a fine layer of sand. The pharmacy was where he remembered it. There was no one in the shop except a white-coated man bent over a counter on which stood a line of large green jars and bottles. He was writing slowly in a ledger.

Baudelaire went straight to the counter and waited. The man seemed oblivious of his presence and continued with slow strokes of a metal-nibbed pen to embellish the ledger with copperplate writing.

Baudelaire knocked gently on the counter. "A bottle of laudanum, please," he said.

The pharmacist looked at him. "Your condition?"

"Bad chest," said Baudelaire with an impressive cough.

The pharmacist reached under the counter for a small brown bottle and placed it in front of him.

"Can I have a larger bottle, please?"

The pharmacist said, "Not without a prescription."

Baudelaire placed his hands on the counter and leaned over, pushing his face close to the pharmacist.

"I have the money. Give me a larger bottle."

The pharmacist picked up the bottle and held it next to Baudelaire's face. "You know what this is?" he said. "Liquid opium. Classified as a dangerous drug. You can get a bottle of this size for medical purposes without a prescription—and that's all. Now, if I knew your doctor—"

"He's in Paris. But you know my mother: Mme Aupick. She lives here. In the villa on the hill."

"Ah . . . ! Mme Aupick's son. The poet," he said. "You will still need a prescription, I'm afraid."

Baudelaire grabbed the bottle, scattered some coins on the counter, and headed for the door.

8

Like many women, Jeanne Duval had concluded at a very early age that fashion began at the feet and that shoes were a woman's most important ally in life. She walked slowly across the drawing room of her new apartment, looking at a long line of footwear on the floor, much as a commanding officer might inspect his troops.

The shop had been kind enough to send her a dozen pairs of their new stock, taking care to establish that she was indeed a resident of a suite of rooms in the Hôtel de Lauzun. She had already tried on every shoe and found that all but one pair fitted perfectly. They looked quite beautiful on feet that were not as small as they might be yet were graced with well-shaped ankles.

Having walked along the line several times, pausing only to lift the odd shoe to the light, the better to judge its style and color, she reached a conclusion that had been forming in her mind since the shoes had first arrived.

There were shoes here for every occasion: sensible brown

morning shoes, dark-red leather shoes designed to impress a friend at lunch, lighter shoes with little heels for afternoon tea, heavier shoes for the street and for shopping, knee-length boots for walking in the park, and at least two pairs of satin slippers for the evening. She would therefore need all eleven pairs, leaving out only the pair that seemed too small. On further reflection, she realized that a cobbler might well be able to stretch those to fit her. She would simply have to buy them all.

There was the sound of a key in the lock. She looked up. The front door opened and Baudelaire walked in carrying a small posy of flowers. He closed the door quietly. Duval stood on one foot, wriggling the other into a shoe. Baudelaire looked at the line of footwear that stretched across the room. He frowned and held out the posy.

"Thank you," she said. "Oh!"

She pulled out the small brown bottle of laudanum nestling in the flowers.

"You should see your mother more often," she said.

Baudelaire wasn't listening. He was staring at the empty space on the wall where his mother's portrait had hung.

"What have you done with that painting?" he asked.

There was a loud knock on the door. Duval slipped on the other shoe and held out her foot for his approval.

"You like them?" she said.

He ignored her and continued staring at the blank space on the wall. She walked through the drawing room to the front door. She opened it and stood back as a procession of men entered the apartment, carrying first a desk, then a dining table, four chairs, a chaise longue, and three side tables.

Baudelaire looked on in silent amazement. "Where did

all this come from?" he said. Realizing the question rather missed the point, he added, "Did you *buy* all this?"

"What does it look like?" she said.

"It looks like you've been spending a fortune on furniture," he replied.

She put a finger to his lips. "It's not a fortune and I haven't spent a franc. It's a housewarming present from your mother. Please thank her very much for me."

Baudelaire lashed out with his feet at a chair being carried past, causing two of the men to drop it and back away toward the door.

"All right, all right," said Duval. "Mama will go back on the wall." She gave him a quick kiss. "No more tantrums, please."

"But how much did all this cost?" said Baudelaire.

"Probably less than you and your friends lose at cards in a night. Did you expect me to live here without furniture? Now, help me arrange these things."

"I've got a better idea," he said, and walked to the drinks table, where he poured equal measures of laudanum and red wine into a glass.

Jeanne Duval had few women friends. Those with men friends didn't trust her. Women looking for men saw her as a competitor. Her sexual allure was too obvious. Her lustrous long dark hair, voluptuous figure, and the sun-kissed coloring conferred by mixed-race parentage gave her exotic looks that had proved irresistible to a long line of thoroughly unsuitable admirers.

They would turn up at the back door of Le Rêve with small bunches of flowers that had clearly been sold off cheaply by a florist at the end of the day. They promised a smart carriage to take her to the grand restaurants on the Right Bank— but the carriages were always just around the corner and the name of the restaurant seemed to escape them. She was patient with these stage-door suitors, because most had at least paid some small amount to see her perform. With others who made cruder suggestions of a purely commercial nature, she was ferocious. Men who made such offers were lucky to escape with a few facial bruises.

When she had arrived in Paris on that potato cart three years previously, Duval had dreamed of making her way in society. She had a vague idea of working in a fashionable salon and learning the skills of designing and selling haute couture. It would be a fitting profession for someone of her family background.

Her father, after all, had been a wealthy coffee planter whose family was reputed to own substantial farmland in the south of France. She carried his name and she had been told that the Duvals were once a well-known family in the Toulon area. She presumed that the land had been lost in the Revolution, and she had no intention of making herself known to her father's relatives, even if she could find them. But she was sure that at least one-half of her bloodline stemmed from the landed gentry of old France, and therein lay her ambition to prove and better herself.

She was not, she told herself, just another Caribbean waif and stray washed up on the shores of France. Her family— and, yes, bastard she might be, but it was her family—had been important people in the south: lawyers, doctors maybe, and certainly landowners. This knowledge gave her both self-confidence and a sharp ambition.

Unfortunately, while the Revolution and the Terror that followed had destroyed the old economic and political order, it had done little to change social attitudes in what remained a conservative, Catholic society. When she presented herself at some of the large businesses and famous shops in Paris, it was obvious that prospective employers did not see an attractive Creole lady with all the charm that can be mustered in one dazzling smile. They saw instead the bastard child of a Frenchman who had long since abandoned the product of some drunken liaison. And when she implied close connections to the Duval family in the south, people shrugged in disbelief.

It was on one of these occasions, in a newly opened perfumery on the rue de Rivoli, that Duval met the woman who was to become the only friend she had in Paris. Her job interview had ended as usual in a brief and dispiriting rejection. Duval was waiting in the shop for the rain to clear when she heard one of the women behind the counter being rebuked by the very lady who had been so dismissive of her own hopes. The cause of the rebuke seemed to be trivial, but Duval could see the young assistant was close to tears. Once the officious manager had left, Duval offered a consoling remark and the two women began to talk. A little later, in a café around the corner, a friendship was formed.

Simone Clairmont came from a small village in the Pyrenees and would probably have remained there for the rest of her life had not a distant cousin in Paris helped secure her a position in one of the new perfume shops that had opened on the Left Bank. Initially overwhelmed by the contrasting squalor and opulence of the capital, she quickly settled into the drudgery of a shop assistant's life and tried hard not to admit to herself that she had been much happier on the family's small farm in the mountains.

At least at home she would have had no difficulty finding a husband. There were plenty of young men tied to their fathers' farms in her area of the Pyrenees who would welcome a bride with a small dowry. Here in Paris, men were more demanding. It was not that she was unattractive, but her features seemed to have been assembled in a haphazard fashion. In the mirror she saw a sharp, masterly nose, a chin that thought too much of itself, two plump country cheeks, and shy, hazel-brown eyes. Her auburn hair was cut to shoulder length. I may not be pretty, she told herself, but I am not unattractive. What really pained her was the lack of a full figure, which was so fashionable at the time.

She was slender rather than thin, she told herself, and she wore her dresses at a length to make the most of her finely shaped ankles. At least she had been told her ankles were well turned, but that was the view of an elderly aunt in Simone's hometown. Here in Paris one lady's ankle seemed very much like another and the eyes of the men she met seemed more interested in a lady's figure above the waist. So she placed two medium-size lavender sachets beneath her bodice and acquired both a shapely bosom and an attractive fragrance.

At first Duval and Clairmont were not entirely truthful as they discussed their lives in Paris. Both claimed a wider circle of acquaintances than either possessed. And both were a little casual with the true facts of their ages. Duval claimed

to have given up counting birthdays but said she thought she
was thirty, while Simone was certain she was only twenty-
four. In fact, as they finally revealed to each other amid a
gale of desperate giggles, Duval was thirty-two and her friend
twenty-eight.

"We're old maids," said Simone.

"Age is all in the mind," said Duval. "Besides, what man
will ever know how old a woman really is? Who's going to
tell them?"

The two women met once a week for coffee and window-
shopping on a Sunday afternoon. The expeditions always
ended with tea and a consoling talk about their lack of money,
men, and prospects. On those occasions, the older woman
talked freely while her companion listened, enthralled and
slightly shocked by stories about the decadent milieu in
which her friend made her living. This week Duval had news
of special importance to impart and, having alluded to its
scandalous nature, she made Simone wait while the waitress
laid the table and poured the coffee. When Duval finally
told her about the young man who had become her lover and
who set her up in a suite of rooms at the Hôtel de Lauzun,
Simone was beside herself with excitement.

"I'm such a country mouse compared with you," she said.
"My life is so dull."

"You are a lucky country mouse," said Duval. "Where I
grew up people were happy just to wake up alive every day.
And every day they had to fight to stay that way— Oh, isn't
that beautiful!"

The women were peering at the window display of a large
shop, which announced itself as Salon Clichy in gold lettering over the door. A row of mannequins sported a range of

outfits from ball gowns to nightwear. What had struck Duval was a flowing white dress in the center of the window. She walked toward the entrance of the shop and opened the brass-handled door. Simone grabbed her by the arm.

"We can't go in there," she said.

"Of course we can—come on."

"Are you sure?"

Duval looked at her friend pityingly. "Yes. Come on."

They walked in and began to examine the dresses on display. Duval lifted the skirt of a white dress with a silver bow at the waist that appeared to be a copy of the one in the window. She ran her hands over the material, feeling the cotton-lined silk between her fingers. A woman assistant appeared at her side.

"Can I help you, madame?" she said.

"This is lovely. Who is the designer?"

"Frederick Levant. He's new. This is from his first collection. You like it?"

"Silk?" said Duval.

"Yes, madame."

"From?"

"China, madame."

"And the lining?" asked Duval.

"Egyptian cotton. But I am afraid . . ."

"What?"

The assistant shrugged her shoulders and looked at Simone as if for support.

"It is . . . rather expensive," she said, almost in a whisper.

"Quality comes at a price. I love it. What do you think, Simone?"

"It's beautiful, but . . ."

Duval smiled at the assistant. "I'll try it on."

"Madame, it's—"

"Expensive, I know. You told me. Where is the changing room?"

"Erm . . . It's three hundred, madame."

Duval turned to Simone, who saw sudden anger in the set of her friend's face. "Simone, did I just say I wanted to try this on?"

Simone looked nervously at the assistant and cast a quick glance at the door.

"You did, but she did say it was . . ."

Duval was not listening. She was striding through the shop, waving a beckoning hand at the assistant to follow her.

A few minutes later the heavy blue curtains of the changing room parted and Duval emerged. Simone put her hand to her mouth with a little gasp. Her friend looked elegant, almost beautiful. The dress glowed as it fell in a silken sheen from shoulder to ankle. The scalloped front looked scandalously revealing in the shop but would be a sensation on a ballroom floor, she thought. The assistant fussed around, smoothing the material down. Duval turned in a slow circle.

"It's wonderful. A perfect fit," said Simone.

"You don't think the cut is a little low?" said Duval.

The assistant adjusted the line of the bust slightly. "No, madame. I think your admirers will be very happy."

"What do you think, Simone?"

"I think your new friend will be entranced," she said.

"I'll take it," Duval said, and went back into the dressing room, followed by the assistant.

Simone looked at the well-dressed shoppers around them. She was embarrassed. Her friend did not have the money to pay and Simone knew such a shop would not accept credit. She feared a terrible scene and rather wished she could just go home and resume her drab and unexciting life. A bowl of soup and the latest romance novel in her ill-heated room were suddenly more appealing than an afternoon shopping dangerously with her new friend.

Duval emerged from the changing room trailed by the assistant, who began to wrap the dress in a cardboard box.

"Madame would like to pay now?" said the assistant.

"No."

The assistant stopped wrapping the dress and looked sharply at Duval. "No?"

Duval had crossed the floor of the shop and was staring at a long black cloak displayed on a mannequin. The cloak had a hood and was slightly open, revealing a bright silver lining. Duval opened the cloak to inspect it.

"This is beautiful," she said.

"Sealskin, madame, and the lining is silk."

"I'll try it on."

The assistant lifted her shoulders and dropped them with a theatrical sigh. She took the cloak off the mannequin and held it out as Duval slipped it over her shoulders.

"It's just the right size," said Duval as she looked at herself in a full-length mirror. She turned to her friend.

"Very elegant," said Simone.

"And no doubt very expensive," said Duval.

"Five hundred," said the assistant, with her hands on her hips and a look on her face that said she hoped this absurd episode would soon end.

"I'll take it," said Duval, opening her bag. She produced a printed address card and gave it to the assistant. There was a slight pause while the card was examined carefully, first one side and then the other.

The assistant frowned. "This is Mme Aupick's card."

Duval smiled and nodded. "My future mother-in-law."

The assistant looked at the card again and handed it back with a deferential little bow.

"Congratulations, mademoiselle."

Later that afternoon the two women drank strong coffee and ate marbled cake in a patisserie close to the Sorbonne.

"You didn't tell me you were getting married," said Simone.

"I didn't know myself until I saw that dress," said Duval. "More cake?"

Charles Baudelaire stood in the bedroom, fully dressed, with a black silk cravat tied around his head, masking his eyes. His cane and a leather portfolio lay on the bed. The room was lit with candles on either side of the bed. He turned his head at a voice from the bathroom next door.

"Don't take it off. No peeping."

The door opened and Duval came through, wearing the white silk dress. She had golden slippers on her feet. She walked up to him and lifted the mask over his head, threw it on the floor, and stepped back.

He looked at her solemnly for a few seconds and then walked slowly around her. She remained motionless. He completed the circle and said, "It's beautiful, the work of a true artist."

Duval gave a little skip of delight. "Let's go to La Chandelle. Everyone will be there."

"No," he said.

"Why not?"

"It's not appropriate."

"Meaning you don't want to be seen with me in front of your fashionable friends?"

"Meaning nothing of the sort. You gave me a nice surprise. Now I will give you one. Stand still."

He stooped, picked up the mask, and slipped it over her head.

"Don't move," he said, and left the room.

She heard noises from the drawing room next door and raised her head to listen. He returned holding the sealskin cloak and his sword stick. He drew the sword and placed the neck of the cloak on the tip of the blade, then let it swing in front of her. She turned her head to and fro to follow the movement in the air.

"What is it?" she said. "A present?"

He let the cloak brush against her face and she recoiled, tearing off the mask angrily.

"What are you doing? That's my new cloak! Put it down!"

Baudelaire dropped both sword and cloak on the floor. "It's not *your* cloak, is it? You bought it using my mother's name—false pretenses I think the police call it."

She bent down and picked up her cloak, throwing it onto a chair. "Don't lecture me about false pretenses. You're supposed to be a poet, aren't you? So where's all this poetry?"

Baudelaire flipped open the portfolio on the bed and pulled out a sheaf of handwritten pages.

"That is my poetry," he said. "That is my truth. That cloak cost five hundred francs. You bought it by telling the shopgirl we were going to be married! That is your lie."

"You steal from your mother all the time," she said. "Anyway, it's a lovely cloak. What's the matter with you? A sudden fit of morality, is that the problem?"

He put the sheaf of notes back into the portfolio, picked up the cloak, and threw it at her.

"Don't do that again," he said. "My mother is not stupid."

"Nor am I," she replied.

"I suppose Mother paid for the furniture as well?"

"You don't give a damn who bought the furniture."

"That's childish."

"You bring me here, tell me the apartment is mine, give me a key, and then vanish. Two days I have been here on my own. Not a word. I buy a table and a few chairs and suddenly you turn up and make a scene. Don't give me 'childish'!"

"Well, stop telling people we are going to get married!"

"Then you stop playing little games! Go off and write your filthy poetry— Oh yes, I've heard all about that—no wonder no one reads that rubbish. At least people listen to my songs."

Baudelaire thrust his face at her. "You can't even write your own name, can you?"

"I write my own songs!"

"They're not songs; they sound like the gurgle of gutter water."

She whipped round, stormed across the room, opened the portfolio, pulled out the sheaf of papers, and tore them in half, throwing the pages into the air.

They looked at each other across the bed, her panting in her white dress, him trembling at the sight of his torn poems on the floor.

He lunged at her. She darted sideways, stooped, picked up the sword, and turned. Breathing hard, he looked down at the point of the blade held against his chest. He brushed it aside with the back of his hand and dropped to his knees to pick up the torn pages.

"I wouldn't bother," she said. "No one is ever going to read them."

9

Poulet-Malassis hurried through the streets that November morning anxious to be on time for his appointment. He carried a valise and an umbrella, both of which slowed his progress through the crowds. He was not yet in the front rank of publishers in Paris, but his father owned one of the oldest printing presses in the country, dating back to the sixteenth century. In spite of such antique equipment, the family firm continued to publish both popular novels and the more serious work of young writers.

On his father's death, he had taken over the business at the age of twenty-eight. Two years later he had established a reputation as someone who was prepared to take a risk with new writers. As the young publisher quickly discovered, this was not a profitable business strategy, and he made sure that the firm continued to sell large numbers of what he regarded as trashy books for shopgirls.

Yet his ambition remained undimmed. He, Auguste Poulet-Malassis, heir to one of the oldest publishing businesses in France, was going to find the writer—playwright, poet, or novelist, it didn't matter—who would help the firm return to the commercial success and status it had enjoyed under the ancien régime. In those days, his father had produced beautifully bound books on history, art, and travel, which he sold successfully to the court of Louis XVI.

Poulet-Malassis intended to repeat the success. The best way to do this, he decided, was to join bohemian society and frequent the cafés and restaurants that young artists and writers seemed to regard as a first, rather than second, home. He would seek out talent where he had the best chance of finding it—and that meant living the life of the writers he hoped to commission.

As he was gifted with a quick wit and discovered both an appetite and a head for strong drink, it was not long before the publisher became an accepted part of the circle of writers and artists who spent their lives in cafés such as the Momus, the Tabourey near the Théâtre de l'Odéon, and a squalid place near the Saint-Sulpice church in the Latin Quarter called the Hôtel Merciol.

The bohemians dedicated themselves to the proposition that their art prevailed over such mundane necessities of life as earning money for food or clothes or rent. They took their calling seriously and looked down with contempt at the students from the Sorbonne, who played the role of impoverished artists by day and retired to comfortable homes in the suburbs at night.

The bohemians were able to sustain their quixotic lifestyle thanks to an understanding with the proprietors of their preferred cafés. The arrangement allowed them to treat such places as their private clubs, to exclude those they considered unsuitable company, and to enjoy open-ended credit. In return, the group would accept the presence of the tourists, the curious, and the hangers-on who wished to observe or sample the bohemian lifestyle. These paying customers kept the cafés in business and allowed the bohemians to pursue their ideal, namely that artistic success could only be achieved through commercial failure and poverty—and, in extreme cases, early death.

As he became familiar with this demimonde, Poulet-Malassis noted with amusement that the bohemians saw no contradiction between their ideals and the fawning admiration they bestowed on those of their number who had become rich and famous, such as Victor Hugo and Alexandre Dumas. Both writers had begun the decade of the 1840s as anxious for a free meal with wine at their chosen cafés as any other struggling artist. Success had not severed their bonds with fellow bohemians, however, much to the relief of the café proprietors. Not only did such famous men pay for their food and drink, but they were also generous in providing for their less fortunate companions and attracted even more tourists anxious to see famous writers in the flesh.

What the publisher was looking for was the next genius to emerge from this bohemian underworld, someone whose work he could profitably sell to a wider public as high art with popular appeal. The trick would be to engage a writer who could take the current fashion for Romantic art and turn it into something darker, more sensual, without alienating the public. And Poulet-Malassis thought he had found his man.

• • •

Baudelaire sat at the desk in his apartment writing with one of the thick nibbed pens that had only recently replaced quills. His hand moved swiftly over the paper. Every few minutes he would pause, chew the wooden end of the pen, scratch his chest, and then resume writing. As he finished each page, he pushed it onto the floor and drew a fresh sheet from the top drawer of the desk. The floor around him was strewn with sheets of paper on which lines of spidery hand-writing had scarcely dried. Poulet-Malassis sat on a chair in the corner of the room with his valise on his knees, reading through a pile of papers.

"I have the first draft here—can we work on that?" he said.

"No," said Baudelaire, without looking around.

"Well, may I give you an opinion?"

"If you must," said the poet.

"You have insulted the Church, made a mockery of the authorities, and portrayed women as . . . as . . ."

"As what exactly?" said Baudelaire.

"As sexual mannequins. Life-sized dolls dressed in the creations of your filthy, feverish mind."

Baudelaire laughed and turned in his chair. "So you like my little poems?"

"They're depressing, anguished, and sad. But I love them. They're fresh, earthy; they speak to the hidden depths of humanity; and, legally speaking, they're almost certainly ob-scene."

"Stop talking like a lawyer. You're going to be my pub-lisher, I hope. When will you bring them out?"

"We may need a lawyer when we do. Say next spring."

"Spring! It's only just fall. Bring the date forward. I need the money."

"We can offer an advance . . . a small advance."

"How much?"

"Say, two hundred francs."

Baudelaire sank his head into his hands.

"Two hundred francs! Dear God, that's hardly a couple of dinners at the Trois Frères."

Poulet-Malassis got to his feet and navigated his way across the sea of paper. He bent down and whispered in Baudelaire's ear.

"If you want money, my friend, write about nature: plants, flowers, trees, rivers, and mountains. That's what's selling these days. Not agonizing poems about death and damnation on the backstreets of Paris."

"Why are you whispering?"

"Because it's a secret, but one you don't seem to understand."

"I have no feelings for trees except for the warmth their logs provide in winter," said Baudelaire. "The countryside is simply mud and peasants. And it is always damnably cold too. As for plant life, the only vegetable that has ever been any use to me was a cucumber, and I would rather not tell you why."

"That's all right by me. We shall break with the past. But what are we going to call this collection? We need a title that will bring them through the door—once inside they will be surprised, shocked even, but they will go on reading. . . ."

"Since you would prefer me to be a pathetic, nature-loving Romantic, I shall call it . . . *The Flowers.* . . ."

"Excellent. *The Flowers* . . . I like it."

Baudelaire looked at his publisher and saw a younger man eager to please, desperate to succeed; a husband with a wife and two children somewhere in the suburbs; a businessman with the honor of a family firm to restore; a witty drinking companion who happily paid for the drinks in those long nights at the Café Momus; but he did not see a publisher who had read and fully understood his poetry. He did not write about the world Poulet-Malassis knew or even about a world familiar to his friends at the Momus.

His friends were simply acting out their own private fantasies, using free drink and cheap drugs to lose themselves in an endless melodrama in which every scene held up a mirror to their empty lives. They disgusted him: all of them, including the little grisettes, those girls who hung around, willing to bed anyone for the price of a meal and a glass of wine.

But was he any different? He drank with them, laughed and argued with them, took the same girls back to those sordid rooms at the Hôtel Merciol, where the sheets were stained and stiff with dried semen—sometimes three girls at a time.

They all loved it. They thought they were living the bohemian dream. They would spend whole days in a daze of hashish and nights talking revolution over bottles of rotgut wine. They were his brothers and he was just like them. He was a hypocrite. He disgusted himself. That was the truth. And that's where he found his poetry, in his dark, secret self, the self that would spend the day in his mother's elegant apartment and the night walking the backstreets, going to the houses where love was for sale and where he would buy a girl for an hour or so. He had been warned of the risks, but he didn't care. If he contracted venereal disease then so would every unknown poet and artist in Paris. It was all right for established writers such as Alphonse Lamartine and Charles Sainte-Beuve. They had made money and acquired mistresses. He admired these men for their success and in turn they recognized the talent in his earlier poetry. They would drink and dine together and at the end of the evening they would depart for the pleasure of a warm woman—wife, or mistress, it didn't matter—in a comfortable bed while he sought solace on the street. His monthly allowance rarely stretched beyond the first week. If he had no money for a brothel, he would pick up a grisette from the café and take her to the Merciol. They all did that. But was he really one of them? No. He was different. The difference was his despair. He wasn't really one of them at all.

"*The Flowers of Evil*," said Baudelaire.

Poulet-Malassis had watched Baudelaire for some months. The poet stood out among the drably dressed café crowd with his extravagant taste in clothes. He dressed like a dandy and indeed was happy to be described as one. His friends admired his eccentric dress sense as much as his insistence that sensual pleasures of sight, sound, and touch were as important as those of the flesh.

The publisher had heard about Baudelaire's poetry from several of the café crowd, but every time he had tried to arrange a meeting the poet had demurred, saying he was not ready and that he had more work to do. Then he would vanish and return a few weeks later to resume his sybaritic lifestyle.

He was said to have given readings in several cafés. Small

literary magazines had published some early verses, but Poulet-Malassis had been unable to persuade the poet to show him any of his work. Then a week ago a large brown package tied with ribbon and sealed with wax had arrived at his publishing house.

Inside were ninety untitled poems. Poulet-Malassis had glanced at them casually, planning to read them that night, but the first few lines told him they were quite different from any poetry he had ever read. He sat down in a state of excitement and read them all there and then. They were extraordinary. They offered such a savage contrast to the prevailing fashion for Romantic poetry that he doubted they would have any commercial value. The poet wrote about alienation, despair, and damnation as if they were central to human existence—scarcely the subject matter to attract a wide readership. But Poulet-Malassis saw the poems were also all about love.

"*The Flowers of Evil,*" he said. "Not exactly a title to appeal to our readers, is it? You may have something with the flowers, though. *The Flowers of Passion* perhaps, or *Flowers of Love*?"

"Love is a crime," said Baudelaire.

"Not a title I would care for," said Poulet-Malassis.

"Love is a crime that requires an accomplice. That is what is so infuriating."

"Nice line, but it's not a title. So you're in love?"

"Far from it," said Baudelaire. "But the fact is, she makes me happy. No, correction: she reminds me of a time when I was truly happy. Not the same thing at all. She's little better than a whore, of course. Maybe that's why I love her."

"And just who is this society slut?"

"No writer can have a society woman as a companion. They talk too much; they think too much of themselves. No, a writer needs either a good whore or a housekeeper to look after him, and I've got the whore."

"So you've fallen for a whore?"

"Lust is a passing fever, my friend; love is a long disease."

"I see. So we're feeling a little feverish?"

"Shall we just agree on the title? *Les Fleurs du Mal.*"

10

The bar at the Hôtel Meurice was marble topped and backed by a large gilt mirror, so that patrons could not only admire themselves but also see who was entering the room behind them. A clock was set above the mirror. Situated on the rue de Rivoli overlooking the Tuileries, the Meurice was one of the grand hotels of Paris and much favored by English visitors.

The founder, a coachman in Calais called Meurice, had made his fortune when wealthy English visitors returned to France after the defeat of Napoléon in 1815. Meurice quickly realized that, above all, the English wanted somewhere to stay in which they would be assured of comfort, brown beer, and staff who spoke English.

Thus the enterprising Meurice welcomed the cross-Channel arrivals in Calais with his self-taught English and put them on a coach for the thirty-six-hour journey to Paris. There they disembarked at his hotel, where all staff had been taught English. In return for this service, Meurice charged prices handsomely higher than those of any other hotel in Paris. This did not trouble his English visitors. They were happy to pay for the privilege of being able to order bacon and eggs for breakfast in their native language.

The Meurice, therefore, was not a hotel favored by the bohemian crowd across the river in the Latin Quarter. In fact, many of them, given the choice, would probably have voted to burn it down.

The one exception was Charles Baudelaire. He entered the Meurice with a feeling of real pleasure at the sight of the gilded furniture, elegant curtains, and liveried servants. Behind him he left the reeking, mud-spattered streets. Here, amid floral displays that breathed their fragrance over richly patterned Persian carpets, he felt at home. He recognized the absurd contradiction between his dress style and love of opulent beauty and the bohemian life he enjoyed—and "enjoyed" was the mot juste, he told himself—with his friends.

He saw himself as an outsider who could share the drunken reveries of his circle while maintaining a certain independence of mind. That said, he had come to share their increasingly hostile view of a society dominated by the court of King Louis Philippe. Baudelaire had raised his glass on many a drunken night to cries of treason and regicide in the Café Momus once the owner had gone to bed—usually with one of their grisettes by way of payment for the bar bill.

Baudelaire understood too that the political energy that now galvanized the bohemians was partly the result of their collective artistic failure. Very few of his friends had achieved any recognition from the critics in the Paris press, let alone commercial success. Failure fed talk of the need for change, not just of the monarchy but of the whole social order—from the merchant class that was bleeding the poor to the editors and publishers who ignored the work of struggling artists. They were all failures, he told himself, and only drink and drugs made that bitter knowledge bearable.

He walked through the hotel lobby, replying in English to the hall porter who asked if he needed help. Since his mother had been raised in London and had learned fluent English, she had passed the gift of that language on to her son. Baudelaire enjoyed being mistaken for an English tourist and he was well aware that, with his silver-knobbed sword stick and top hat, he looked the part. He also enjoyed the very occasional opportunity to speak the language. It was another thing he liked about the Meurice.

As he turned into the bar he immediately saw Jeanne Duval sitting on a stool with her back to him. She was accompanied by a man. From behind he could see her companion was well dressed. In the mirror he saw them both, hands on their drinks, heads close together, talking and smiling. The man whispered something to her and she laughed, placing her hand on his arm. His hand slid around her waist, drawing her closer to him, so that her stool tilted slightly.

Baudelaire walked up to the bar and slid onto a stool beside Duval. She looked up, frowned, and glanced at the clock. The man took his arm away.

"You're early," she said.

Baudelaire nodded at the man and said, "The clock's slow. Who's this?"

"Just a friend. Pierre, this is Charles Baudelaire. He's a poet. Charles—Pierre Martin. He's, ermm . . . what do you do again?"

"I'm in the theater," he said, and offered Baudelaire his

hand. "I have heard all about you. Your work is magnificent."

"You haven't read a word I've written," said Baudelaire. He nodded at the clock. "It's almost eight."

Martin took Duval's hand as she slid off her stool.

"Forgive my friend," she said. "He is a little overwrought."

Martin kissed her on both cheeks and said, "Just the two of us next time?"

She looked at Baudelaire and said, "Why not?"

"And just who was that?" said Baudelaire, loud enough for the departing Martin to hear.

"I told you, a friend. Anyway, now you're here—early for a change—what do you want?"

"I'd like to know why we are meeting here, for a start."

"I like it. It has style."

"It's the most expensive hotel in Paris."

"You think I'm paying?" She raised her glass to the barman. "Another glass of champagne, please."

The barman took the glass and looked inquiringly at Baudelaire, who nodded.

"You know what I want," Baudelaire said.

"First things first. You threw me out of my apartment—remember, the one you said was mine?"

The barman placed the two glasses of champagne on the bar top. He picked up a cloth and began polishing an already-gleaming flute-shaped glass. The conversation across the bar promised to enliven a dull evening.

"You've still got the key," Baudelaire said.

Duval dipped into her purse and brought out a small brown bottle. "And I've still got this. This is what you want, isn't it?"

She opened the bottle, poured some liquid into his glass, and replaced the bottle in her purse. The champagne bubbled into a froth and turned a dark brown. He drank, coughed, and reached for her bag. She pulled it back across the table. "And you've got something I want."

"Don't ask me for money," he said.

"What are you doing tomorrow night?"

"Going out with Mama and my stepfather."

"Going to . . . ?"

"Why?"

"Because you're going to a wedding ball on the Champs-Élysées." She handed him another drink. "And you're taking me."

"That's not possible."

"Everything is possible," she said, patting her purse.

11

In a large salon lit by many chandeliers, the ball was in progress. An orchestra played on a stage at one end while guests descended a sweeping red-carpeted staircase at the other. They handed one footman their cards, which were passed to a second footman, who bellowed out the names of the arrivals. The newly married couple received their guests at the foot of the staircase. Beside them waiters offered drinks on silver trays. Tables laid with crystal glass and silverware on white cloths lined both walls.

The married couple were finally making their way to their table when Baudelaire appeared at the top of the staircase. He was dressed in a black evening suit and carried his silver-knobbed cane. Beside him Duval wore her long white dress with the silver bow. An emerald, or what looked like an emerald, hung from a chain around her neck. Her black hair had been tied back, and long teardrop diamanté earrings fell on either side of her face. Baudelaire handed the footman his card.

"M. Charles Baudelaire and Mlle Jeanne Duval," the footman announced.

As they walked down the staircase, several heads had turned, but three guests at a table close to the orchestra showed a particular interest in the pair. Baudelaire and Duval took drinks from a waiter and walked slowly along one side of the ballroom. There was no question now of the stir they were causing. Lorgnettes were raised and small opera glasses slipped from evening bags.

Baudelaire bowed to the occasional acquaintance while searching the room for his table. He saw his mother seemingly deep in conversation with her husband, the general, and a third guest, a young woman. Taking Duval by the hand, he walked toward the table. The orchestra began to play a waltz and the dance floor filled up.

For a second or two Caroline Aupick feigned ignorance of the presence of her son. Then she looked up, apparently surprised. Her husband puffed on his cigar and lowered his head to examine the glass of wine before him.

"Good evening, Charles," she said. "I thought you were coming alone."

"I changed my mind."

"Would you care to join us?"

"No thank you, Mama. May I present Mlle Jeanne Duval."

Duval stepped forward and put out her hand. There was no reciprocal gesture from Mme Aupick. She let her hand fall back to her side.

"What a beautiful dress, Mlle Duval."

Duval looked pleased, mistaking the nature of the compliment. "Thank you. It's from the Salon Clichy."

"I know where it's from, Mlle Duval," said Mme Aupick.

"They have a new designer, Frederick Levant. He—"

"Frederick is a very talented young man, but I fear his business will fail."

"Really? You think so?"

"I do. He is too expensive. Fine clothes need not cost a fortune." She turned to her son. "I want you to meet one of our guests, Apollonie Sabatier."

Baudelaire knew the name but couldn't place it. She was young, with a fresh-faced milk-and-roses complexion and bright auburn hair falling in long ringlets to her shoulders. She looked at him and smiled. He took her hand, kissed it lightly, but said nothing. There was an awkward silence. Baudelaire turned to say something to his stepfather, but his place was empty. A cigar burned in an ashtray beside a half-drunk glass of wine. Mlle Sabatier looked away in silent embarrassment. Baudelaire picked up the half-smoked cigar and dropped it into the wine. He turned to his mother.

"My compliments to the general, Mama."

He put his arm around Duval's waist and steered her onto the dance floor.

A group of men stood smoking by their table, watching as the dancers flowed past, moving to the music like synchronized puppets. Baudelaire was dancing awkwardly with Duval, bumping into other couples. One of the men leaned forward, beckoning the others to do likewise, and whispered. They all laughed, holding on to one another as they guffawed.

A woman's voice silenced them. "Share the joke, gentle-men," said Apollonie Sabatier.

The group straightened up, coming to attention like sol-diers in front of an officer.

"We were just saying what a well-suited couple Charles Baudelaire and his new friend make," said one.

"Really? Personally, I think it's ridiculous bringing your whore to a ball."

Apollonie Sabatier walked off, leaving behind her a regis-ter of facial expressions from surprise to shock. The group of men immediately resumed their huddle.

Baudelaire held Duval close, shuffling slowly sideways across the floor, while those around them whirled to a fast waltz, the long dresses of the women opening into white clouds and the black tails of their partners flying between them like swallowtails.

"Your mother doesn't like me," said Duval.

"You can hardly blame her," he replied.

"She thinks I'm a whore. They all do. Look at them. The men want to fuck me and the women want to kill me."

Baudelaire stopped dancing, did a little jump, and threw his hands in the air.

"Hey! That's beautiful," he said.

"What is?"

"What you just said."

"Why?"

"Because it's true," he said. "Everyone here tonight is tell-ing lies. This whole charade is a lie. And you have just told the truth."

Ignoring the whirl of dancers around him, he kissed her passionately. She turned her head, breaking off the embrace, and pushed him away.

"You're embarrassing people. Come outside."

The music washed into the garden from the ballroom, where dancers could be seen through misted windows. They walked slowly across the lawn.

"This is really strange," said Duval.

He looked at her questioningly. "Why?"

"I don't know who you are."

"Of course you do."

"I know you're a poet; at least that is what everyone tells me," she said.

"What about you? I know you're a cabaret singer, but nothing more."

"So we are strangers. Good. Let's stay that way."

"We are hardly strangers. You're living in my apartment."

"The apartment you threw me out of?"

"And you are wearing the dress I bought you."

"The dress your mother bought me."

"And . . . ," said Baudelaire, leaning forward to whisper in her ear.

Duval looked shocked. "Such pleasures still leave us strangers."

"Exactly: I know nothing about you."

"Why should you?"

"Because I am curious."

"Very well. I come from Haiti," she said. "My father was

a French plantation manager and my mother a slave. That's all you need to know."

"But what happened? How did you get to Paris?"

She put a finger to his lips. "As they say in the casinos—*rien ne va plus.*"

"What about those scars on your back?"

She looked surprised for a second, then walked away, her voice trailing behind her.

"I was whipped. In public. In Port-au-Prince. The main square. It was raining. They stripped me and tied me to the leg of a cart. I felt the blood and the rain run down my legs. There were red puddles on the ground. The crowd cheered. At every lash they cheered."

"Why? What had you done?"

"It doesn't matter."

Baudelaire caught up with her and turned her toward him.

"You're shocked?" she said.

"Of course. How old were you?"

"Sixteen."

"That's shocking."

"Not really. It happened all the time. It was always the same. A white man with a whip and a black stripped and tied up. Always in public. What was shocking was that I . . . I found it . . . well, exciting. The crowd, the crack of the whip, my blood on the ground, the rain on my skin."

He took her face in his hands. "Pain and pleasure are royalty in the kingdom of lust."

Duval shook her head loose. "A line from one of your dirty little poems?"

Baudelaire didn't seem to hear her; he was looking at a young man on the far side of the garden, wearing full evening dress and smoking a cigar. "I want you to do something for me," he said.

"I'll do it for myself if I so please," she said.

"And you will be pleased. See that man over there?"

"Yes."

"I'd like you to . . ." He whispered to her.

She looked at the man and then back at Baudelaire. She opened the palm of her hand, spat into it, and slapped him hard across the face. He reeled back, tripped, and fell onto his back. She stood over him briefly, seemingly intent on kicking him, then walked away.

12

A light rain was falling on the rue du Bac and the café was crowded with ladies taking a midmorning break from their shopping. It was warm inside and there was an agreeable odor of damp garments, perfume, and coffee. The ladies were well dressed and the waiters suitably attentive. Jeanne Duval and Simone Clairmont were sitting at a corner table. Duval had unbuttoned her sealskin cloak, displaying the silver lining. Simone wore a sober gray dress.

"He's a squalid brothel creeper lucky enough to be born into money," said Duval. "He only wants me for his whore. Trust me, I know the type."

"Have you read his poems?" said Simone.

"Of course not."

"You should. They're beautiful, very sad—full of dreams of death. He is not living in this world, you know. He's somewhere else."

Duval looked at her friend sharply. "When did a country

girl start reading poetry? And anyway, how did you read his poems? They haven't been published yet."

"Magazines have printed some of them. I'll show you if you like."

"Don't bother. He will never make any money: poetry is supposed to be about love and beauty."

"Not with him. He's different. I think he will be famous."

"I don't care what he does," said Duval. "He can go and find himself a whore. That's all he wants. I've got a decent cloak and a dress out of that mother of his and that will do me."

Simone pointed at the emerald on the pendant.

"And a few sparklers to go with your nice new clothes?"

Duval sat back and laughed, her hair falling over her shoulders and her white teeth flashing in the dim light of the café. Those around her paused from their conversation to stare.

"Wait till his mother gets the jeweler's bill!"

Baudelaire, hatless, coatless, but still carrying his sword stick, pushed open the door of Le Rêve and walked straight past the man with the scarred face at the desk. He strode through the main room, where people were gathering for the evening show. He jumped onto the stage and went into the wings.

He didn't bother to knock on the dressing-room door but pushed it open with a crash. A woman with long dark hair stood with her back to him. Céleste was fastening her into a red dress. Baudelaire stood swaying in the doorframe. Céleste turned, as did the woman, both looking startled. For a

moment Baudelaire stared at them, trying to make sense of
what he was seeing.

"Where is she?" he said.

"Get out!" said the woman, reaching for a pot of makeup.

"She's long gone," said Céleste. "Now leave us."

Baudelaire searched bar after bar that night, concentrating
on those advertising musical entertainment or cabaret shows.
He combed the Latin Quarter on the Left Bank and then
worked through the cheaper clubs in the lightless streets
behind the Louvre. He felt obliged to have a drink or two in
every place he visited, and by midnight he was weaving wearily past a small two-story house with a flaring torch outside.
He raised his sword stick, placed it against the door, pushed,
and walked in. He found himself in a gaslit, smoky bar like
so many others. Young women were serving customers at
tables, and men were rolling dice and playing cards.

Baudelaire went to the bar, drew a small notebook and a
pencil pouch from his pocket, and laid it on the counter. He
fished a black crayon from the pouch and began to sketch.
The girl behind the bar pointed to a wine bottle and Baudelaire nodded. She poured a glass and set it down beside him.
Without taking his eye off the notepad, he reached for the
glass, drained it in one gulp, and resumed the sketch.

The face and upper body of a young woman took shape
on the page. She had a bow tied on top of black hair that had
been netted to fall to the base of the neck. She wore dark
hooped earrings. Her long-lashed eyes glanced sideways,
away from the artist, with an infinite sadness that found further expression in a wistful whisper of a smile on a wide

mouth. She wore a high-collared blouse with a bow tie. Her breasts were exaggerated, pushing out almost in separate directions over a belted wasp waist.

He finished the drawing and showed it to the bar girl, who was waiting impatiently for payment.

"Have you seen her?" said Baudelaire.

The girl shook her head. She rolled up the sketch and handed it back.

Behind him a voice said, "She's up at the Gare Saint-Lazare."

Baudelaire turned to face a middle-aged man, who from the suit he was wearing seemed to be the manager.

"Thank you," said Baudelaire, "but where?"

"There's a place called La Mer by the station. Watch yourself; the police are in there all the time."

Two crude paintings of mermaids framed the inner doorway of La Mer. Beyond was a horseshoe-shaped bar and a woman dressed as a mermaid serving drinks. She wore a tight green sheath dress on which scales had been crudely painted. Above her waist she was unclothed, but long black hair reached down to cover her breasts. Her face had been painted with green makeup.

As the woman moved around the bar, drinkers leaned forward, trying to touch her. She swatted them off like flies with flicks of her hands. Men sat smoking opium pipes on benches along the walls, which had been painted brown and amateurishly decorated with gulls, fishing boats, and leaping dolphins to form an unlikely backdrop. Two women, also dressed crudely as mermaids, moved among the drinkers and dope smokers, setting down pewter mugs of drink.

Baudelaire took in the scene for a minute and walked to the bar. He was very tired and very drunk. He beckoned to the mermaid to order what he promised himself would be the final drink of the evening. The mermaid moved toward him and stopped. They looked at each other. The mermaid began to laugh.

Jeanne Duval was still laughing the next morning. She couldn't help it. The sight of the supposedly great poet, ashen faced with drink, swaying at the bar of a dope den, staring unbelievingly at a bare-breasted mermaid, was more than amusing—it was great comedy.

His face had frozen in fury when he finally recognized her, and a night's sleep had done nothing to soften the expression. She looked at him sitting in their apartment—well, her apartment, if you believed him. It was almost noon and he was slumped in a chair, wearing a robe and sipping a glass of wine. And still looking furious. It served him right. If he treated her like a whore, she would behave like one. He was a spoiled brat, she realized, a mummy's boy who would sink into a sulking rage if denied exactly what he wanted. She started to laugh again and threw herself on the chaise longue.

"It's not funny," he said. "I spent three weeks looking for you."

"You should have left me alone. I come from the gutter, remember?"

"Which is where I found you."

"Thank you," she said.

"You had no right to vanish like that."

"Mermaids swim where they want."

She stopped laughing, got to her feet, picked up a small satchel, and walked to a table. She ran a finger over a number of bottles, chose one, and poured two glasses of wine.

"Come here."

Baudelaire looked at her sulkily and did not move. Duval took a small white linen bag from the satchel, opened it, and sprinkled white powder into the wine. Baudelaire got up and walked toward her.

She knows I can't resist, he thought. In this disgusting world crammed with everything that is ugly, the only thing that can make me smile is a little opium, an old and terrible mistress; and like all mistresses she lifts you to heaven one minute and betrays you the next.

Duval made him happy too. He didn't know why. He had slept with dozens of women—wealthy ladies from fine families, mistresses of the famous, and then there were the whores working out their lives in the brothels of the Left Bank. Why were they different from her? He didn't know. And he didn't care.

13

Revolutionary fervor gripped Paris in the first months of 1848. Ordinary people knew that their fathers and grandfathers had forged history in the Revolution and the Terror that followed. But where were the fruits of their sacrifice? In the taverns and cafés of the poorer parts of the city, the question could be heard repeatedly: for what had their forebears stormed the Bastille? Many hundreds had died that day in 1789 when a prison infamous for torture and maltreatment of its inmates had fallen to the mob. Fifty-nine years later, what had been achieved?

The Great Revolution, the rise and fall of Napoléon, the overthrow of the restored monarchy, and further uprisings against various Bourbon offshoots of the ancien régime had left the people of the city very much where they were before: impoverished, powerless, and at the mercy of a corrupt elite backed by the army and police. Even after working a fifteen-hour day, people did not have enough money to put food on the table for their families. The daily lines of people waiting for bread handouts from local churches lengthened across the city.

A return to the barricades was inevitable. People talked of nothing else. A speaker only had to mount a wooden crate on a street corner for an angry crowd to gather. Publishing houses were churning out adulatory histories of the 1789 Revolution. Established writers such as Chateaubriand sneered at these efforts to "gild the guillotine," but public opinion and his fellow writers were against him. In the summer of 1847 the grand old man of French poetry, Lamartine, predicted that the monarchy of Louis Philippe would face a "revolution of contempt."

That autumn Alexandre Dumas staged a successful play, *Le Chevalier de Maison-Rouge,* that extolled the triumphant nationalism of the Revolution and ignored its blood-soaked excesses. The king, meanwhile, spent more and more time at various hunting châteaux around Paris and at his official residence at Saint-Cloud—a good twenty miles from the city. His absence emboldened the mob and enraged the Parisian shopkeepers, who depended on lavish royal expenditures for much of their income.

On the Left Bank the bohemians talked only of revolution. Baudelaire was initially cautious and resisted joining the general clamor for a republic to replace the monarchy. Although he had published little poetry, his art criticism had won warm approval from café society in the Latin Quarter and also from the elegant salons of the Right Bank. This was a considerable achievement, and he was listened to with respect when he poured scorn on the Paris mob.

"They're just children," he said. "It makes no difference

to them who rules France. King, emperor, or a Jacobin ty-
rant like Robespierre—what does it matter to the mob?"

Le Vavasseur raised his bulk from the back of the room.

"Are you saying we shouldn't care about what is happening in the street?"

"I'm saying it is easy to call for the overthrow of the king
from the comfort of a coffee shop."

"Meaning only starving peasantry have a right to political
views?"

"An artist can have no political convictions," Baudelaire
told them loftily. "His art is his revolution. Beauty is the
ideal to which the artist must aspire. He achieves that ideal
through great painting, poetry, and prose."

"Charles, you talk pompous nonsense. Sit down and have
a drink."

And they laughed at him, just as they teased him for
dressing like a dandy while fleeing his creditors. Baudelaire
conceded that he and Duval had had to give up the expensive rooms in the Hôtel de Lauzun and were now living in
cheaper lodgings. It was also true that he was forced to move
regularly to avoid his creditors. He was, he reflected, a man
on the run from the ignorant parasites who would not give
him time to achieve the success that was due to him. He
would become famous and they would get their money. It
was a question of time, but as his favorite clock reminded
him, it was always later than you thought.

As the moment of truth approached for the king and his
government Baudelaire's outward contempt for the revolu-
tionaries concealed a growing excitement. He felt history
was on the move and he did not want to be left behind. It

was in Paris that he found his poetry, and if the city was about to enter another violent convulsion that redefined the political order he wanted to be part of it.

That was one reason why, when the barricades went up and the killing began, Baudelaire would play a much more prominent role in the revolution of 1848 than most of his contemporaries—to the surprise of his friends, and the rage of his mother.

The only person not surprised by the spectacle of a poet on the barricades was Jeanne Duval. They had argued long and fruitlessly about the inevitability of revolution. She reminded him that she had lived through one; she had seen the killing and the blood-smeared walls against which prisoners had been shot. She didn't want to live through that again.

"Why can't this country just change?" she asked. "Why does it always have to be so bloody?"

"Because this is France," he said. "Don't you understand our history—what happened in '89?"

"Of course I understand. Without '89 we would not have freed ourselves in Haiti, but our revolution was thrown away; it became anarchy. My father fled, my mother was murdered, and I had to escape."

"And they whipped you."

"Yes, I was whipped."

"When?"

"When, where, why, what does it matter? You just want the details, don't you?"

She knew he enjoyed that story. She had told it to him many times. How many lashes? Who delivered them? What did the crowd do? He always asked those questions and listened intently to the answers. What did that make him, a sadistic voyeur? It didn't matter. She forgave him, as he forgave her. His wild, irrational nature entranced her. He lived the life of a hedonist but gave vent to a flinty morality that damned the excesses and hypocrisies of the age. He had contempt for politicians as much as for the mob yet yearned for direct action to bring about change.

One day late in January that year, he and Duval were walking the streets as usual, warily conscious that anarchy was close at hand.

They passed a noisy crowd around a speaker on the corner of a street near the pont Marie. Fists punched the air as the speaker whipped up his audience with bellowed questions. Soldiers of the National Guard in red and white uniforms with muskets over their shoulders slouched around the crowd. Baudelaire watched them carefully. The soldiers were listening with evident sympathy to the shouted list of grievances that were feeding the fury of the crowd.

Duval stood beside him dressed in her sealskin cloak. She held his arm tightly. She didn't like mobs. She had seen too many in the violent days back in Haiti. She was glad Baudelaire was dressed inconspicuously in black for a change but carried as usual his silver-knobbed sword stick.

"Did the Great Revolution finish the monarchy?" shouted the speaker.

"Yes!" yelled the crowd.

"Did Madame Guillotine slice off that bastard king's head?"

"Yes!"

"And has another Bourbon king crawled his way back to the throne of France?"

"YES! YES! YES!"

"And do we know what to do with him and his slimy family?"

"The guillotine!" yelled the crowd.

Duval shivered. These people were desperate, she thought; they wanted blood, just like the slave mobs back in Haiti. There might be good reason for their anger, but the blood on the streets would soon be theirs. She tugged at Baudelaire's arm. They pushed through a press of people into a street leading to the Seine. The roar of the crowd followed them as they walked to the river and turned onto a broad footpath.

"It's the same old story. It's going to be a revolution without a revolution. Robespierre used that argument to justify the Terror," said Baudelaire.

"I think you're hiding behind your cynicism. You're frightened of what you really think."

"Wrong. I have no political convictions, because I have no ambitions for my country. Politicians crave public approval for their good works. That makes them cowards. They fear failure. They compromise. They trample on their own good intentions."

"Don't be such a poseur, Charles. Do artists really not care about history? Doesn't it matter to you that in thirty years France has been through revolution, terror, and empire, only to return to the monarchy the Revolution was supposed to end? Are these just minor distractions while you contemplate the pursuit of beauty?"

That was the trouble with women, he thought. They always know more than you think and talk more than they should. He had picked up his Black Venus in some backstreet cabaret club and now she was becoming his critic. She'd be trying to write poetry next.

They were walking under the arch of a bridge being built over the newly embanked river. A group of men dressed in rags, their faces begrimed with dirt, were lying under the arch. They could be refugees from the countryside, homeless, or convicts on the run—Baudelaire didn't know which. But he knew they stank of sweat, urine, and shit. Their smell was a weapon.

Baudelaire took her arm and turned her to face him. He was a little rough, but she knew how frustrated he became when trying to express ideas that opened up in his mind like wildflowers after rain. He became excited and angry when people didn't see what he was trying to say. He always claimed he only found his voice when writing, and especially when writing his poetry. Great ideas broke over him like waves, he said, but his spoken words were no more than empty shells on the shore.

"Glorious empires are founded on crime and violence," he said. "Look at Napoléon. He enslaved Europe. Look at the English, greedily guzzling backward countries in the name of Christian morality, but actually doing so for profit. Don't tell me it makes any difference to a peasant whether he is ruled by a French dictator or an English king. He is born in misery and dies in misery. And in between this is how he lives!"

Baudelaire swung her round to face the group of beggars. She shook him off angrily. There was a murmur among the

men and they got to their feet, sensing an opportunity to secure the price of their next meal from the strangers suddenly
in their midst. They began shuffling closer.

"That's it, is it?" she said. "The suffering mass of humanity can rot in poverty for all eternity while you and your artistic friends contemplate man's immortal soul?"

Baudelaire looked at her, this woman he had rescued from
misery, upon whom he had lavished clothes and jewelry, and
who was now turning against him. What had he told Poulet-
Malassis? An artist needs a whore or a housekeeper and he
had rightly chosen the whore? Well, he was wrong.

"You're from the gutter. You wouldn't understand," he
said. "You would open your legs for this lot if they gave you
a sou."

In the distance the roars of the crowd could still be heard
demanding the guillotine for Guizot, the prime minister.

She pushed him away and was about to follow through
with a well-aimed kick when he raised his cane and pointed it
at the men. There was a low collective growl from the group,
who were beginning to think that events in the city had presented them with an opportunity for rather more than their
next meal.

The five of them slouched forward slowly like hyenas and
began to circle them, two at the front and three moving behind.

Duval took his arm, tightening her grip.

"Don't say anything. Leave it to me," he said.

The leader of the gang wore a long, greasy ponytail and
had a livid scar that ran down his cheek from his right eye to
the beard line, a saber slash from a battle long ago. The men
murmured among themselves as he stepped forward and

touched Duval's cloak, opening it to show the shiny silk lining. She slapped him as hard as she could, a stinging blow that hurt her hand. The man stepped back, rubbing his cheek and grinning toothlessly at her. The murmuring rose to an angry growl. Then all five men attacked.

Baudelaire leaped forward, holding his sword stick like a club. Before he could use it a blow from behind felled him. He sank to the ground in a flurry of fists. His sword stick rolled away over the edge of the path into the line of reeds. Two men knelt down. One lifted his head by the hair and banged it against the ground. Then they went through his pockets, tearing off his pocket watch and finger rings.

Three men backed Duval against the arch. Two of them pinioned her arms behind her back while the man with the scar tore open her cloak. He ripped the bonnet from her head and snapped the emerald pendant from her neck. His hands ran over her body like rats, groping, pinching, and squeezing.

She screamed, but he clamped a hand over her mouth. She bit hard and heard a string of curses. The man with the ponytail looked at his bleeding hand, clenched it in a fist, and punched her. She turned her face, taking the blow on her cheek, and slid down the wall. She felt them pulling her boots off. Her bonnet was stuffed in her mouth. All five men were around her now, opening their filthy trousers and arguing among themselves in a dialect she did not understand.

Baudelaire came to, shook his head, ran his hands over his torn clothes, and looked at them. There was no blood. He looked toward the arch. Duval was bloodied, her clothes torn, but she had half got to her feet with her back to the wall. He looked around but couldn't see the sword stick;

then he rolled over several times in her direction. He got up unsteadily and charged, flinging himself at the group with a roar of anger.

The men fell back and scattered, only to regroup and encircle him. Duval was forgotten for a moment. She crawled away toward the river, toward the reed bed.

The gang was in a tight circle around Baudelaire. They pushed him, kicking and struggling, back against the wall. The scarred man produced a knife and spat on the blade. He wiped the knife against his trousers and walked up to Baudelaire.

The roar from the crowd in the distance was getting louder. Cries of, "Death to the king and all tyrants!" floated down to the river and found a muttered echo from the men now poised in a semicircle around their victim. They urged their leader into action speaking now in a common gutter patois.

"Kill him! Stick the knife in and watch him squirm! Slit his throat—quick!"

Duval was on all fours now, pushing her hands into the reed bed. She thought she had seen where the sword stick had fallen, but it wasn't there.

Two men held Baudelaire's arms as the gang leader stepped up.

"You hear that?" he said, nodding in the direction of the crowd.

Baudelaire, still struggling, spat at him. The scarred man stepped back, wiped the spittle from his face, and raised his knife.

Duval's hand closed around the handle of the sword stick. She drew it from the reed bed, got to her feet, and pressed the silver button. The knob popped up and she drew out the shiny eighteen-inch blade.

The men had pulled Baudelaire's head back, exposing his neck to the knife that was now pressed against his throat.

A hand from behind gripped the scarred man's ponytail and pulled hard, yanking his head back. He twisted and turned and felt the sharp point of the stiletto sword resting for a second against his upper back. Twisting his head farther in the last murderous moment of his life, he saw Duval behind him. The sword slid into his back and straight through his body as she pulled him onto the weapon. The man gave a deep sigh as he sank to the ground.

Duval pulled the stiletto sword from the twitching body. The blade was dripping with blood. The remaining four gang members stared at her in horror. They seemed paralyzed with disbelief. Baudelaire looked at her, mouth open in amazement. The men suddenly came to life and fled, stumbling along the riverside, looking back as they ran to confirm what had just happened.

Baudelaire stepped away from the wall and brushed himself down. He seemed unnaturally calm. Duval had dropped the bloodied blade and was beginning to shake and sob. He put his arm around her and looked down at the dead man.

"Oh God, what have I done?" she said.

"You had to do it. He was going to kill us both," said Baudelaire.

He bent down and picked up the sword blade. He walked over to the reeds fringing the path and pushed it several times into the mud; then he slid it back into the scabbard. She began to rearrange her clothing and do up the few buttons she had left.

"Take me home," she said, and began to cry again.

"Just let me get rid of him," said Baudelaire.

He used his feet to roll the corpse toward the river, pushing it through the reeds into the water. Then he looked around carefully. His watch lay on the ground, but the rest of his jewelry and hers had gone.

She huddled into him as they began to walk away. They saw the body floating past them down the river.

14

Baudelaire was late. He walked fast along the boulevard, pausing occasionally to look at his pocket watch. After the attack he had taken Duval back to their lodgings, where they had both drunk generously laced wine. He never knew where she got it from and he didn't ask. He just paid. She was suffering from shock and complained of stomach pain. She had taken more laudanum and some pills and fallen into a deep sleep. He should have stayed with her, he told himself, because the whole city seemed on the edge of an abyss. Crowds of people who ought to have been at work were milling around aimlessly. National Guard troops were stationed at all major road junctions and he could see regular army soldiers positioned on the rooftops of government buildings. But he had an urgent appointment.

He thought over the extraordinary events of that morning. His father had always told him that his old sword stick would come in useful one day. But he hardly thought his mistress would use it to save his life. She had done it so calmly! And the blade slipped in beautifully! He was slightly jealous. It should have been him sliding the sword so cleanly through those disgusting rags into the gang leader's back. He wondered what it felt like, to kill a man like that. She knew now. He still couldn't quite believe it. His Black Venus was now a murderess! The bastard had left her no choice, of course, but that wasn't the point.

Caroline Aupick and Apollonie Sabatier were taking afternoon tea at a carefully prepared table. Pretty china teacups and a silver sugar bowl and milk jug had been placed on a white linen tablecloth. A small china cake stand rose in three levels, each offering different pastries. A maid poured the tea. The drawing room of the Aupick apartment had French windows that gave on to a small south-facing terrace. Apollonie looked radiant in the soft winter light that streamed through the windows. Her hair glowed like burnished copper and fell in silken curls around her face. Her face was round, with a clear pale-pink complexion that would have looked well on a girl ten years younger. Her eyes were gray-green, and spoke of an older and wiser woman than her looks suggested. She sipped her tea.

"I am sorry. He's late. It's always the same," said Caroline Aupick.

"I have never met an artist who paid any attention to time," Sabatier said.

There was a knock at the door and the maid entered to announce that a guest had arrived. Baudelaire walked in and went straight to his mother, bending down to kiss her lightly on both cheeks.

"You know Apollonie Sabatier," said Mme Aupick.

"Of course," he said, and lowered his head in a small bow to the lady.

"We met at the ball, I think," she said.

"Indeed," Baudelaire said, and walked to the windows.

"Sit down, Charles," said his mother. "We're having tea."

"There is going to be a revolution, Mama," he said. "Very soon. Maybe tonight. There are soldiers everywhere."

"It's midwinter," said Sabatier. "It's too cold for a coup. They'll wait until July, when it's hot and people remember the Bastille."

Baudelaire sat down and took a cup of tea offered by his mother. He smiled at Sabatier.

"You are looking lovely," he said. "Quite beautiful. Perhaps you should leave Paris. Stay with Mama in Honfleur."

His mother sat back in her chair and smiled her approval.

Sabatier blushed at the compliment. "Thank you. I'm not afraid of the mob, M. Baudelaire."

Baudelaire rose to his feet, spilling his tea. He began to pace the room.

"Nor me," he said. "Bring on the mob. Let them storm the Tuileries and rip those Bourbon pigs to pieces. Let them tear up the streets of Paris and hurl paving stones at the grotesque apology of a police force. Excellent. I shall witness the whole ludicrous spectacle with delight."

Sabatier looked surprised. "I didn't know poets delighted in violence."

Baudelaire flung himself back in his chair.

"There is a certain charm in the surreal, Mlle Sabatier.

There is nothing more absurd than the sight of the great unwashed of Paris destroying one dictatorship, then bowing down before another. Infantile destruction, I think they call it."

Caroline Aupick frowned. Her son as usual was getting overexcited. The last thing she wanted to talk about that afternoon was politics.

"Well, I shall be going to Honfleur," she said. "I have lived through one revolution. Another doesn't worry me. You are right: the mob is absurd. But Paris is impossible. The shops are shut. No one is working. Perhaps, Apollonie, you will accompany me to the sea and stay for a while. You too, Charles. I will expect you there. We will have time to talk. You never come these days."

Baudelaire returned to the window. So there it was, he thought, Mama's arrangement for my future. I am to spend a few weeks in Honfleur making love to Apollonie Sabatier. A respectable mistress, a woman with taste and refinement, well known in the literary world. She has an eye for talented young artists and chooses many as her lovers. They come and go, but they always remain friends. Yes, Apollonie is that rare woman whose sexuality is enhanced by her kindness. They say she will only invite those she has slept with to her Sunday lunches at the rue Frochot apartment. She rather enjoys the sexual frisson this creates among her guests. But nobody seems to mind and she has no enemies. Someone sculpted her once, nude from the waist up. There was quite a scandal when the bust went on display. Those firm, rounded breasts drew big crowds. And now they are to be mine for the rest of the winter. If I can stand a month by the sea. A month away from my Black Venus. But I shall get my money. And the pharmacist may prove more helpful this time. He'd better be. It could be worse.

He turned. "Excellent, Mother," he said. "I look forward to it."

There was little for sale at the vegetable market at the eastern end of rue du Vieux-Colombier, close to the Luxembourg Gardens. Long lines had formed at stalls offering nothing but potatoes, cabbages, and parsnips. Vendors had raised prices to impose a crude form of rationing, but this served only to exasperate their customers further. A vendor broke off an argument with a woman at the head of a line for the few remaining cabbages and onions and clambered onto his barrow to address his customers.

"Nothing is coming in from the country!" he shouted. "There is no transport. That is why the prices are high. So if you don't want to pay, make way for those that do."

The woman who had been at the head of the line shouted back at him, "Your kind will pay for this—and soon!"

The stallholder jumped down and picked up an onion. "No, madame," he said. "You'll pay for this—now, if you want it! If you don't, there's plenty behind you who will pay."

The woman left and Duval stepped forward to take her place.

"Three onions, please," she said.

The man put the vegetables in a straw bag and handed

them over. She gave him some money and walked away fast through the crowd. Baudelaire pushed past people to catch up with her. She did not turn her head but increased her stride.

"It's only for a month, for God's sake," he said.

"You think I don't know?" She spat out the words, not deigning to look at him.

"Know what?" he said.

"Who you're going with."

"I am not going with anyone. I'm staying with my mother, and God knows that will be a penance. And I can get some stuff there."

"You're going to be with that Sabatier woman, aren't you?"

"Who told you that?"

"Your mother's maid, if you must know. On instruction, no doubt. It's your mother's charming way of telling her son's whore to get lost—because she's found a better whore for you. A white milkmaid of a whore."

Baudelaire pulled her to a halt.

"You're all I want," he said. "But I have to go away with Mama. It's the only way I am going to get my money—or some of it. Do you have any stuff on you?"

"And your whore?"

"She's not a whore. She's not mine and, yes, she will be there."

"I am going to see her—to tell her there's only one thing that makes you happy."

She dipped a hand into her satchel and pulled out a sachet, opened it, licked a finger, and dipped it into the sachet.

She smeared white powder on her tongue and wiggled it at him, then closed her mouth.

"The taste of love on the tip of my tongue. That's all you want, isn't it?" she said.

Baudelaire seized her and started kissing her.

15

The two sleeping figures seemed almost one in the semi-darkness. Their heads lay on the same pillow and their bodies formed a single shape beneath the blankets. A gray light filtered into the room through closed shutters. The sound of a loud explosion woke the sleepers. A second later the shutters rattled in the shock wave. Ragged cheering broke out in the street. There was another explosion and more cheering. Baudelaire sat up suddenly, shaking off the sheets. Duval stirred beside him. He leaped out of the bed naked, opened the shutters, and looked down.

A large crowd had gathered around a barricade of up-turned carts, furniture, and wooden beams. They were hacking up paving stones and cobbles. Many of the crowd were throwing missiles over the barricade at a group of soldiers gathered at a crossroad. The troops seemed uncertain how to respond. One soldier ran up to the barricade and threw a grenade. The iron sphere, the size of a coconut, threw off a trail of sparks and smoke as it arced through the air. The crowd scattered as the grenade landed and rolled down the street before exploding. Amid more cheering, the crowd regrouped.

Baudelaire closed the shutters, locked them, and ran around the room picking up his clothes. He dressed with frantic haste. Duval raised herself sleepily in the bed. The sound of shooting could be heard from the street.

"Where are you going?" she said.

"It's started. Stay here."

"I thought you said the mob was absurd."

"They are. But I still want to get rid of this bastard king." He opened the door.

"Hey, you forgot something!" she said, pointing to his sword stick in the corner.

"Keep it. I need a gun."

In the few minutes it took Baudelaire to dress and reach the street, the mob had surged beyond the barricade and begun looting a bread shop close to the crossroad. The soldiers had vanished, although one or two of the crowd seemed to be deserters who had taken off their National Guard uniforms. Baudelaire looked wildly out of place in a yellow waistcoat, velvet evening jacket, and brown trousers.

The looters moved on to a clothes shop. People were staggering out with armfuls of clothing. Baudelaire stopped a man carrying a box of dresses.

"There is a gunsmith's on rue Harcourt," Baudelaire said. "Five minutes from here. If we're quick, we can get there first."

The looter dropped the clothes and turned to the crowd. "Follow me to the gun shop!" he yelled.

There was already a crowd when they arrived at the gun shop. They had broken down the wooden grille over the front and were now smashing the windows. A row of modern rifles stood amid the shattered glass. As the looters started passing out the weapons, Baudelaire shouldered his way through the throng to the front of the line and grabbed a rifle, wrestling it away from two other looters. From inside the shop people were passing out handguns, hunting knives, and ammunition.

Baudelaire walked down the rubble-strewn street with the rifle in one hand and a bandolier of ammunition around his waist. Broken glass crunched under his feet. Bodies were lying everywhere, some on the street as if they had suddenly gone to sleep, others hanging halfway out of the very shopfronts they had been looting.

There was no sign of any wounded. Those who could move were helped away, while those who remained were shot out of hand. The looters paid no attention to their dead comrades but continued picking over the furniture, ruined clothing, and household goods that covered the sidewalks. At the far end of the street troops were pulling down a barricade.

So this was what a revolution looked like, he thought. It was madness. They said the king would be gone before nightfall. Exactly what they had all been calling for, but then what? Another Napoléon would be acclaimed by the shopkeepers and landowners. There would be a massacre of the mob. Those who survived would drag themselves back to the slums. Law and order would be restored. A revolution without a revolution. This was history as farce. So why was he involved? What was he, a poet in search of the higher beauty, doing here? He was here because this was the ideal time for revenge. Madness? Yes, maybe he was a little mad, like everyone else in Paris this February of 1848.

A shout from across the street stopped Baudelaire. He saw Poulet-Malassis walking toward him with a bundle of manuscripts and some books under each arm. Baudelaire ran to meet him.

"What are you doing here?" he said.

"I might ask you the same question. And that gun?"

"I am going to say good-bye to my stepfather. A final adieu," said Baudelaire.

Both men moved off the street and ducked into a deep doorway beside a shop as a volley of shots scattered the looters.

"General Aupick?" said the publisher incredulously.

"He's in charge of them," said Baudelaire, nodding to a group of soldiers.

"What, with a gun?" said Poulet-Malassis.

"Nothing says good-bye like a bullet. He's a three-star general—my contribution to the revolution."

"I am sure the mob will be most grateful," said Poulet-Malassis. "Where exactly are you going to find this three-star general?"

"He'll be behind one of the barricades, directing the troops."

"You're completely bloody mad: running around the streets trying to shoot a three-star general because he married your mother! Now, give me that gun and go home, and while you're at it, take these and put them somewhere safe."

The publisher thrust a bundle of manuscripts and books at him. Baudelaire shrugged, took them, unslung his rifle, and handed it over. The two men peered out of the doorway and looked carefully up and down the now-deserted street. It was quiet, although distant explosions and occasional gunfire could be heard.

They stepped into the street and almost immediately half a dozen looters turned the corner ahead of them, pursued by several soldiers. Poulet-Malassis and Baudelaire flattened themselves back into the doorway as the pursued and the pursuers ran past.

"We had better stay here for a while," said Poulet-Malassis. "If it makes you feel any better, I am going to publish your poetry next year. Your *Fleurs du mal,* as you insist on calling them. So when we get out of here, go home and finish them."

"The king will be dead or in exile by nightfall and you want to talk about poetry!" said Baudelaire.

"I rather think most of the mob will be dead or in jail by nightfall. And no doubt we will have another Napoléon in the Tuileries in a few weeks. Now to my question: will you be ready?"

Baudelaire sighed. In the nicest possible way, his publisher was mad. But then the whole world had gone mad. He had eighty finished and revised poems ready. He needed at least thirty more. But the creditors were being bloody-minded as usual and his mother wanted him to spend time with her on the coast. And that was how they left it. Poulet-Malassis

concealed the gun under his coat and walked in one direction and Baudelaire in the other.

The soldiers did not stop him as he walked home through
the wreckage of the Latin Quarter. As he was wearing his
strange clothes and had a bundle of papers under his arm,
they took him for a professor from the Sorbonne.

He was lucky. Those looters who had not been killed or
dragged away by their comrades had been tied to drainpipes
or gas-lamp brackets, their faces smeared with their own
blood, and left to die.

Baudelaire looked with pity at these poor creatures. His
mother had told him that in London until recently captured
pirates would be staked out on the Thames foreshore at low
tide and crowds would gather to drink beer and watch them
drown as the tide rose. "Come hell or high water" was the
saying. It was barbaric, she had told him. And here in Paris
we are doing almost the same thing. It was madness, but the
madness has ended, he thought, and so has mine.

For a moment he really had wanted to shoot the bastard;
years of resentment had bubbled up like lava from an old
volcano—exactly the same rage that sent the mob to the barricades. And it would have been a perfect opportunity. Aupick was a brave old soldier. He had always worn his uniform,
even in the heat of battle during those years in Algeria; firing
an anonymous bullet from some barricade would not have
been difficult. Then Baudelaire could have had his mother
back. They could sort out his debts, maybe live together
again.

An impossible dream, of course, like those of the miserable slum poor who had fought for a better life on the barricades. I am a writer, a poet, an artist, he told himself, a man of letters, not a revolutionary. In any case, the revolution is over; the mob has been crushed. The troops are said to be shooting any civilian they see with any kind of weapon, especially a gun. He hoped poor Poulet-Malassis would be all right. He should never have given him that gun.

Baudelaire reached the door of his lodgings in an old house on rue du Sentier. The days of comfort in a suite in the Hôtel de Lauzun had long gone. He had been reduced to a single ground-floor room pervaded by the stench and noise of the street. Jeanne Duval was in the roadway remonstrating with a group of men who were passing furniture through the window and loading it onto a cart. This had been a regular feature of the sixteen years they had lived together. Some things never change, he thought, my bastard creditors, to start with.

16

Cheap hotel rooms always looked like this. The paint on the walls was a dirty white and had begun to peel like bark from an old tree. There was just enough room between the bed and the wall for a small table on which sat a candle that had almost burned down to the wick. A cracked mirror hung above a small corner basin. The bed was low and the mattress sagged down, almost touching the floor.

A few flies circling just below the ceiling appeared the real occupants of the room. Dust lay in a thick layer on closed shutters that allowed in a low light. Baudelaire lay naked from the waist up on the bed, staring at the circling flies. Duval was washing laundry in the basin. She pummeled and squeezed the clothes with an angry vigor quite unrelated to the task in hand.

"It won't be for long," he said.

"A day would be too long in this rat hole."

"We will be out of here soon. I'm going tonight and I'll be back with the money in a few days."

"Leaving me here? Thank you very much."

"What do you want me to do?"

"Get an advance from Poulet-Malassis. He wants to publish, doesn't he? He'll give you money."

Baudelaire shifted up the bed and opened his arms to her.

"Come here."

"No. First some money, a new apartment, clean clothes. Remember those things?"

"All right, all right, but let me have some stuff."

Duval balled up the wet washing and threw it at him.

"Get it yourself," she said, and left, banging the door.

Like his father before him Auguste Poulet-Malassis ran his business from the first two floors of a house in the rue de Buci, close to the Latin Quarter. The ground floor was occupied by old, inefficient flatbed presses that had long since been overtaken by more modern machinery. Partly for sentimental reasons and partly because they still produced high-quality printed pages, he refused to replace them.

At the back of the building, in a room built over the garden, the bookbinding took place. Here the pages were stitched and glued together in two separate kinds of binding. The most popular and the cheapest were thick cardboard. The higher-priced limited editions were bound in buckram and were offered first to wealthy private book lovers—whose names were on a list left to him by his father.

The printing operations started early, at six o'clock in the morning in the summer, and continued until four in the afternoon. By that time the smell of glue, ink, and old cloth had permeated the building. Some visitors wrinkled their noses in disgust at this malodorous printers' brew, but Poulet-Malassis delighted in a fragrance that brought cherished reminders of childhood and his father.

The publishing offices were on the second floor, up a steep staircase that had been lined with bookcases on one side, making an uncomfortable passage for those seeking business with the publisher.

Baudelaire caught sight of a volume of Lamartine's poems halfway up the stairs and paused to inspect the book. Lamartine had become politically involved in the revolution that month and seemed destined to play a commanding role in shaping a new constitutional arrangement. But as ever the mob was ahead of the politicians. That May the rallying cry on the streets was: "Better an end with terror than terror without end!" The February uprising had failed to dislodge a despised Bourbon monarch, Louis Philippe. Grand old men of letters such as Lamartine had joined forces with progressive politicians to create a new constitution and a peaceful end to a bankrupt monarchy. They wanted reform. Baudelaire knew it wouldn't work. He didn't want it to work. There would be another bloody upheaval that summer. Lamartine and his friends would then get the revolution they deserved, not reform. The year 1848 was going to be another year of revolution in France—and maybe in Europe. Baudelaire glanced at the first poem and smiled. Lamartine was no better a poet than a politician.

Baudelaire had not been to his publisher's offices before; nor, indeed, had he made an appointment. He saw a young clerk, no more than a boy, fast asleep at a large desk, with his head cradled in his arms. An open ledger lay before him, with a pen placed beside an open inkwell. The pen had dripped several small spots of ink onto the green leather of the desk. Looking at the fresh writing on the page, Baudelaire judged that the clerk had succumbed to sleep in the middle of a sentence. He coughed, but the boy did not move. Baudelaire gently shook his arm. The boy raised his head, barely glanced at him, and picked up his pen to resume work.

"Monsieur Poulet-Malassis, please," said Baudelaire.

The clerk did not look up. "Not available," he grunted.

"Make him available," said Baudelaire. "It's Charles Baudelaire. Tell him it's urgent."

The clerk laid down his pen with a sigh. "M. Poulet-Malassis is in prison. He was arrested two days ago for carrying a gun in public. He was lucky not to have been shot." He returned to his ledger.

Baudelaire looked appalled. "Is he all right? Where is he being held?"

The clerk looked up. "Is he all right? I doubt it. And we have no idea where he is being held. Now, if you wouldn't mind."

Baudelaire retraced his steps down the narrow staircase.

17

Low tide at Honfleur had revealed a long stretch of sand speckled with strutting seagulls. Apollonie Sabatier was running barefoot up the beach alongside a small dog, which continually jumped up at the swirl of white petticoat beneath her light-blue dress. She stopped as the dog broke off to chase seagulls. She was alone on the sands in the winter sunshine. Caroline Aupick, who was drinking coffee under the awning of an elegant café on the seafront, thought Apollonie was bound to catch a cold. Her feet must be frozen. Caroline turned to her son, who was also watching the solitary figure on the beach, and said, "Order some more coffee, Charles. She will be here in a minute."

The coffee arrived at the same time as Sabatier and her Chihuahua. Baudelaire rose and kissed her hand. She remained standing and put the dog on her chair beside him. He looked at the animal dubiously and put out a hand. It snapped at him.

"How is Paris?" she asked, sipping her coffee.

"Calm," he said. "They have buried the dead. The king has fled. We shall have President Napoléon shortly, and in a year or so there will be a coup and he will declare himself emperor. It's a tradition in that family."

Sabatier looked at him over the rim of her cup. The flamboyant figure she had met briefly at the ball had changed. The face was more lined, the forehead creased in a permanent frown, and the clothes were darker, more somber. Perhaps his mother had been right: he had put his wild days behind him.

"You don't seem to care, or does your nonchalance deceive us?" she said.

"I hate the Bourbons, of course. But then I hate the mob. They're so stupid. They never learn."

"You must tell me all about it. But excuse me for a minute. Would you watch the dog for me while I get the sand off these feet?"

She walked into the café.

Baudelaire looked at the dog suspiciously. He held out his hand again, but the creature bared a surprisingly large set of teeth and gave a growl.

"She's a lovely lady, Mama. Lovely," he said.

"She suits you. And you're right. She's a lady. She will steady you, Charles—give you an anchor in your life."

"I quite agree, Mama," he said. Taking advantage of the fact that his mother was staring out to sea and refusing to talk directly to him, he gave the neighboring chair leg a surreptitious kick. The dog almost fell off but regained its balance and glared at him.

"She will be the making of me. But women are expensive to keep, and I . . ."

Caroline Aupick was following the progress of a red-sailed fishing boat that had just turned out of the harbor and was sailing in front of them a few hundred yards offshore. The boat was close rigged against a strong west wind and heeled over, showing its hull.

"Spend some time here with us and we will work something out," she said.

"But, Mama, I need a new apartment in Paris."

Now it was his turn to look out to sea as she swung round to face him. At moments like this he knew so well the expression on her face and the tone of voice that went with it: the pain of a loving mother yet again disappointed by her son's behavior.

"What happened to the last one?"

"They took it back."

She sipped her coffee, removed a small silk handkerchief from the sleeve of her dress, and dabbed her lips. He watched the red-sailed fishing boat firmly on course for the open sea. He could just see two or three fishermen on deck. He felt a flicker of envy: they were out at sea all day, and often all night, hauling in the silver treasure of the deep—far from mothers, lovers, and creditors.

"Very well," she said. "You shall have a new apartment and perhaps a larger allowance. I want to see you settled. Apollonie can give you the peace of mind you need. When are your poems to be published?"

Baudelaire shifted in his chair, leaned over, and took his mother's hand.

"There's been a slight problem. My publisher is in prison."

She pulled back, releasing her hand from his.

"What on earth for?"

"They've charged him with sedition, apparently."

Caroline Aupick looked up at the awning as if in sup-
plication, raised her hands, and dropped them to the table.
There were times when she behaved like an actress at the
Comédie-Française, thought Baudelaire.

"Well, can't you get another one?" she said.

Apollonie Sabatier returned and Baudelaire got to his
feet. The dog stood up on the chair to greet her, wagging its
tail. She picked it up and held it in her arms.

"Will you walk with me to the village?" he said to her.

"Of course," she said, "and we can take Fleurie?"

"Why not? I am sure Fleurie would love a long walk," he
said. "Mama, will you excuse us?"

They walked down the seafront and turned into a cobbled
road that ran along the river to the harbor. The dog, no longer the playful animal from the beach, trotted behind them.

Honfleur was a harbor town that was struggling to recover from the ruin of its trade because of the blockade imposed during the Napoleonic wars. The harbor was partially
silted up and much of the trade had gone to Le Havre along
the coast. There was still a safe anchorage for the few day
boats that brought a harvest of fish from the Channel every
evening in good weather, but the old fish market, like the once
brilliant array of shops and restaurants, had gone.

As they passed St. Catherine's church Sabatier slipped her
arm in his, a gesture that seemed natural to both of them.
They talked of how his mother had inherited her villa in the

town, the fast-changing Channel weather, the fact that he had not eaten fish since the goldfish pond incident in childhood, and then back to the weather again.

Outside the pharmacy at the end of the high street, Baudelaire made an excuse and detached himself. While she waited, she consoled Fleurie, who was clearly upset by the presence of a stranger at her side. In a few minutes he emerged carrying a small bag. He seemed angry and did not take her arm as they resumed their walk.

"Just a little something for my chest," he said. "But they never give me enough, damn them. Damn them all! Stupid bourgeois imbeciles!"

Apollonie looked at him in surprise.

"I'm sorry," he said. "My nerves are not good."

Every day for the next two weeks Baudelaire and Apollonie Sabatier took their morning walk and lunched in the town before returning to the villa. In the evenings they played cards or joined small dinner parties at which Caroline Aupick would entertain neighbors or friends. She used these occasions to present her son and his new lady friend to Honfleur society as a couple. She had given them adjoining bedrooms and would inquire solicitously every morning at breakfast whether they had slept well. Both lovers were aware that she had stage-managed the affair, and both seemed happy to let the relationship blossom under her roof.

Baudelaire was surprised, not so much by his mother's evident desire to initiate and thus control the affair but by the fact that Apollonie proved such a willing partner in the plan. They must have discussed it, planned it together, he thought—if not in so many words, then certainly the affair was the result of an understanding between them.

And who was he to object to such an arrangement? By any measure, Apollonie Sabatier was perfect. She had been the mistress of Théo Gautier and thus knew everyone in the literary world. She understood the pain that great artists must inflict on themselves, and those they love, to create lasting beauty.

She was intelligent and beautiful. In the bedroom she tantalized and teased Baudelaire, showing him little tricks that he had never imagined in the sexual repertoire of a well-bred lady. Gautier was famous for his carnal appetite and his taste in exotic perversions. Clearly she had learned a lot from him, not least that in bed the only rule was pleasure.

Baudelaire had even been moved to write poems for her. He found that astonishing. He had never thought he would be able to work in the suffocating atmosphere of his mother's seaside villa. Yet he did and the work pleased him. They were good poems—strong, rhythmic, and sensual—although devoid of the passion he had brought to his Black Venus cycle. He showed them to her. She was flattered and very admiring. She told him that he was a great poet and his name would live forever.

So why then did he strain at the leash to leave? Why could he scarcely wait to get back to Paris? Mama was clever. She made him wait. He knew she wanted him to fall in love, as if he ever could. He paraded his passion for Apollonie before his mother like a matador with his cape. Just as the bull believed the red cape was the real enemy, so she believed his passion really was love. So she gave him the money, or a large part of it—four thousand francs in notes. Not a banker's draft. He had insisted on that. His creditors would have pounced on any bank where he presented a draft.

Then he was gone. He told Apollonie he would go ahead and organize the apartment they would share. She knew it was a lie. He could see that in her eyes. But she said nothing. She had lived with artists and writers for too long to be surprised by any act of passion or betrayal. Sooner or later his mother would also know it was a lie. That was obvious. That would cause them both pain. He loved her, as he always had and always would. But he deceived her for one simple reason that she—and maybe he himself—would never understand.

What he came to understand in Honfleur just added another layer to the knowledge he already possessed. It was like a new stratum on an old rock that showed its age through layers laid down by time. He could not do without her—his Black Venus, his true muse. The biggest joke of all—well, a delicious irony rather than joke, he told himself—was that he could never have written those poems to his snow-white, firm-breasted milkmaid by the sea if it had not been for his Black Venus.

18

Jeanne Duval prowled around the main room looking at the new furnishings. He had bought chairs, tables, and a good-sized desk, and the paintings were watercolors, which were just becoming fashionable and thus commanded high prices. She could hardly resent the money he had spent on the apartment. She had had her fair share of the fine food and the wine that went with it.

She wore a dark navy-blue dress whose silken texture shimmered in the light of two gas lamps. The green emerald pendant lost in the murderous attack beneath the bridge had been replaced by a heart-shaped ruby on a silver chain. Polished ebony hoops, studded with what looked like small diamonds, hung from her ears. Charm bracelets on each wrist were spangled with tiny carvings, gold, silver, and ivory. Her black hair was swept back in a netted bun. She ran her fingers over the tabletops, lifted a plate off the wall, and examined the potter's name on the back. She bent down and looked closely at the signature on a painting.

Baudelaire watched her anxiously. He poured two glasses of wine for them.

"You like it?" he said.

Duval sat down on a chaise longue and kicked off her shoes.

"Did you write poems for her?" she said. "When you'd finished pleasuring her in that big bed your mother provided."

"I write poems only for you."

"Liar," she said quietly. "Read me the poems you wrote for her."

Baudelaire raised his glass and drank almost half in one gulp.

"No," he said.

"So you did write poems for her?"

"I did it to please Mama. But they were no good."

"Read a poem you have written for me, then."

"Of course. But first things first," he said.

He was almost pleading, a little boy demanding a favorite treat from his mother. Duval dipped into her satchel and opened her sachet. He refilled his glass, crossed the room, and placed the wineglasses on a table at her side. She poured a little powder from the sachet into both glasses. She swilled the wine around and then raised it to him. He took his glass, clinked it against hers, and murmured, "Santé!" They both drained their glasses.

"My poem, please," she said.

Baudelaire began pacing back and forth.

"Very well. But this is for you; it is you, in fact. It's a beautiful palace I built for you, so move in and make it your own."

"What is it called?"

" 'Les Bijoux'!" he said.

"My loved one was naked and, knowing my heart,
Was dressed only in the music of her jewelry . . ."

Baudelaire paused and looked at her without expression.

Duval stood up and slowly unbuttoned her dress at the side. She stepped out of it, revealing a petticoat beneath. She raised both hands to the nape of her neck to unfasten her hair. Her bracelets jingled like tiny bells and flashed in the low light.

"Read it again," she whispered.

"My loved one was naked and, knowing my heart,
Was dressed only in the music of her jewelry . . ."

Duval released her hair from the bun so that it tumbled over her shoulders. She let her petticoat drop to the floor. She put her hands behind her back and unhooked a tight-ribbed corset. She leaned forward to unlace her boots. The ruby pendant swung in an arc before her and flashed in the light. The bracelets continued to jingle as she fiddled with her bootlaces.

Baudelaire gazed at her, transfixed, then continued:

"When the jewels make their mocking music,
In a sparkling symphony of precious stones,
I find in the harmony of light and sound
A passion that brings me ecstasy."

Duval was naked but for her boots. She turned her back to him and put one foot at a time on the chaise longue, pulling the tongues forward and sliding the boots off. He saw more clearly now the thin white scars that ran across her lower back and buttocks. They looked like creases on her light-brown skin and they seemed to wrap into the cleft of her buttocks.

"So she lay upon a divan preparing to be loved,
Smiling on my lust, as it rose like the tide of a distant
sea."

She turned to face him and sat down on the chaise longue, leaning back with her knees apart. Baudelaire knelt beside her and ran his fingers through the long dark strands of hair that fell over her breasts.

"Her eyes are fixed on mine with the dreamy look
Of a tame tigress; she moves from one position to
another . . ."

Duval locked her eyes on him and pushed herself up the chaise longue until she sat on the back, legs splayed. She leaned toward him, placing her hands on her knees, so that her breasts swung forward with the ruby pendant.

His voice sank almost to a whisper.

"Her legs, her arms, her thighs, polished as if with oil,
Uncoiled with swanlike grace before my eyes;
Her belly, loins and breasts, the fruit of my vine,
Thrust themselves forward, more tempting than devil
angels,

To trouble my restless soul and shake me
From the crystal calm of my solitude."

Duval stood up and stepped off the chaise longue. She raised her kneeling and still-clothed lover to his feet. She pushed him gently onto the chaise longue and straddled him, her hands pressing down on his shoulders. Bending over him, she rocked gently from side to side, so that the ruby pendant and diamanté ebony earrings swung over his face and her breasts brushed back and forth over his mouth. His eyes followed the jewels and the strange patterns they threw on her skin.

"Write me another poem," she said.

He put his hands on her breasts and pushed her gently away.

"Of course," he said. "But first things first."

She shook her head. "Call it 'The Albatross,' " she said. "I want a poem called 'The Albatross.' "

"If you wish, but why?"

"Because I saw one long ago on the ship to France. It was a young bird and lost. It circled the ship for days even when a gale blew. And I feel like that albatross, born to fly on storm winds and never able to find sanctuary here on earth."

Baudelaire raised himself suddenly, almost throwing her off the chaise longue.

"Who told you that?"

"No one. That's just the way I felt then—and now."

He walked to the window. "What happened to the albatross?"

"It flew into the rigging one night. We found it on the

deck in the morning. It could hardly move with those great wings."

"And?"

"One of the sailors killed it with a boat hook. To put it out of its misery, he said. The captain was furious."

"He had every right to be," Baudelaire said. "The albatross in flight is majestic, awe inspiring—but on the ground it can hardly drag itself along. But you shouldn't have killed it. Bad luck."

Duval lay back on the chaise longue.

"It didn't bring me bad luck, did it?" she said.

19

The boy clerk was asleep in exactly the same position when Baudelaire returned to his publisher's offices. The uncapped inkwell, the dripping pen, and the open ledger implied that great work had been done that morning before sleep had stolen over him. Happy child, thought Baudelaire. He has a job and somewhere to sleep, which is more than most slum kids can hope for. Baudelaire breathed in deeply. The pungent smell of ink and glue had wafted up the stairs with him. He set down his portfolio on the desk and coughed, first softly, then louder. The boy raised his head, regarded the visitor blankly, picked up his pen, and returned to his work without a word. Baudelaire waited and then coughed. The boy did not look up.

"He's in there," he said, nodding to a door on which had been inscribed in gilt letters "M. POULET-MALASSIS."

The publisher's office was lined with bookcases and the floor strewn with piles of books that rose shakily toward the ceiling like leafless, long-unwatered plants. Baudelaire threaded his way through them and stood before a large oak desk, at which Poulet-Malassis was writing furiously in another ledger. His left arm had been heavily bandaged and was in a sling. There was silence as the pen flew back and forth across the page, leaving a trail of indecipherable writing. He was not having much luck with clerks, publishers, and their ledgers that morning, thought Baudelaire.

"Good day," he said.

Poulet-Malassis looked up and pointed at him with the pen. "You very nearly got me killed."

"I didn't ask you to take the gun."

"You wouldn't be here if I hadn't. Now give me the proofs."

He gestured at the portfolio. Baudelaire drew out a sheaf of papers and handed them over.

"Now, this is the final version, isn't it?"

Baudelaire nodded.

"You've added sixty poems—yes?"

"Yes. What happened to your arm?" he asked.

"They broke it in prison. In Brest, of all places. The jailer who did it said it was to stop me publishing any more socialist books. He seemed to think I write the books I publish. And he got the wrong arm."

"I'm really sorry. I didn't know I—"

Poulet-Malassis waved his good arm at him. "Of course you didn't. No one did. Sit down. I want to read these in sequence, to see how the new work fits with the old."

He squared the sheaf of papers on his desk and began to read.

Baudelaire looked around. The only chair in sight was piled high with books. He walked over very quietly, moved the books onto the floor, lifted the chair to the desk, and sat down. He pulled out his watch. It was a quarter past ten. He watched the publisher work through all one hundred poems, the first full edition of *Les Fleurs du Mal.*

Poulet-Malassis looked briefly at those he had read before and set them on one side. The others he studied with care, occasionally tipping his chair back to look at the ceiling, scratching his nose, and then coming forward to scribble in a small notebook. Toward the end of the first hour, he became excited and, oblivious of Baudelaire's presence, began to talk to himself.

"Yes!" he exclaimed. "Very good. No, dear me, no, no we can't have that. Beautiful; yes, that's good; now what would he mean by that?"

Finally he threw down his pen and stood up. Baudelaire did likewise. It was almost noon. Poulet-Malassis shuffled the papers back into a neat pile.

"You do know some of this work is obscene, don't you?" he said.

Baudelaire drew himself up. "I know nothing of the sort. I—"

"All right, spare me the great-art-rises-above-man's-jurisdiction lecture. I've heard it all before. Fact is that at least ten of the latest poems will probably get me sent to prison again. Then they'll break my other arm."

"So what are you going to do?"

"I am going to publish them, Charles. The first time I saw these poems I told you they were extraordinary. And now you have built on that. There is a rhythm and sequence to the volume. It's wonderful. It won't be popular and it probably won't earn me any money, but there's an emotional power here that will make your name."

"Thank you. And I am sorry about your arm."

Poulet-Malassis looked at him and frowned. "I'd like to believe that. Now, a small point. You have dedicated a cycle of poems in the volume to a Jeanne Duval."

"That's right."

"May I ask who she is?"

"She's my companion."

"Your mistress?"

"Yes, but it's difficult."

"You mean she's not your only mistress."

"I didn't say that. Anyway, I don't see what this has to do with the book."

"I am trying to suggest that a dedication to a society lady—or maybe an established artist like de Vigny or Victor Hugo—might be more helpful."

"I couldn't have done it without her. In fact, I wouldn't have done it without her."

"Right, that's settled. It is now December. We will publish in one month. I promise you decent paper and an engraving of your choice on the frontispiece. I suggest a first run of one thousand, three hundred copies. We will price the book at three francs and you will receive twelve percent. Agreed?"

Baudelaire murmured his thanks. "Yes. You are very kind. Thank you. One small point . . ."

"Which is?"

"You mentioned an advance of two hundred francs. Could we make it, say, three hundred?"

Poulet-Malassis raised his injured arm. "It cost me five hundred francs to get out of jail."

Baudelaire nodded. "Yes. Of course. I'm sorry. So the two hundred is still on offer?"

Poulet-Malassis laughed. "Women are expensive, aren't they? Especially that one," he said. "Yes, the advance is with Albert outside. Try not to spend it all in the first week."

The man was vaguely familiar as he brushed past her on the steps of a small three-story apartment building in Le Marais, one of the less fashionable parts of the city. Duval looked at the retreating figure and glimpsed the prominent nose set on thickset features, that walrus mustache, and the pince-nez spectacles. She had seen a sketch of the man in those literary magazines she occasionally leafed through.

She'd heard one of Baudelaire's friends call her illiterate, but that was not true. She could read perfectly well. To her mother's joy, the kitchen maid in the plantation house in Haiti had taught them both during the long afternoons when the plantation owner—her father, she reminded herself—was occupied with whichever girl was the favorite of the moment. It was writing she found more difficult. No one had taught her that. She still made the cross when asked to sign any document.

She entered the building and took the stairs to the third floor. She was about to knock when the door of the apartment opened and a maid appeared, holding an umbrella. They looked at each other in surprise.

"I was expecting M. Gautier," the maid said. "He left his umbrella."

Then Duval remembered. It was Théophile Gautier who had almost knocked her down. A writer, critic, and famous lover. They didn't put that last description in the magazines, but that's what Baudelaire always said.

Duval walked into a well-furnished hallway as the maid backed away from her. "I've come to see Mlle Sabatier," she said.

"She's busy. Who shall I say is calling?"

There were two doors off the hall and a staircase leading to another floor. Duval tried one of the doors, opened it, looked in, and then closed it.

"Excuse me," said the maid. "Would you wait here?"

Ignoring the protesting maid, Duval walked up the stairs. She opened the door to the bedroom without knocking.

Apollonie thought that either her lover had returned or the maid had forgotten her training. She was seated in a robe at a mirrored makeup table. She saw Duval in the mirror and flushed with anger. She turned, stood up, and drew her robe tight around her.

"It is usual to knock on someone's bedroom door," she said.

"As your last visitor did, I am sure."

The maid was standing behind Duval in the doorway, wringing her hands.

"You can go, Marie," she said, and turned to Duval. "I know who you are—what do you want?"

Duval walked up to Sabatier and brushed the back of her hand over her cheek. Sabatier breathed in deeply but did not flinch or move.

"He was right. Your skin is white as milk and soft as silk. You're lucky."

"Let me repeat the question . . . ," said Sabatier.

"I know. Why did I come? What do I want?"

"Exactly," said Sabatier.

"What I really want right now is a cup of coffee."

"But that's not what you came for."

"Obviously not."

"Wait here," said Sabatier. She opened the door into a side room and left.

Duval walked around the room, examining the paintings. She stopped at a portrait of Sabatier, nude from the waist up. She peered at the signature. "Courbet 1848."

The side door opened and Sabatier reappeared fully dressed.

"The coffee will be here in a minute. Now, perhaps you would explain."

"I wanted to see you. We have something in common."

"I don't think so."

"You know we do."

"I know nothing of the sort."

"Do you love him?"

The door opened and the maid came in with a tray of coffee and cups. She put it down on the table and left. Sabatier began pouring the coffee.

"You take sugar?" she said.

"No. Do you?"

Sabatier shook her head in irritation. She placed a cup on a table next to Duval and sat down holding the other.

"I don't love him, if that's what you want to know," Sabatier said.

"He's passionate about you."

"All men like the idea of love. But they confuse it with something else: lust. And you know all about that, don't you?"

"I know how to make him happy."

"Of course you do. That's why he stays with you."

"Why wouldn't he stay with me?"

"Are you really asking me that? After what you have done to him? You've dragged him into the gutter, spent all his money."

"Ah! The milkmaid has sharp teeth."

"All Paris knows about those special little pleasures you give him, and I am not talking about the bedroom. You understand me?"

"Yes, I do understand you—you and your muddy little mind and milk-white skin. You filthy hypocrite. Remember those letters your lover Gautier wrote to you? All Paris has seen them. They are obscene. Did you really do all those things?"

Sabatier stood up, trembling and white-faced. Her coffee cup rattled loudly on the saucer.

"The men in my life do not need opium to make love to me. That is the difference between us. Now get out," she said.

Baudelaire had been at the printer's since early morning, following the production through from the typesetting to the first roll of the presses. He watched as the damp printed sheets were laid in wicker baskets by small boys and taken to the binding room at the back. It was June 25, 1857. *Les Fleurs du Mal* had finally been published.

Poulet-Malassis watched his author and friend fuss over the machinery like an old hen. He was frankly surprised they had got this far. Baudelaire had handed in the final version of his manuscript in February and since then the poet had been revising, changing, correcting, deleting, and amending the first full proof. When the second proof was produced he started all over again, often changing the very alterations he had already made.

It was nine years since they had met, seven years since Poulet-Malassis had seen the first poems, seven years to get a slim volume into the bookshops, seven years in which his company had earned little, and seven years in which his partner and brother-in-law, Eugène de Broise, had complained endlessly.

"Why are we doing this?" de Broise kept asking. "This man Baudelaire takes opium, he is an addict, and he goes around with that half-caste drunk." "Read the poems," Poulet-Malassis would say. "I have read the damn things," de Broise would reply. "And they're sordid; they're going to get us into trouble. They're unworthy of a great publishing house like ours." And so it went on.

The real problem was that the publisher knew his partner was right. *Les Fleurs du Mal* would probably ruin them both. But he had to do it. If he didn't publish the work, nobody would. The poems would be scattered like confetti among the poet's papers after his death. France would lose the glory and the beauty of the greatest poetry in her language.

The first copies were ready that evening and Baudelaire was joined at the publishing house by his friends Le Vavasseur, Buisson, and Prarond. Together they packed up the books ready for dispatch to every important poet in continental Europe, England, and the United States. Tennyson, Browning, and Wordsworth were sent copies accompanied by a handwritten note from Baudelaire—in English. Victor Hugo received his copy weeks later in Guernsey because of the erratic postal service in the Channel Islands. Longfellow's copy was sent to his home in Cambridge, Massachusetts, and arrived in America in the remarkable time of three weeks.

Hugo would be the first to respond. He had never met Baudelaire but had heard of his reputation as prophet of the high art, a writer who defied convention to express in poetry an eternal truth about man's struggle for salvation in the face of damnation. Those were Hugo's words, and Baudelaire cried when he read them many weeks later.

"Finally someone understands me," he told his friends, "and not just anyone—the great Victor Hugo."

20

On the night of publication the author gathered with his closest friends at the Café Momus. Poulet-Malassis had given Baudelaire twelve free copies, which had been casually stacked on the table amid the candles, bottles, and glasses. Jeanne Duval was dressed in her favorite red dress, but she sat at a corner table away from the celebrations and refused pleas to join the drinking and singing.

For one thing, she hardly knew his friends: the blond giant Le Vavasseur, Dozon, the poet and translator with a passion for Slavonic languages, Prarond, Buisson. They called themselves journalists, but they never appeared to do any work and they always seemed to have money for drink and hashish. She despised them: rich young men talking about poetry and preaching revolution almost in the same breath.

Only a few yards from the café there were women and children struggling to survive in the slums. If they ventured into the Momus, they would be given the odd coin to satisfy the collective conscience of the revelers and then shooed away.

Baudelaire and his friends would go back to talking about revolution.

Well, they had had their revolution and much good it had done them. The 1848 uprising had been savagely suppressed by the army, the king had fled into exile, and the National Assembly had created a republic under an elected president. And whom had the people of France elected to be their first president? None other than Louis-Napoléon, nephew of the late emperor. It was said that many of the peasantry voted for him thinking that Napoléon the Great had somehow returned. And then history proved again that the present never escapes the past. After two years in office the president, in a brief and violent coup, installed himself as emperor. The result was another Napoléon on the throne of France. The Second French Republic had ended and the Second French Empire had begun. The ashes of the great Napoléon, lying in state in the crypt under the dome of Les Invalides, might well have stirred with silent laughter. In 1804 Pope Pius had crowned him Emperor of France in the cathedral of Notre-Dame. After military defeat, exile, the creation of a republic, and his own death on Saint Helena in 1821, France had returned the imperial crown to his nephew. The pages of history were being turned backwards.

Nothing had changed for the poor of Paris, or in the Momus, for that matter. The bohemians were still talking about revolution, only this time they were baying for a parliamentary democracy like the English, whatever that was.

Baudelaire detached himself from his friends and came over to her.

"You're looking sad—come and join us!"

"Thank you, but no. I like it here."

"These are your friends too, you know."

"No, Charles, they're not. They're with you. This is your night. Enjoy yourself."

"It's your night as well. These poems are for you."

"So you keep telling me."

"Aren't you pleased?"

"Of course. Now go back. Be with your friends. They're waiting."

But she was not pleased. She was fearful. She was losing him. It was fifteen years since she had first seen him in the audience at Le Rêve, and he was leaving her. She was sure of it. He didn't know, of course. But his friends did. That's why they were so pleased he had finally published his poetry. They thought he could turn his back on his muse, on his big-breasted slut with her slinky dark looks and the frizzy hair that had to be carefully ironed straight every morning. They thought they could put her back on the boat to Haiti, a slave child returning to the plantation and the lash. They hated her; she was sure of that.

And who were *they*? His friends, his publisher, and his bloody mother. But the greatest barrier between them was that book, those poems. They were for her; they were about her: the wellspring of genius from which the poetry sprang was the inner cycle of poems about her—the dark songs of lust, desire, and damnation, as he called them.

Her breasts, her belly, what he charmingly called her loins, the long shuddering moans she made as she reached orgasm—it was all there. And how did he describe her? "My ebony-thighed witch, daughter of the shadows." Charming!

He talked of her "coal black eyes, the chimneys of your soul."

My eyes, chimneys indeed! What did he call that poem? "Sed Non Satiata," as if that meant anything to anyone.

Then there were endless references to her as cruel, unfeeling, a tigress, and the repeated descriptions of her breasts. He was obsessed by them. He had given her the sketch he had done when he was searching the clubs of Paris. That said it all. He had drawn her breasts way out of proportion to the rest of her. The moment she had met his mother at the ball she realized why. He must have buried his face in that maternal bosom from childhood, breathing in the milky perfume, feeling his very being enclosed in that soft warmth.

He did the same with her. He always tried to go to sleep with his head pillowed between her breasts. That was all right for him but very uncomfortable for her. And he never washed his hair. And what about that poem called "Le Léthé"? She was the tigress of the first verse, it was her skirts in which he wished to bury his head, breathing in her "moldy sweetness," and in the last verse it was her "charming nipples on those pointed breasts" from which he wished to suck hemlock.

And there you have it, she thought. My poet, my lover, my companion, wishes to suckle poison from my breasts. Where does that leave me? His Black Venus? No, more like something between a witch and a vampire.

Strangely, he was jealous, childishly so. Another man only had to look at her admiringly in the street—as frequently happened, because she made sure there was much to admire—and Baudelaire would accuse her of having had a liaison with him or exchanging some secret signal to arrange a meeting. That was another good reason to keep clear of his friends. They all wanted her. They looked at her the way dogs look at a bitch in heat. She had her affairs, of course, just as he did.

She found consolation in chance encounters, the casual embrace of a stranger, but she never gave herself to his friends.

Baudelaire called over to her. "Where are we living now?"

"Why?"

"Le Vavasseur wants to know."

"And you've forgotten?"

"I am a little confused—is it the Hôtel Concorde?"

Of course you're confused, she thought. We've moved probably eight times in as many months, and here you are with your shiny new book and your friends, and you're drunk and you cannot remember where you woke up this morning.

"I have an apartment, remember?" she said.

"Of course," he said, and turned back to the group.

"She has an apartment. That's where I live."

"Where is it?"

"God knows. Somewhere cheap, maybe Le Marais."

"Charles, you don't even know where you live?" said Le Vavasseur.

"What does it matter? My Black Venus will take me home."

"I don't think so," said Le Vavasseur, nodding over Baudelaire's shoulder.

Baudelaire turned and looked at the corner table. Jeanne Duval had gone.

21

Albert raised his head from the desk, wondering what had woken him. He shook his head drowsily and was about to resume his slumbers when he heard his name from within the publisher's office. Albert knew his master's moods well. The rage that had rattled the closed door meant only one thing. He reached into the lowest drawer of his desk and drew out a bottle of cognac and a crystal glass.

"Albert!" came the shout again as he opened the door.

Most of that morning's *Figaro* had been thrown onto the floor. It was July 5 and the first review had appeared. The publisher had his hands on the page containing the review, which he tore in half as Albert placed the bottle on a side table and poured a glass. Albert bent down and picked up the torn pieces.

"Go on, read it," said Poulet-Malassis.

Albert placed the two halves of the paper on the desk and began reading. The review, signed in the single name of Bourdin, went straight to the point.

" 'Never have so many brilliant qualities been squandered! There are moments when one doubts the sanity of M. Baudelaire, but there are others when one has no doubts at all. The poems are for the most part the monstrous repetition of the same words and ideas. Never in the space of so few pages have I seen so many breasts bitten, chewed even; never has there been such a procession of demons, fetuses, devils, cats, and vermin. The whole volume is an asylum full of the inanities of the human mind, of all the putrescence of the human heart—' "

"That's enough," said Poulet-Malassis.

Albert looked up. "Who is this Bourdin?"

"No one has ever heard of him. And no one ever will. He's just a hack brought in to do the dirty work. This was planned. They've always hated him."

Poulet-Malassis balled up the torn page and lobbed it into the wastepaper basket. He picked up the bottle of brandy.

"Get yourself a glass," he said. "We might as well all get drunk."

That morning, in the apartment he shared with Duval in a little street in Le Marais, Baudelaire wrote to his mother.

Dearest Mama,

You will probably have seen today's Figaro, *that of July 5, before you get this. All I can say is that it didn't take long for the wolves to close in. We published on June 25 and exactly eleven days later that paper has condemned my whole work as an obscene monstrosity. That madman*

*Billaut at the Ministry of the Interior was behind it. He
had failed to get a conviction against Flaubert's* Madame
Bovary *in the spring and was looking for a new victim.
Well, he found me. As you can imagine, I am distraught.
No, more than that, I am enraged. I fear I now face prosecution, because the* Figaro *attack was obviously intended to prepare public opinion for an obscenity trial.*

*I would love to have kept this from you, but that
would have been absurd. Please don't worry. I have pow-
erful friends like Lamartine and Sainte-Beuve. They will
not stand by and watch the state crush an innocent artist.
They will stand up for me. And I have broad shoulders.
I long to see you in Honfleur when this is over.*

> *Your loving son*
> *Charles*

Albert was as usual asleep when the two officers from the
Ministry of the Interior reached the top of the narrow staircase. They regarded the sleeping assistant briefly and then
one bent down to whisper in his ear.

"Police!"

Albert woke up, rubbed his eyes, and took the documents that were thrust into his hands. The two visitors left
without a word of explanation, but the documents were clear
enough when the publisher examined them in his office. The
entire print run of *Les Fleurs du Mal* was to be confiscated,
and both he and the author were to face trial on charges of
publishing obscene material likely to endanger public morality. The trial was set for August 20 in the Palais de Justice.

• • •

Baudelaire was defiant. He believed this would be the making of him. His friends would give evidence on his behalf, the trial would fail, and he, the artist wronged by a philistine government, would become famous. He had told his friends many times that the true artist must turn his back on the quest for wealth that made greed a god for much of society. But the fact was that Baudelaire was desperate for success and the fame that went with it. Now the sensational Parisian scandal in the summer of 1857, in which he would face and refute charges of obscenity, would finally bring him the public recognition he deserved.

He felt certain he would be hailed by writers across Europe for taking a stand against censorship. His work as a critic, as a translator of Edgar Allan Poe, and above all as a poet would be seen as redefining European literature. He would be recognized as the man who broke the hold that Romanticism exercised over the public imagination. And in time he would win recognition as the first of the modern poets, as Manet and Monet were the first of the moderns in their field. This was his due. For this he had worked and suffered.

"On top of all this, you want to get rich, don't you? Be honest," said Jeanne Duval, who had heard these wild ambitions many times and was listening now to the poet in full flow in a café around the corner from the publishing house.

"I will be honest," he said. "I despise money. I treat it with contempt. But I want it. All the time."

"Sounds like the women in your life," she said, and laughed.

"There's only one woman in my life," he said.

"That's a lie," she said. "There's your mother, for a start. Give me another drink."

They drank more wine. On a linen napkin Baudelaire scrawled the few lines he would send to his mother in a letter later that night explaining how the forthcoming trial would be a turning point in her son's life. Duval picked up the cloth and read it out loud.

" 'I beg you to see this scandal, which is creating a sensation in Paris, as the foundation of my fortune,' " she said.

Baudelaire smiled at her. "It's true," he said.

"You hope for too much," she said. "And you trust your friends too much. I fear for you."

22

In the heat of mid-August, the Palais de Justice, the central criminal court on the île de la Cité, was not a pleasant place. Sensible law-abiding Parisians chose to avoid the place at any time of the year but especially so in the summer. Ten fluted columns of granite rose at the entrance of a building that had been built and rebuilt since medieval times, with the apparent intention of cowing all who entered under the crushing weight of architecture.

There was an inhuman aspect to the echoing anterooms, offices, and archives, enclosed by tiled floors and vaulted ceilings. The six courtrooms, with their ancient wooden benches, dark green walls, and grimy barred windows that could only be opened partway, were just as depressing.

The prison cells within the Palais were empty now, but it was here during the Revolution that the condemned had been held before being herded, blindfolded and bound, onto a wagon for the journey to the guillotine in the place Vendôme.

The legacy of those savage days clung like a layer of ashen dust to the ill-lit corridors and courtrooms.

The judges, lawyers, and court officials usually returned with reluctance from the long summer recess that ended with the Feast of the Assumption in the second week of August. During the six-week vacation, the city jails had filled up with minor criminals, pickpockets, rapists, and thieves of every kind. Major cases of murder, conspiracy, and occasionally treason were not scheduled to be heard until the fall, allowing the senior counsel and judges the opportunity to remain in their country houses until the cooler weather. Normally, there was no interest in cases that were heard at the Palais de Justice in August and the public galleries would be empty. There was little reason for anyone but a close relative to apply for the blue carnet that allowed individuals entry to one of the six courtrooms.

In the summer of 1857 all that changed. On August 20 the public gallery of court number one was packed. Outside, a line of people, mostly women fanning themselves beneath parasols, stretched some four hundred yards down to the Seine. They were hoping that the oppressive heat would force some of the frailer occupants in the public gallery to leave early. Within the Palais, clerks, ushers, messengers, court officials, and lawyers moved about their business with unusual urgency.

In a crowded anteroom to the court, Charles Baudelaire and Poulet-Malassis held scented handkerchiefs to their faces as they were jostled and pushed by the other defendants. Most had been arrested on the street for thieving, indecent assault, attempted or actual rape, and a range of offenses committed with violence. As the publisher observed to his author when they were first ushered into the room, scarecrows in the fields were better dressed and smelled much sweeter than their fellow accused.

Baudelaire did not acknowledge the remark. He was dressed entirely in black, from the silk bow at his neck to his shoes. The funeral attire made him look even paler than usual. His face seemed more deeply lined and the expression one of sorrow.

What had overwhelmed him was not the prospect of the trial, nor even the unlikely event of a guilty verdict. He was prepared for that. What he had not been prepared for, and would never forgive, was his betrayal by friends and those well placed in the literary world to help him. Almost without exception those who had once praised him, Lamartine, Théophile Gautier, Sainte-Beuve, had now turned their backs in his hour of need. The old gang from the Momus had stood by him, Le Vavasseur and Prarond especially, but they were of no use at the Palais de Justice.

What hurt most was that Charles Sainte-Beuve, his friend and colleague for fifteen years, had refused to write a letter commending *Les Fleurs du Mal* to the presiding judges. Sainte-Beuve was highly influential, a noted newspaper columnist and critic, and was well respected by the government. He had also privately praised *Les Fleurs du Mal* when he had been sent a proof copy. Yet he simply refused to repeat the praise, either to the judges or to the ministry. He was frightened of offending the minister, terrified that he might lose a government grant.

Those editors and critics on Paris newspapers who had warmly praised Baudelaire's recent translation of Edgar Allan Poe were suddenly not available and refused to see him or respond to his correspondence. The dramatist Prosper Mérimée, whom Baudelaire thought he had known well, even went so far as to say that he would not lift a finger to prevent Baudelaire from being burned at the stake, except to advise the minister of justice to burn his poetry first.

Given the level of invective from established writers, it was not surprising that members of the popular press were virulent in their attacks on the poet. One editorial set the tone for the coverage when it claimed that Baudelaire was the author of "filth and horror." The press also went after Jeanne Duval. They called her a half-breed and said she was the evil influence on the poet's work.

By the end of July Baudelaire was in despair as he wrote to his mother:

I have always championed the cause of press liberty and as you know have railed against censorship. I can stand the vile abuse of the gutter press, although I would rather spend time with a sewer rat than a journalist. But what enrages me is the Judas behavior of those editors and critics who know full well what my work is worth and who have often praised me in print.

They are frightened, craven cowards, gutless fools who think they will gain some advantage by crawling to the ministry. What they really fear is me and my art. I have left them behind. They know it and they hate me for it.

The door to the anteroom opened. There was a general surge toward the small clerk who had appeared at the entrance.

"M. Baudelaire," said the clerk in a loud voice.

Poulet-Malassis pushed through the crowd, followed by Baudelaire.

"I think every cutthroat in Paris is here," the publisher said. "We will probably join them in jail tonight."

In the middle of the room, Baudelaire put a hand on his friend's shoulder and said, "There's one thing I haven't told you. I have a surprise witness."

"He'd better be good," said Poulet-Malassis.

Baudelaire and Poulet-Malassis were ushered into the dock and told to stand. The public gallery stretched along one side of the court in two rows. It was thronged with well-dressed ladies, all of whom were fanning themselves against the heat. There were two tables in the well of the court stacked high with documents. At one a middle-aged man with a gray wig was busy writing. A sign in front of him stated: "M. PINARD: PUBLIC PROSECUTOR." At the second sat an elderly lawyer with a lopsided wig gazing vacantly at the public gallery. A sign on the table identified him as M. Chaix d'Est-Ange, acting for the defendant. On a raised dais at the end of the court, behind a long mahogany table, sat three high-backed chairs.

Baudelaire scanned the faces in the gallery and was surprised to see Apollonie Sabatier. She smiled as she fanned herself, her long auburn curls moving slightly in the draft. Baudelaire smiled back. She was probably there at the suggestion of his mother, but he was pleased to see her. Apart from anything else, she and the other society ladies added much-needed glamour to the drab courtroom. There was no surprise at their presence. The popular press had treated the obscenity trial against the poet and his publisher as one of the great events of that year and had alluded endlessly to the sexually explicit content of *Les Fleurs du Mal.* The respectable ladies of Paris were not going to miss the opportunity to see judicial punishment meted out to the perpetrator of such filth. The fact that no one had been able to read the text, since all but a few copies had been seized shortly after publication, only heightened their interest.

"The court will rise!" bellowed the court clerk, and the whole room came to its feet. Three judges, gowned, bewigged, and with the florid look of men who enjoyed a schooner of sherry with their breakfast, took their seats. Pinard bowed to the bench and looked at the court clerk, who nodded. Pinard turned back to face the judges.

"The case is simple, Your Honors," he said. "The defendants created and published work of such obscenity that it makes all previous trials of this nature look trivial. There is also a charge of blasphemy that concerns references to the Virgin Mary."

Pinard spoke without pause for almost half an hour. He did so without enthusiasm, in a low, dull voice that seemed to be directed at one of the soot-stained windows above the heads of the judges. He cited legal precedents, previous cases of obscenity, and past judgments. He explained in painstaking detail the provisions of the law relating to obscenity under the Napoleonic Code.

The public gallery wilted with disappointment. This was not what they had come to hear. The prosecutor's heart was clearly not in the case. The three judges had sunk back in their chairs without any apparent interest in the proceedings. Then, without changing his tone or the tenor of his voice, Pinard warned the court that he would have to quote from one of the most offensive poems in the volume under discussion. Would Their Honors like to clear the court? There was a collective intake of breath in the public gallery and much shaking of heads. Their Honors came to life, briefly conferred, and said they would not. There was a sigh of relief from the gallery.

The poem, said Pinard, made repeated and entirely gratuitous references to breasts, buttocks, loins, and thighs. The ladies in the gallery sat upright. Their fans fluttered audibly, like a flock of frightened birds. Some looked as though they might faint with excitement.

Pinard's mouselike demeanor changed. He looked at the judges, then at the gallery, then back to the judges. His tone hardened. Here was the warrior lawyer determined to defend public morality whom the ladies of Paris had come to see. He held up a copy of the poems and boomed, "I shall read this obscene passage from an early poem by this author and ask you to judge it against the Christian code, which has been the foundation of our public morality for a thousand years."

There was a buzz of expectant conversation throughout the court.

"Silence!" cried the court clerk.

There is always a low hum of noise in a crowded place when silence is commanded by authority. People whisper to one another, shift in their chairs, move their feet around, and blow their noses. But in this case the silence was almost a sound in itself. Even the hoarse cries of the wagoners and carters in the surrounding streets ceased.

Pinard looked around at his rapt audience. He held them in suspense for a moment longer and then bowed his head to the book.

" 'I smoothed oil into her thighs with sensuous strokes, watching her nipples harden and her loins glisten with the soft dew of love,' " he read, then raised his head triumphantly. "What are the mothers and daughters of France to make of that?"

As far as Baudelaire could see, the mothers and daughters of France loved it. There they were in the gallery, lightening their lives with a little sweet pornography. They sat with their bosoms heaving, and no doubt thinking unspeakable thoughts. That's what they made of it. The judges couldn't get enough of it either. As for Apollonie, she blushed in a very pretty way and looked at him from under those long eyelashes. She knew, oh yes, she knew, he thought.

The oldest of the three judges beckoned Pinard toward the bench.

"Perhaps, M. Pinard, you could provide further evidence from other poems—so that we might get a balanced view, you understand," he said.

"Of course, Your Honor," said the prosecutor. "This is from 'Le Léthé,' one of the most disgusting poems in the entire collection."

"Excellent," said the judge, ignoring sharp looks from his two colleagues. "Proceed! Proceed!"

Once again Pinard held the volume of poems like a conductor poised with his baton. Every eye was on the book as he swung round to display the entirely innocuous cover. Then he read: " 'I want to hide my throbbing head in the sweet perfume under your skirts and breathe the moldy sweetness, the fading fragrance of a dying rose.'

"I think it would be gravely upsetting for those in the public gallery, and especially the ladies present, if I were to continue," said the prosecutor. "The court will acknowledge, I am sure, that the two extracts constitute a breach of the obscenity law as promulgated under the Napoleonic Code. I rest my case."

There was a sigh of disappointment from the public gallery. The ladies wanted a great deal more meat on the bone they had come to gnaw. Mlle Sabatier looked prettily at both defendants and rose to leave. Baudelaire caught her eye. She smiled and sat down again.

The defense began without adjournment or pause in the proceedings. The judges were anxious to conclude the hearing within a day and, as the court clerk advised the defendants, they wished to deliver their verdict in the afternoon.

Baudelaire listened to his lawyer with concern, then despair, and finally incredulity. Chaix d'Est-Ange whined and wheedled, pleading mitigation in the name of art. He told the court that Baudelaire was an honest artist trying to plumb the depths of the human soul. His address had little effect. Two of the three judges seemed asleep. The ladies in the gallery were getting restless.

The lawyer banged the table in front of him and bellowed, "To sum up . . ."

The judges woke from their doze and the ladies in the gallery sat up and smoothed the skirts of their dresses.

"At a time when France is enjoying the fruits of liberty in the Second Empire, is it not a futile waste of time to prosecute an artist who is barely known beyond a small coterie of poets and writers, whose erotic scribbling is to be found in a volume that will be read by hardly anybody?"

So much for my defense, thought Baudelaire. The idiot has virtually admitted my guilt but has pleaded mitigation on the grounds that no one bothers to read my poetry. Imbecile. However, he would surprise them all. Although he was not allowed to testify, he was permitted to call a witness.

"We are to hear a witness for M. Baudelaire, I understand," said the judge. "Send him in."

The doors at the back of the court opened and Jeanne Duval walked in and threaded her way through the officials below the public gallery. The ladies in the gallery craned their necks for a better view. Duval was wearing a white dress that reached from neck to ankle. She entered the witness box. The defense lawyer wearily got to his feet again. It had not been his idea to call this witness; indeed, he had counseled against it.

"Your name, please?" he said.

"Jeanne Duval."

"Occupation?"

"Cabaret artist."

There was laughter from the gallery. Duval looked sharply at the rows of bonneted ladies, who smirked back. She caught the eye of Apollonie Sabatier, who looked away.

"When did you first meet M. Baudelaire?" said the lawyer.

"At Le Rêve cabaret club."

"How did that happen?"

"He saved me from a fight that had broken out."

There was laughter from the gallery.

"It was no laughing matter. Two men died in that fight. M. Baudelaire was most gallant."

"Then what?"

"I had nowhere to live. He found me somewhere to stay."

"So he looked after you?"

"He did. I was penniless."

"You might say he saved your life. . . ."

"In a way, yes."

"And in return?"

"I gave him warmth, love, and inspiration."

There was further laughter from the gallery. The ladies forgot the heat and the discomfort of the wooden benches. They forgave Pinard for his failure to read all of the poems that had been deemed obscene. The appearance of Duval was an unexpected bonus. "So you became his mistress . . . his muse?"

"Those are your words, not mine," she said.

"But you don't disagree with them?"

"M. Baudelaire was a deeply unhappy man. I think the only time he had really been happy in his life was when he was a child. Childhood was his paradise. He spent his life trying to regain it."

"You are saying you helped re-create that paradise?"

"I think I was very different from anyone he had ever known. I helped take him out of himself. I gave him unconditional love."

"Love or lust?"

"There is nothing wrong with a little lust. Ask those ladies in the gallery."

There was a flutter of fans. Sabatier hid a little laugh. Around her, the ladies tried their best to look outraged.

The senior judge who had been so keen to hear readings of the poems intervened to say he failed to see any merit in the defense's line of questioning.

Chaix d'Est-Ange replied that he was trying to show the court that M. Baudelaire was a sensitive and generous man who cared for those less fortunate than himself. Far from being the pornography the press had described, his poetry was rooted in compassion and a deep understanding of human nature.

"You have made your point," said the judge. "M. Pinard, your witness."

Pinard rose, smiled, and bowed to the gallery; then he turned to Duval with a theatrical frown.

"You say you are a cabaret artist, Mlle Duval?"

"That is right."

Pinard stepped around his table and approached to within a few feet of the witness box. He looked at the gallery and then at the line of judges. Finally he turned to face Duval.

"I say you are a whore, a woman who has dragged a good man into the gutter and inspired him to write this filth."

There was a collective intake of breath in the court. Then the murmuring of shock from the gallery and the crash of a chair as Chaix d'Est-Ange sprang to his feet. He was still trying to find suitable words of protest when Baudelaire shouted from the dock.

"That is an outrage. This woman is a witness, not a defendant!"

"Silence!" cried the clerk as an indignant clamor bubbled around the courtroom.

The senior judge beckoned the prosecutor to approach the bench. Pinard strode confidently across the court and bowed his head respectfully.

"As a prosecutor you are entitled to question the moral integrity of a witness—although, if I may say so, your language was a little, shall we say, flamboyant."

Pinard smiled.

"However, it is equally the right of the witness to respond. So if you will resume your place, the court will ask Mlle Duval whether she has anything to say."

Duval stiffened, clenched the edge of the witness box, and remained silent for a few seconds.

"I would like to ask a question of the prosecutor," she said.

"Proceed," said the judge.

Duval stared at Pinard, who shrugged and examined his nails.

"You count yourself a Christian, M. Pinard?" she asked.

"Mlle Duval, my job is to ask the questions in this court. Yours is to answer them."

"You heard the judge, monsieur," said Duval. "I have a right to ask a question. Are you or are you not a practicing Christian?"

Pinard flushed and addressed his answer to the bench.

"My religious faith has absolutely nothing to do with the witness, Your Honors. But since she insists, I see no reason not to tell the court that I am a practicing Christian—unlike the witness, I suspect."

"Thank you," said Duval. "Now, perhaps you can tell the court what a practicing Christian was doing in the Salon d'Or on rue du Vieux-Colombier on the night of June 24 this year?" She turned to the bench. "You may be interested to hear that the specialty of this house—which has since been closed by the police—was very young virgins from North Africa, some no more than ten years of age."

In the momentary silence that followed, various thoughts flashed like sparks from a fire through the minds of those in court. The ladies in the gallery realized that as witnesses to the scandalous exchange they would become the most desirable guests at every social occasion in Paris that fall. The judges balanced the uncomfortable thought that the inevitable publicity might suggest a lack of order in their court against the fact that the morning session would have to break early for lunch. And Pinard realized that a slut from the gutter, a half-caste from the Caribbean, a woman without manners, morals, or social refinement, had probably ended his career.

A general hubbub erupted in the court as those in the gallery rose to shout at both Pinard and Duval, although it was hard to tell what they were trying to convey to either. The judges had also stood up, using their gavels on the table before them in an attempt to restore order, while the court clerk and several minions struggled to talk above the din.

Baudelaire, in the dock, looked stunned. Pinard was bellowing obscenities at Duval. She remained calm and utterly unmoved by the scenes around her.

A few minutes later, the judges announced that their verdict was to be given at a later date and the court was adjourned for the day.

23

The Café Orpheus, close to the Palais de Justice, was used to customers with unusual requests. Judicial victims and victors would gather there with friends and relatives to celebrate or bemoan their fortune at the ends of their cases. So the staff was not surprised when Baudelaire swept through the glass-paneled doors in the middle of the afternoon, followed by Jeanne Duval, Poulet-Malassis, and Chaix d'Est-Ange, and demanded a bottle of vintage champagne, four glasses of Napoléon brandy, and a cat, alive, not stuffed.

Baudelaire took care to seat Duval and his publisher first and then flung himself into a chair beside them. He was restless with excitement, raising himself repeatedly to check the progress of the order. Chaix d'Est-Ange quietly pulled his own chair up to the table, aware that it would fall to him to break the bad news.

Baudelaire looked impatiently at the bar. The single question he wished to ask Duval required everyone to have a drink in their hands. There was as yet no sign of the drink, but the house cat, a brown Burmese with a white scar across its fore-head, had been placed on the floor beside the table. The animal, resentful of its sudden removal from the warmth of the kitchen, tried to escape, but Baudelaire scooped it up and held it in his lap, stroking it and looking at the quizzical face that stared back at him.

"In ancient Egypt, cats were thought to have magical powers because they killed rats and frightened away snakes," he said. "The pharaohs mummified their cats so they would accompany them to the afterlife."

"Maybe you should get one," said Duval, stroking the cat.

"I have one already—it pads softly through my head, making music as it purrs. It's my head cat. It brings me luck."

He jumped to his feet and whirled around the table, danc-ing with the cat in his arms, as a waitress arrived with the champagne and four glasses of cognac. She stepped aside in amazement as Baudelaire twirled around her with the cat held aloft. Choosing her moment, she darted to the table, set down the glasses and champagne, and fled. Baudelaire placed the cat on the table and collapsed breathless into his chair. The cat arched its back, raised its tail, and calculated the jump it would have to make to escape from the madman who had hurled it around the room.

"Which shall we drink first?" said the lawyer.

"Champagne is the drink one gives a lady. Brandy is for heroes. And as this lady is a hero, I suggest we drink them both," said Baudelaire.

He opened the champagne, poured them all a glass, and raised his to Jeanne Duval. She raised hers in turn and clinked her glass with his. But she said nothing.

"In the words of an English poet, here's to my *belle dame sans merci.*"

He drank the champagne in one gulp and reached for the brandy. The cat mistook the gesture and leaped from the table, landing elegantly on its feet, and disappeared toward the kitchen. Baudelaire frowned, briefly considered recapturing the animal, and then turned to Duval.

"So tell us. How did you know?" he said.

She smiled. If she loved him at all, and she doubted it, it was at times like these, when he became wildly excited, consumed with curiosity, desperate for information, overjoyed at what had happened or was about to happen. These were moments of great passion, when he lost himself in an idea, an event, or a line of poetry and when it seemed there was nothing he would not do to express his exuberant belief that life had finally smiled on him, that a corner had been turned, that success and fame awaited him—even dancing with a cat.

"It won't help, of course," mumbled the lawyer into his brandy. "It will go against us."

"I have friends in low places," she said.

"Wonderful. I love it. The sheer hypocrisy of the man—and those judges. Did you see their faces? They looked terrified. Because they all have something to hide—young girls, little boys . . ."

He made a fist and beat out a drumroll on the table.

"It won't help," said the lawyer again. "They'll crucify you after this."

Poulet-Malassis had said nothing throughout the exchanges. He sipped his champagne reflectively and said, "I fear our legal friend is right."

Baudelaire ignored them both. "But tell us, how did you know and why didn't you say anything?" he demanded.

Jeanne Duval refused all entreaties to explain how she had discovered that the public prosecutor regularly paid large sums of money to deflower young virgins at that exclusive brothel in Paris. All she would say was that Pinard was not the only senior public figure to make use of the service.

As for not telling Baudelaire beforehand, did he take her for a fool? He would have blurted the secret to everyone at the Café Momus.

"You wanted me to tell the court how you saved my life, what a fine upstanding citizen you are," she said. "Well, I did. Then I said what *I* wanted to say."

Chaix d'Est-Ange rose and headed for the door, muttering and shaking his head. Baudelaire laughed, called him an old fool, and ordered more champagne.

The old fool was right. The next morning the court announced that the defendants had been acquitted on charges of blasphemy but found guilty of offenses against public morality. Baudelaire was fined three hundred francs and his publishers one hundred francs. Worse still, six poems were banned and ordered to be deleted from all further editions. Every copy of the edition was confiscated. The fines were punitive and had been deliberately set at a level that neither defendant would be able to pay in the foreseeable future. In theory Baudelaire's monthly allowance could have paid off the fine within a year if he had been careful with the money. But much of the allowance was withheld and paid straight to his creditors. Worse still, Poulet-Malassis had lost his substantial investment in *Les Fleurs du Mal*. In addition to the twelve hundred copies printed, a limited edition of two hundred copies had been produced on fine paper for distribution to important writers and editors. The heavy costs were now irrecoverable.

Baudelaire was devastated. He could not believe or understand how a case prosecuted by a senior public official who had been revealed in court to be a sexual pervert, an abuser of trafficked children, and a hypocrite could have been allowed to proceed.

Admittedly, his lawyer had made a pig's ear of the defense, but the case should never have reached that stage. In exposing the hypocrisy of the chief prosecutor, surely Baudelaire had made the judges realize the hypocrisy of the whole case against him? How could they not see that *Les Fleurs du Mal* was an evocation of the struggle between good and evil that has afflicted mankind since Creation? That was what made the work a moral statement. As for the language, well—had the court not read the erotic verses in the Old Testament, especially the Song of Solomon or the Epistle of Saint Paul to the Romans? And why had his pathetic lawyer not pointed that out to the court?

Jeanne Duval could do little to assuage his rage. She didn't really want to try. The sudden mood swings that took him from triumphalism to tragedy were so sudden, so savage, that there was little point getting involved. Instead, she relished her own brief moment of fame. All the newspapers carried long reports of the trial and verdict, but while heavyweight papers such as *Figaro* concentrated on the case itself, the popular press led with her role in the prosecutor's spectacular and very public fall from grace.

Who was this mulatto charmer, with her dark skin and coal-black eyes, who had destroyed the career of a high official with a single question? How did she know exactly what had been going on at the Salon d'Or? And what other senior figures had enjoyed the *specialité de la maison* there?

The questions multiplied in the press and were repeated in the cafés and taverns of Paris, where there was no shortage of people prepared to offer the answers. The bohemians in the Latin Quarter hailed Jeanne Duval as a campaigning radical who had fought and defeated arrogant authority in the shape of the public prosecutor. In the Café Momus, where she so often sat in the corner while Baudelaire caroused with his friends, she was now the main attraction.

Duval delighted in the friends and admirers who briefly fluttered like moths to her candle. She was even more pleased when she realized that Baudelaire was jealous. As he pointed out to her with some asperity, he had been the victim of a gross miscarriage of justice and yet she seemed to have emerged as the heroine of the story.

As ever, he poured his feelings into a letter to his mother. The barbarians had won, he told her. Poor Poulet-Malassis was a broken man. The fine, the legal costs, and above all the loss of sales had virtually bankrupted him. And he, the man once destined to become the greatest French poet of the century, was a literary outcast. Publishers wouldn't touch him now. He was dangerous. He was finished. He would turn to some prose poems he had long planned, but in the meantime, could he have an advance on his monthly allowance— say two hundred francs—to help pay the fine?

• • •

Once the press caravan had moved on, Jeanne Duval turned to her own future. She was forty-six years old, although she never admitted that to anyone and only occasionally to herself.

Her life with Baudelaire had become impossible. She had left him before, but this would be the last time. Her court triumph had made it easier to make the break, she argued to herself. She was well known and might now be able to acquire the money to bring some stability to her life.

She played with the idea of becoming the kept woman of some wealthy man, not an aristocrat but an entrepreneur who had made his fortune in mining from the rapid rise in the price of coal and iron. There were many such men, especially those who had gambled and won on the surging stock market.

Some of the most famous mistresses in Paris were kept in style and lavished with gifts by their wealthy lovers. The difference between such women and outright courtesans was a fine one, but the distinction—or lack of it—no longer bothered her. Since she had been Baudelaire's mistress for years and received scant reward of any kind, would it not be better to find a rich man she could satisfy before her looks gave way?

She discarded the idea of a liaison with a society gentleman. Apart from anything else, she knew her skin color prevented any such relationship. Rich, titled men were happy to set up girls from poorer classes as their mistresses, provided they had the looks and a talent for perversion—but they wanted women with milk-white skin.

So she would find herself another artist, but this time one who had achieved success and made some money. She was getting old and the endless stress of life with Baudelaire was beginning to take its toll. They had been together now for fifteen years—and neither she nor he, nor anyone they knew, could explain the relationship. She needed him, and not just for money. That's all she knew. They clung to each other in an inexplicable embrace. She satisfied him, satiated his lust, allowed him to seek his pleasure in the strangest ways. He desired most to watch, to be the voyeur—above all, to see her naked with her jewelry, a simple pleasure easily granted.

Occasionally he would shyly ask for a third to join and some youth from the streets would be brought in, scrubbed down until his skin gleamed, and paid a few francs to join them. Baudelaire would watch, sometimes masked, sometimes behind the curtain that divided the bedroom from the drawing room, sometimes sitting in a chair next to them. He would drink laced wine, emitting sighs of satisfaction as she took her pleasure with the boy. Baudelaire found such ménages à trois gave him an adrenaline surge of excitement that was deeply satisfying. The young man would stumble off into the night with a story to tell that none would believe.

Both Baudelaire and Duval took pleasure in such chance encounters and in the long walks through Paris that usually followed. He would talk without stopping on those walks, about art, politics, the venality of the merchant class, and the immorality of the bohemian class. If he found a new gallery showing the work of an unknown painter, he would insist on taking the young artist out for a drink, where they would talk even more.

After the trial, however, Baudelaire changed. He stopped talking and shrank into himself, becoming a caricature of a morose misanthrope. She gave up trying to communicate with him. She had done her best and, frankly, she was bored with the repeated rages, the tears, and the suffocating self-pity that followed the verdict. He was a poet, wasn't he, with the imagination and technique to create great verse? So why didn't he create proper poetry, suitable for the age, without the explicit references to female anatomy that he knew would provoke the authorities?

24

The pendulum clock took pride of place in the window of the watchmaker's shop on the rue de Rennes, close to the junction with the boulevard du Montparnasse. Painted on the face of the clock were the traditional images of God and the Devil, the former a bearded, benign face smiling from the center of a radiant sun, while the latter conformed to the traditional image of a black half man, half monster with horns and a tail and carrying a trident.

A dozen other smaller carriage clocks were placed around the centerpiece. Sunlight streamed through the window, catching the brass weight of the pendulum as it swung to and fro. A shadow fell over the clock. A figure dressed in black bent down, leaning on a silver-knobbed cane, peering intently through the window. His hair was cropped short. He looked haggard and underfed. He placed one hand against the glass as if to reach through the window. He judged the main clock to be early eighteenth century, probably made in Antwerp, the center of the watchmaker's craft in Europe.

Baudelaire knew all the great clocks of Paris. He had a mental map of the church towers, public buildings, and new railway stations that displayed their ornate timepieces to the public gaze. These were the sinister deities of his poetry, their black hands pointing not to the present but to the inexorable fate awaiting mankind in the future. He looked at clocks with the fascination of a condemned man. The time was always later, and death was always closer, than you thought.

The backdrop to the display was pulled aside, an arm reached through, and a new clock was positioned among the others. The arm withdrew and the face of a shop assistant appeared, hovering over the clocks and inspecting the new arrangement. The face looked up at the figure on the other side of the window. The two men stared at each other. The shop assistant's face vanished. Baudelaire stepped back from the window and pulled out his watch. He was going to be late.

He turned and walked around the corner into the boulevard du Montparnasse. The far side of the street was being demolished; a whole block of broken buildings, once shops and houses, was disappearing. Gangs of men were swinging sledgehammers and picks at the remaining walls and throwing buckets of water onto the steaming rubble. Paris was changing around him and he had hardly noticed. Boulevards had been bulldozed through the slums, broad avenues across which it would be impossible to raise a barricade. Emperor Napoléon III and his city planner, Baron Haussmann, knew what they were doing.

Mature plane trees had been planted on either side of these thoroughfares. This in itself was a huge undertaking, requiring the extraction of grown trees from the forests around Paris and their transport into the capital on specially constructed wagons. Four- and five-story apartment blocks had risen behind the trees, changing the face of the city. Even along old boulevards like Montparnasse, a highway since medieval times, the buildings were being torn down.

Baudelaire lengthened his stride as he walked through the clouds of dust billowing from the demolition work. He wanted to buy that clock as a gift to his mother. She was widowed now and living alone in Honfleur. He had grieved for her when the general had died that spring, but with the trial approaching he had had little time to help her mourn.

As for the general, "good riddance" was his uncharitable view. He conceded that his stepfather had made his mother happy, but the man had refused to talk to him for years and had even continued the estrangement beyond the grave. Aupick had left his stepson nothing in his will. Baudelaire needed money—and not just to pay a percentage of the fine the court was now demanding on pain of a further hearing and imprisonment. He needed money for everything—the clock for his mother, a small allowance for Jeanne, and the basic food and drink to enable him to finish his current translation of Edgar Allan Poe's masterpiece, "The Black Cat."

Baudelaire's earlier translations had won praise and established him as an important critic and translator. The royalties were regular, if not substantial. The recognition meant much more than the money. He craved that above all. Maybe now important literary magazines such as *La Revue de Paris* would pay attention to his poetry.

But time was against him. He was thirty-six and looked thirty years older. He rarely saw his friends. Le Vavasseur had joined the army and gone to Algeria. Buisson had taken his stutter to America and apparently could now speak quite clearly in English but still stammered in his native language. Saddest of all, Prarond was dead, found still warm in his bed by his mother's maid. In fact, the suggestion was that he had been in bed with the maid and the heart attack had been brought on by strenuous early-morning activity.

The maid was fired but had turned up weeping at the graveside. Baudelaire's friend was dead at the age of thirty-two. That left only a few close companions. Édouard Manet was one, a young painter of great talent who had joined their circle at the Momus. Baudelaire immediately saw that this bearded young man, who had forsaken a privileged background to live the life of an artist on the Left Bank, was a fellow revolutionary. Manet used his brush as Baudelaire did his pen to demolish the old cultural order. The two of them would sit up until dawn in the Momus taking hashish with their wine and agreeing on the sterile realism of recent classical art and the shallow sentimentality of Romantic poetry. Manet argued that there was no point to an artist painting in exact detail what anyone could see for themselves. "Our work as artists is to awaken in people the imagination to see what is not apparent to the naked eye. That is where our genius lies," he would say.

Manet's belief in his genius was absolute and he saw the same extraordinary talent in his new friend. Baudelaire had praised his work in several magazines devoted to the arts and Manet in turn had expressed admiration for *Les Fleurs du Mal*—especially the banned poems. He had told the bohemians that one day soon he would paint a nude that would shock society as much as Baudelaire had done.

Life is a casino, Baudelaire thought. Here is Manet, defying his contemporaries to create what he calls impressionis-

tic works of art about life on the streets of Paris. Then there
is Buisson. One minute he cannot get a word out; the next he
is talking perfect English. Prarond is in the arms of a maid;
he ejaculates and dies—a life left at the height of satisfaction.
And Le Vavasseur, the golden giant, is now carrying a musket
in the desert—only two months ago they were taking a little
hashish and wine in the Momus and talking as they always
did, about the poet's place in the world and whether poetry
mattered at all.

"Tell me exactly what you write about," Le Vavasseur had
asked.

"It's difficult to put into words," he had replied.

"There you are, the poet who cannot express himself—
how are the rest of us to understand you, then?"

Baudelaire had been irritated. Le Vavasseur had never
been one of his more sensitive friends, but still . . .

"The mystery of man's destiny, that is what I write about,"
he had said.

"And love?" asked Le Vavasseur.

"*That* is the mystery," replied Baudelaire, and they drank
and smoked their hashish and talked until the chairs were on
the tables and the gas lamps had been dimmed.

And now his friend was wearing a kepi and fighting the
Arabs.

Life was indeed a casino. The house rules were simple.
Time spun the roulette wheel and rolled the ball. You placed
your bet. You lost. You grew older. You always grew older.

He looked at his watch again. He was going to be very
late for Manet, even supposing he could find his studio.
Baudelaire and the painter had become good friends during
their drinking nights at the Momus. When the wine ran out

absinthe was their drink of choice, and it was he who had suggested Manet paint a portrait of an absinthe drinker. The painting had been a success. Baudelaire's friend was going to be famous, and now he had agreed to do a portrait of Jeanne Duval. They hoped to sell it and share the profits.

Édouard Manet had rented a studio in Montparnasse to take advantage of the much lower rents than those charged in Montmartre, on the other side of the city. Fashionable and successful artists such as Monet had set up their easels in Montmartre and charged accordingly. For artists who had yet to sell a painting, and in some cases who had yet to complete a painting, the southern side of the city offered a cheaper alternative. A bowl of soup and a *coup de rouge* cost half as much around Montparnasse as anywhere else in Paris, or any other major city in Europe. The artistic colony who gathered there did not exactly starve in their garrets. Most could not afford a garret in any case, but as Monet pointed out in a controversial magazine article at the time, they rejoiced in their poverty because it added to the air of artistic martyrdom that they cultivated so assiduously.

Manet was different. He was gaining a reputation but had chosen to rent a studio in Montparnasse close to his friends in the Latin Quarter. His studio comprised a single large room on the top floor of a house that had not yet been designated for demolition. The tall bay windows and skylights provided the light he needed. There was a stove in the corner next to a washbasin. A chaise longue and a stool were the only pieces of furniture. The sole luxury was the door. It had been specially made of thick mahogany, with heavy brass hinges to take the weight. The hinges had been oiled so that the door swung open silently. Good light was the first requirement of an artist, Manet was fond of saying, but silence came a close second.

When Baudelaire finally arrived, he found the artist at his easel finishing a pencil sketch of his model. Jeanne Duval was lying with her back against the upright end of the chaise longue wearing a long white dress, from which appeared two slippered feet. There was black-lace edging around the bust and the dress flowed out over the chaise longue. Her hair fell to her shoulders and there was a small crucifix tied tightly to her neck. She wore red earrings. The familiar gold pendant that hung from her neck seemed a forlorn creature lacking its natural habitat. Behind her, the artist had arranged a diaphanous white curtain as a backdrop. Manet had positioned Duval to give no prominence to her figure. The voluptuous woman who merely had to breathe in deeply to command the attention of a crowded room had been transformed into a small, sad face in a sea of white. She looked demure and thoughtful, and a little lost.

Manet did not turn toward Baudelaire but waved a hand in his direction. Duval smiled and put a finger to her lips. Baudelaire walked softly behind the artist and inspected the sketch. He neither understood nor liked what he saw. The whole point of the portrait was that Duval had achieved some notoriety following the court case. She was, as one of the more scurrilous papers had pointed out, a moral hazard herself, since she clearly inhabited a milieu familiar to patrons of houses of ill repute such as the Salon d'Or. That was what would interest buyers. Yet here was a woman who looked as if she could have been a schoolteacher. She seemed devoid of passion and, to be frank, he thought she looked much older than her years, although he never had found out exactly how old she was.

Baudelaire began to pace the room. He inspected the stove, which was lit and gave the room warmth. He stared out of the windows at the drab urban landscape beyond. He sat down briefly on the stool, then walked over to look at a number of sketches hung on hooks along the wall. All were portraits of unknown people, a series of faces staring out at the artist.

Manet stepped back from his easel and waved a brush at Baudelaire.

"Would you stop moving around like that!" he said sharply.

"Charles! Go and get a coffee or something," said Duval.

"Why do you have to take so long?" he replied. "You've been here all day and you haven't even finished a sketch!"

"What you really mean is why I am painting her portrait and not yours?" said Manet.

"Exactly!" said Baudelaire, and it was true. He had approved the moneymaking plan, but only reluctantly. He, the wronged author, was surely the better candidate for a portrait by the coming artist of the day.

Manet put down his pencil and walked over to his friend, arms wide open. "Come here," he said.

Baudelaire reluctantly allowed the artist to embrace him. Manet stepped back.

"The trial made you both famous," he said. "Courbet has painted you—not a good portrait admittedly, because you never kept still. And now I am painting your delightful companion, the lady all France has heard about. They wish to see what she looks like in the hands of a great artist. And you will both make money out of it, I promise you."

Baudelaire pointed to Duval. "But that is not the woman I know nor indeed the woman France wants to see. You've made her look like a schoolteacher. Where's the passion, where's the look that can enchant a whole restaurant?"

Manet turned to his friend, clearly very irritated.

"I am trying to create a portrait. How I do it is my business. I don't write your poetry, so please don't try to paint my portraits."

"It's ridiculous," said Baudelaire. "Who do you think is going to buy a painting like this?"

"What are you trying to say?" said Duval, rising from the chaise longue again.

"You would be surprised what art hangs on the walls of the wealthy," said Manet.

"All right, I am wrong. So a painting of my friend, my what?—lover, muse, call her what you will—is going to sell for a fortune. Well, good luck, but for God's sake don't turn her into some dessicated spinster."

"You're being childish," said Duval. "You're just jealous."

It took Baudelaire an hour to walk to the Bibliothèque Nationale from Manet's studio. By the time he reached the Latin Quarter his temper had cooled and he decided to break his journey at the Momus for cognac and coffee.

It was true that he was jealous of Duval. He had good reason to be. He knew she took occasional lovers and pretty much slept around as she pleased. She made no secret of that. He was sure many so-called friends had slept with her. Men found her exciting and they were right; she was a free spirit sexually. She never charged for her favors, at least not in any conventional sense, but she was very free with them. She was quite open about it and told him he was just as free to behave as he wished.

"So what is the point of staying together?" he had demanded.

"Because I satisfy you," she had said. "I don't make you happy—no one could—but I make you less unhappy."

"And I give you money," he had retorted. "I clothe you, feed you, support you—what thanks do I get for that?"

She had laughed, always that rich, dark laugh that bubbled up to mock him at moments like this. "Money?" she had said. "You don't have any money. You scrounge it from your mother when she's not looking. And what you give me wouldn't keep a beggar in rags."

The stacks of the Bibliothèque Nationale were arranged over several stories, separated by flooring made of iron grilles that allowed light and air into the miles of shelving. Thus it was possible to look up from the lowest corridor and see daylight from the skylights at the top of the building. A chair and desk with a lamp were placed at regular intervals along the corridors for the benefit of researchers and authors.

Access to the stacks was restricted to members, who had to provide references and evidence of a fixed address, as well as paying an annual fee. Courbet and Gautier had provided the references for him, and his mother had agreed to pay the fee. It was here he came both to find rare volumes from past centuries, usually poetry or histories, and to be able to read in peace. Silence was requested throughout the stacks and the only noise was the occasional rustle of a book being pulled from a shelf or footsteps on the iron grilles.

Baudelaire always looked up when he heard the metallic sound of a boot on the grille above him. When one of the women assistants walked on a floor above, it was possible to look up through the grilles and see the flash of an ankle and lower legs in a swirl of petticoat. Sometimes, if the woman paused, he could see more—the outline of thighs, the white blur of undergarments.

There in the peace of the library stacks, with an early edition of François Villon open at his table, peering up through the skirts of an unknown woman, he would satisfy himself quickly and easily. Sex, he had always thought, was not about what you saw but what you imagined. Carnal pleasure arose not from the act itself, satisfying though that was, but in the mind, where women would tempt and tease him but ultimately submit. Orgasm was just a fleshly end to a flight of imagination, the final act of a play in the theater of lust.

He always gave himself the leading role in such fantasies and tried to populate them with women he had seen on the street, in a shop, or behind a bar. There was never a role for Apollonie Sabatier. Try as he might, she would only appear as a distant figure, clad in white. She would smile at him, but the image would quickly fade.

In such dreams he always returned to one woman.

A week later, the portrait of Jeanne Duval was almost finished. Manet had not allowed her to see the work in progress, and at the end of every sitting he had carefully covered up the canvas. Now it was time for her first viewing. She was nervous. Manet was already well known and she was sure he would soon become famous. He had found a patron who had bought *The Absinthe Drinker*. But Baudelaire, who knew her better than anyone, had hated the early sketches, and she feared he was right. She had never liked the pose, lying back adrift in a flowing white dress like some virgin spinster. And she could not understand why Manet had placed that silk curtain behind her.

Manet removed the cover with a flourish.

"Come and look," he said. "Take your time. No one likes their portrait on first viewing; in fact they usually hate it."

She walked nervously around the easel as he stepped back. She looked, then stepped back herself, colliding with him. She frowned and smiled weakly to hide the frown. She bent down to look more closely. The brush strokes close up looked rough, almost coarse, and carried no hint of the way they would harmonize into an image when viewed from a distance. Why had he painted the feet so small? Why was the hand so disproportionately large? And the dress—well, it seemed to overwhelm the painting; it was almost as if he was painting the dress and not the person.

"I think it's very good . . . the skin tones are perfect . . . ," she said, trying but failing to conceal the doubt in her voice.

"But you hate it. Don't worry, everyone does, as I said. . . ."

"I just don't think it's me," she said. "You've painted a society lady. I'm not like that, am I?"

"I painted what I saw," he said, "but an artist always sees a truth in people that they do not see themselves."

She looked at it again. No, this was not her. This was someone else; maybe he had some other, older, woman in his head from an earlier sitting. Where was the woman who inspired those beautiful poems of lust, longing, and loss? What had happened to the figure she was so careful to accentuate with a tight-belted waist? She was proud of her breasts. Even at her age, they had not fallen; they were firm and she showed them off beautifully in the dresses she made Baudelaire buy for her. Why had he ignored them? He was as red-blooded as the rest of the bohemians; she knew that. And yet he had suppressed her sexuality.

"Maybe you should take another look," she said and went back to the chaise longue and sat down on the far side with her back to Manet.

He replaced the cover on the painting and said nothing.

"You are famous for your paintings of nudes, M. Manet. . . ."

"Thank you," he said.

She unlaced her dress, pulling it down at the front and exposing her back. She turned, stood up, and let the dress fall to her feet. Without taking her eyes off him, she slipped out of the petticoat and stood naked before him. She lay back on the chaise longue.

"This is how I want the ladies of France to see me," she said.

Baudelaire had come to believe that the reason Manet had painted his mistress in such an unflattering light was to disguise his own passion for her. The moment he saw the sketch he had formed the view that there was an ulterior motive. How could anyone looking at that portrait suppose that Manet had any desire at all for Duval? He had flattened her figure, made a small, mouselike caricature of her face, and allowed two black-slippered feet to emerge from that absurd dress like a couple of wayward moles.

Baudelaire had no reason to return to the studio that day, apart from the thought that gnawed away at him: that his friend Manet was going to join all the others in having her briefly for his own—a plaything for an hour, a night, or even a few nights. At the end there would be no tears on either side, just a trinket, some perfume maybe, and the promise of eternal friendship. That's how she always wanted it. She broke off such liaisons almost as soon as they started. She refused to be tied down. For all that she needed money, she would never allow herself to be the kept woman of some artist.

And that, he told himself with grim satisfaction, was because she could never leave him. Well, if he discovered what he feared he was about to discover in the studio, he would end it once and for all.

And he did.

The door swung silently inward and there they were, perfectly placed on the sofa. She was naked and kneeling, head down, her dark hair flowing forward over her face, gasping and grunting. He was bent over her, thrusting and sweating, the artist and his model in a time-honored pose. Neither saw Baudelaire. He watched briefly, weighing voyeuristic pleasure against the pain of jealousy. Then he turned and left as silently as he had come.

Duval watched, arms folded, as Baudelaire emerged from the bedroom with an armful of clothing and dropped it into a large burlap sack on the living-room floor. He moved back into the bedroom and returned with a dressing-table drawer, the contents of which he tipped into the sack.

It was only when he came back from the room for a third time with an armful of dresses that she reacted and barred his way. He had already thrown some cheap stuff out of the window. She had let him make his point. Now as usual he was going too far.

"Not those! They're all I have!"

Baudelaire barged past her, but she grabbed him by the arm and swung him round.

"Put them down!" she shouted.

He dropped the dresses on the floor and grabbed the sack.

"I picked you out of the gutter. I made you. But nothing changed, did it? Once a whore, always a whore."

"I saved your life, you ungrateful bastard!" she shouted back. "What did I get for that? The rags you have just thrown out of the window, cheap dresses, cheap shoes, cheap everything—that's all I ever got from you!"

"So why did you stay so long? I've given you the best years of my life."

That was the question she had asked herself too many times. She didn't know the answer; nor did he.

He walked to the window, flung it open, and threw the sack out. That wasn't what hurt her. He had never called her a whore before. That had hurt. He knew she wasn't. The business with Manet was unfortunate and she understood his anger. She initially thought he had just been guessing wildly when he confronted her. He claimed to have seen them in flagrante. She denied it, but when he described exactly what he had seen she had told him the truth. It was a passing pleasure, a moment of lust—and why not? When had he ever denied himself such pleasures? When did he assume the right to judge her?

Anyway, now it was finally over, after sixteen years. She was free. Even at this late hour, she thought, she could remake her life.

25

The leisure steamer cut a crisp white furrow through the placid waters of the Seine as it headed upriver on the first of the afternoon cruises. The main deck was crowded with couples and families enjoying a Saturday-afternoon outing in the early days of spring. The women were holding parasols against the bright sun that bounced glaringly off the water. An accordion player moved through the crowd, a monkey on his shoulder holding out a tin for tips. Sellers of ice cream and sorbet were pursued by children from deck to deck.

An artist painting such a scene of middle-class Paris at play on a weekend afternoon would no doubt have wished to contrast the general air of gaiety with someone who stood somberly aloof from the crowd. He would have found the perfect study in the black-clad figure sitting on a bench at the rear of the craft scribbling furiously. The figure raised his head occasionally to frown at the merriment around him. Charles Baudelaire was writing to his mother.

Dearest Mama,

 You were right. She is nothing but a slut. I have thrown her out—this time for good. She has nowhere to go but I don't care. The irony is that I was evicted the same day I threw her on the street. I now live on the streets myself and spend my days on the river going back and forth on the boats. The day ticket is cheap and I can just afford it. Mama, more than ever I need your help. I have a new project translating a second work by Edgar Allan Poe. I just need to rent a room somewhere. So please forgive your errant son. If I could have three hundred francs, I could pay my fine and find somewhere to live.

 Your loving son
 Charles

Caroline Aupick ordered a strong pot of coffee before opening the letter. She did so with foreboding that quickly became despair. Her son, her only child, was now both homeless and bankrupt. She was a widower in her sixties, with a meager army pension and a small amount of savings from her first husband. She kept the money in the bank at a low rate of interest and refused to invest in railroad stocks as her friends constantly suggested. The stock market was a casino, and if she lost she would be forced to sell the one great consolation in her life—her little house by the sea.

"What am I to do with him?" she demanded of the maid. "He is determined to ruin us."

Mariette was familiar with such scenes. She knew the handwriting on the letter meant another request for money, which in turn would lead to a day of angry denunciation of the feckless youth whose sybaritic lifestyle in Paris laid waste to all around him. That would be followed by sorrowful reflection and an invitation to the priest to join her for an early-evening glass of sherry. The priest would gently remind his hostess that forgiveness lay at the heart of the Christian faith and would feel the need to consume at least half the bottle while doing so. Finally, Mariette would be dispatched to the post office in Honfleur with a bank draft to be sent by registered post to yet another cheap hotel in the capital.

On this occasion, however, Mariette suggested a new strategy. Rather than send the draft to Caroline's errant son directly, she advised sending it instead care of Apollonie Sabatier, thus encouraging him to renew a relationship that might yet be his salvation. Caroline approved of the idea, although she hardly thought it would break her son's obsession with his Creole mistress. In which case, suggested Mariette, why not offer the mistress a small sum to stay away from him for good? It was well known that the woman would do anything for money.

The maid who opened the door to Baudelaire thought he looked more like a scarecrow than the notorious poet who had been invited for tea. He was unshaven and haggard. His hair had been cropped short and his black clothes hung loosely on his frame. She ushered him into a well-furnished drawing room. Everyone in Paris wanted to get a copy of the poems, but the book had been withdrawn and burned, it was said. She had a friend who worked in the ministry and she said she might be able to get a copy. It was hard to think that such depravity had been created by this weary man who looked as if he hadn't slept for a week. She motioned him to a chair and left the room to get the tea.

Two places had been set on a side table. There were pretty china cups, tea plates, small bone-handled knives, and a silver cake stand holding jam sponge rolls that wafted the aroma of fresh baking into the room. There was a silver bell next to the cake stand. The walls were lined with paintings that had been carefully hung almost to the ceiling.

Coals glowed in the grate beneath a large mantel mirror. Beside the fireplace stood an open drinks cabinet containing a decanter of red wine and glasses. Heavy brown curtains had been half-drawn against the fading light of an October afternoon. Two sofas were placed on either side of the fireplace and in the center of the room a gas lamp had been lit on a round table.

He looked into the mirror. A deeply lined face looked back and nodded. They had tried to destroy him. He would respond. He would write more poems and bring out a second edition of *Les Fleurs.* He would educate the oafish, unlettered, newly rich of the so-called Second Empire of Louis-Napoléon and his absurd wife, Eugénie, about the meaning of beauty. He felt like a stage manager raising the curtain on scenes of great opera to a chattering, distracted audience. He had already given them Edgar Allan Poe, the greatest American writer of his generation. He was now writing enthusiastic reviews of the work of another genius, Richard Wagner, whom the French critics had ignored. Above all, France had not yet grasped how artists like Manet, yes, even him, and Monet were transforming the concept of what a great painting should look like.

He turned his attention to the paintings and stepped back in surprise. To the right of the mirror in a gilt frame, Apollonie Sabatier stood naked in a bedroom. She had her back to the artist but half-turned to face him with a look of slight surprise. She was holding a towel to cover her breasts and, from the damp sheen of her red russet hair and skin, looked as if she had just stepped out of the bathtub.

Behind her a double bed had been left unmade, the pillows rumpled and the blankets pulled back to reveal the sheets. Baudelaire walked over and peered at the signature. Of course it was Courbet. The story was clear. After a night of passion with the artist she had woken up, left him asleep while she took a bath, and returned to the bedroom to find him at work with a sketch pad.

A voice behind him said, "Do you like it?"

He turned, startled. Sabatier was smiling at him. She was dressed as if to go out, wearing a long red skirt, a black lace blouse topped at the neck with a bow, and jewelry: green jade earrings, an amber pendant, and two bracelets that glittered with bangles.

"Of course," he said. "It is beautiful, suggestive if I might say so. Sensual."

"Thank you. I only have it for a few weeks. It is to be hung in the Galerie Nationale."

Baudelaire nodded and smiled. "Congratulations. But do you normally pose like this for unknown artists?"

"He is hardly unknown. I think he is going to be a great painter."

"Maybe, but why in the nude?" said Baudelaire.

"Is that not when a woman is at her most beautiful?"

"In this case, most certainly," he replied.

"There will be the usual scandal, of course, when it is shown."

"The ladies of Paris like nothing better—and I suspect it will suit young Courbet as well."

"You're a cynic, M. Baudelaire," she said. "Would you care for tea?"

"Thank you."

They sat down opposite each other. She smoothed her skirts as she looked at him, while he fidgeted nervously and kept sliding his eyes to the portrait on the wall. She rang the bell and the maid appeared with a teapot on a tray. She placed it on the side table, poured two cups, and served them.

Sabatier waited until the maid had left, then said, "Your mother asked me to see you."

"I know. She thinks I am a terrible son—and she's right."

"She loves you very much; you know that?"

"She loves a little boy she once held in her arms. But we have to grow up, don't we? The clock ticks, the hands move, and suddenly we are older."

" 'Life is a casino. Time spins the wheel. You place your bet. Time rolls the ball. You lose and grow older. You always grow older.' "

"Ah, so you read that."

"It was beautiful but sad. Everything you write is sad—it's all about sin, pain, and death. What happened to love? And beauty?"

"I find beauty everywhere in this city, even in the cemeteries. That's where I find love."

Baudelaire rose, walked to the drinks cabinet, and picked up the decanter. He looked at the portrait. "Let's drink—to fine wine, great poetry, and to a lady who has been surprised in her bedroom."

Sabatier smiled and said, "Perhaps the wine first?"

He poured two glasses and handed her one. She took an envelope from her purse and gave it to him.

"Your mother asked me to give you this."

He ripped it open and examined the bank draft. He laughed and waved the envelope at Sabatier.

"A reward for being a good boy!" he said, walking over to the portrait and gazing at it again. "Hmm. Courbet was privileged."

"It was a privilege granted to a fine painter. He believes they will hang that portrait in the Louvre one day—and I will be famous."

"I can make you famous too."

Sabatier laughed. "I only pose like that for great artists," she said.

"Poets and painters are both artists," he said.

Baudelaire looked so serious as he said this that she couldn't help laughing. "And because you're an artist, you think I should just take off my clothes and pose for you?"

"Why not? Courbet painted you with a brush and oil. I would paint you with poetry."

"You don't need me," she said. "You have your own muse."

"Ah yes, I had forgotten. You've met her."

"And you have written poems for her—obscene poems, I believe."

"Have you read them?" he said.

"Yes, Courbet gave me a copy."

"And?"

"I found them moving, passionate."

"Erotic?"

"Maybe."

"They aroused you?"

"Possibly."

"And did they give you a sudden yearning to become that woman?"

"Meaning?"

He pointed to the sofa by the fire. "The woman who would lie there, jeweled hands cupping her breasts, oiled skin glistening with flashes of color as the light of that fire sparkles against her jewelry—that's the woman I mean."

Sabatier stood up, suddenly looking pale.

"My muse has gone—back to the gutter," he said. "Let me paint a portrait of you that will last forever. Courbet may make you famous. I will make you immortal." He turned and looked out through parted curtains at the windows glowing into life across the street as dusk settled on the afternoon.

Sabatier drank her wine and looked in the mirror. She could see Baudelaire with his back to her, staring out at the street. She turned down the gas lamps on either side of the mirror.

The room was in semidarkness, lit only by the glow of the fire and the gas lamp on the center table. She took off her clothes slowly and placed them across the back of a chair. Baudelaire closed the curtains and turned as she lay back on a sofa with her head on one armrest and her legs, parted slightly, on the other. She raised both arms so that her bracelets caught the light from the lamp. She lowered her arms, cupped her breasts with her hands, and smiled at him.

• • •

Although he had promised his publisher that he would avenge the humiliation of his trial by writing more poems to take the place of those condemned as obscene, Baudelaire found himself unable to do so. He could not even find words to express his creative desolation.

He wrote letters to his mother telling her that the foaming waves of imagination no longer broke on the shore, the well from which he drew inspiration had run dry, the starlit heavens in which he had once found such a rich source of imagery had been darkened. Then he tore them up in disgust at such thin, ill-nourished, shallow imagery.

The only money he made was from translating Poe. As he drifted around the cafés and bars of Paris, he found some solace in the expensive bookshops on the rue du Faubourg Saint-Honoré and the rue de Rivoli. He would go in, make an inquiry, and then be handed a new clothbound book with the silhouette of a black cat imprinted on the cover over the lettering: *Histoires extraordinaires par Edgar Poe. Traduit par Charles Baudelaire.* He never bought the book but always managed to persuade the bookseller to place it advantageously in the shop window. Every day he would pass the same shops, making sure that his book had not been supplanted by a newer title.

He often reflected that of all the absurdities of his life the chance by which he had learned to speak and write English was the most extraordinary. His maternal grandfather had been an officer in Louis XVI's army at the time of the Revolution. When the tumbrels began to roll through Paris he had fled with his wife to London, where Baudelaire's mother had been born in 1793. Caroline Aupick was proud of the fact that she alone among her contemporaries could speak English and she insisted that her son learn the language too. In the intervening years, he had forgotten much of his English. "But language is like a bicycle," his mother had told him. "You never really lose the original skills required to use such simple machinery." When he first read Poe's long narrative poem "The Raven," he was enraptured by the musical use of language and the evocation of the supernatural. "Nevermore," croaked the raven repeatedly to the heartbroken dying student. It mirrored Baudelaire's innermost despair; nevermore would he find love or pleasure. His life was ending miserably in failure and poverty. He was certain that Poe's gothic stories of the macabre would find a wide readership in France. The American writer had died a mysterious death in Baltimore a few years earlier and Baudelaire's letters of praise to an author he regarded as his alter ego were returned. He wrote to Poe's publisher asking permission to translate all his work and quickly brushed up his English.

Poe saved him. The translation of "The Raven" was an instant success and other works quickly followed. French readers warmed to such stories as "The Fall of the House of Usher" and "The Tell-Tale Heart." Poe was a poet of the dark underworld, whose stories dealt with the nightmare of murder and bloody revenge, of being buried alive and struggling to survive the plague.

For Baudelaire, however, the poetry had stopped. His work as a translator allowed him a brief respite from his creditors and, more important, meant that he could write to his mother without the usual request for money. But as she told the priest at one of their regular meetings, her son was still determined to cause her anguish. In his latest brief letter to his mother he had said:

I cannot write. I feel as if I have been buried alive, like one of Poe's characters. I am dying.

26

Poulet-Malassis had lodged an appeal against the court verdict. He persuaded the poet to write a personal letter to the Emperor Napoléon and his wife, Eugénie, pleading for a pardon. But the chance of success in either case was remote. The first edition had been withdrawn from sale and he was therefore left with the cost of printing the volume and the advances paid to the author without the immediate prospect of earning any money.

However, the trial had generated considerable public interest, and the presence of so many wellborn ladies in court showed there was a real appetite for the controversial poems. There was a widespread belief that the whole volume was erotic, which was not true, but Poulet-Malassis did not intend to do anything to discourage that view. It would certainly help sell a second edition of the book—should he be allowed to publish one. He might even recoup his losses and make a small profit. But he needed extra poems from his despondent author. The first edition had been thin, with only one hundred poems, and now Poulet-Malassis had lost six of the most explicit.

He would ask Sainte-Beuve, someone Baudelaire still greatly admired, to try to encourage the poet to resume work. And in the meantime he would put together an expurgated version of the first edition, with the titles of the condemned poems printed over blank pages. That would make a mockery of the court decision and prove a selling point for the public. It would still depend, of course, on whether the appeal court allowed publication at all, but Malassis was confident enough to begin planning the edition. Baudelaire would object noisily and there would be the normal scene. But that would strengthen Poulet-Malassis's argument that further poems were needed to create a proper second edition.

To the publisher's irritation, however, Sainte-Beuve refused even to consider a meeting with Baudelaire. He admired the poet and his work, but as a distinguished literary critic he, frankly, had better things to do than play nursemaid to a wayward author.

Jeanne Duval seemed the only hope. Poulet-Malassis was determined to reunite the poet with his mistress. She haunted his life as she did his poems, an unattainable ideal, a woman with a feline sensuality who would never return the love she was offered. In his Black Venus, Baudelaire saw mirrored both his deepest passion and his darkest despair. Surely, Poulet-Malassis argued, in his hour of need the poet would turn again to the woman who had meant so much to him.

Yet Baudelaire would simply not countenance a reconciliation. He blamed Duval for every ill that had befallen him, especially his permanent lack of money. He claimed she was responsible for his inability to meet any deadline for his poetry or those set by the editors of the various journals for which he was commissioned to write literary criticism.

When his publisher asked how Baudelaire could write with such passion about someone who pained him so much, the poet had drawn a sketch showing an attractive coquette with a big bosom and ink-black eyes that stared searchingly from the page. Below the drawing he had written: "Quaerens quem devoret." It was a drawing that said more about the artist than his subject, not least because Baudelaire would tell anyone who cared to ask that the Latin inscription meant "seeking whom to devour."

"That's what she's done to me," he told Poulet-Malassis. "Devoured me alive, left me an eviscerated corpse."

There seemed nothing the publisher could do to rekindle the fire that had once burned so brightly within the poet. Baudelaire was lost in despair.

Jeanne Duval had moved in with her friend Simone Clairmont after the final break with her lover. Little had changed in Simone's life since they had first met. Occasional suitors always proved a disappointment. She had friends, but none, except Jeanne Duval, had become close companions. She was lonely but wore her loneliness lightly. She created a routine around the things that mattered in her life: mass on Sunday, ice cream followed by a demitasse of strong black coffee every Wednesday after work at the Café Tortoni on the boulevard des Italiens, and on Fridays she would queue for a cheap seat at the Théatre Français, where revivals of Moliere's comedies alternated with modern drama. Most evenings she read or wrote long letters to her family at home. She was not unhappy, she told herself, but neither was she happy. Her greatest pleasure came at the end of the working week when she would spend hours in the secondhand book stalls that had begun to appear along the banks of the Seine on weekends.

She had agreed without hesitation that Duval should move in with her, but it was an inconvenient and uncomfortable arrangement for both women. Simone lived in one room dominated by a large bed. They shared the bed, but there was little room for the few remaining clothes Duval possessed. Nor could she pay her friend rent. Duval had long since given up her job at Le Rêve and took care to avoid the cafés favored by the bohemians. Thus she had no income and no opportunity to borrow money from the few people in Paris she knew well enough to ask for a loan.

She would rise late, long after Simone had left to walk the two miles from Neuilly across the city to the Latin Quarter. Around midday, Duval would make the same journey on foot to the perfumery on rue de Rivoli where her friend worked. The two would share a modest lunch—usually weak coffee, a pastry, and maybe an apple. Simone always had to pay for the meal, a cause of increasing irritation and embarrassment to both women. It was not an arrangement that could last.

"I promise I will not impose upon you much longer," Duval said one lunchtime. "I know how difficult it is for you having me around all the time. I have worked out what to do. I need just a little more time."

"I am your friend. I love your company. You can have all the time you want," said Simone. "Really!"

The two women smiled at each other, allowing the understanding implicit in the remarks to go unspoken. The next morning Duval did not join her friend for lunch as usual. She took the shorter walk instead to the Champs-Élysées, near which the houses of the wealthy and the embassies of major countries were grouped.

Poulet-Malassis knew the neighborhood where Jeanne Duval lived. He knew the cafés she used to frequent and the cabaret clubs where she once worked. He was renowned in the publishing world for personally checking every draft and proof of a book word by word, line by line. He brought the same attention to detail to his search for the woman of whom Baudelaire had talked endlessly. When he found her he would offer her money, a reasonable sum. She would understand that. And she would agree.

He employed two boys at his publishing houses whose duties were to carry messages, manuscripts, proofs, and occasionally banker's drafts to and from the homes of writers scattered through the city. These two boys, who were of indeterminate age but looked more like children than young men, were given crude copies of the sketch Baudelaire had made and told to show them to the patrons of every café and bar in the Latin Quarter, street by street.

The stratagem worked. Simone Clairmont noticed a boy showing the pen-and-ink sketch to a series of bemused customers in a café one lunchtime. A waiter seized the sketch, tore it up, clipped the boy around the head with the back of his hand, and bundled him into the street. When Simone followed and dried the boy's tears with a kerchief, she discovered the nature of his mission.

27

Jeanne Duval walked down the boulevard des Italiens, turned into the place de l'Opéra, and then began the walk back to the Latin Quarter on the Left Bank. Her boots were comfortable, the weather cold but dry, and her progress unimpeded by the crowds of pedestrians who would take to the streets in a few hours' time. She walked everywhere in Paris both because she could not afford the price of a carriage and also because she enjoyed the creative chaos of the city center.

Baudelaire had been excited about the changes on the Left Bank, but Duval had paid little attention either to his views or to what was happening around her in the city. Now she realized that the center of Paris looked as if it had been struck by an earthquake. Baron Haussmann, that master of urban geometry, was tearing down the web of medieval alleys and backstreets that had held the central slums together for centuries. Whole areas were reduced to rubble as unbending boulevards were driven through the city, bringing with them shopping parades and apartment blocks. The new highways were clean, asphalted, and clearly lit at night. The rising architecture of Paris was designed to celebrate trade and commerce and free the city from the mob.

As for the wretched poor, they would be removed to the far-flung suburbs. Everywhere wagons creaked through the streets with families perched on their few goods and chattels as they were taken to new homes. Tens of thousands of people were being moved without appeal and with little compensation.

Good, thought Duval as she skirted a gang of a dozen men digging furiously in a large hole at the bottom of the rue Saint-Honoré. She had spent too long in the squalor and stench of the old Paris to mourn its passing. The city would be well rid of the thieves, beggars, prostitutes, and pimps that had infested it since the Dark Ages.

Baudelaire seemed to delight in writing about these people. The man took a perverted pleasure in the sordid life of the slums. Well, she didn't. She knew that for most people life in the dank underbelly of the city meant a brief and miserable existence that finished on a slab at the city mortuary. She swore to herself that she would not end up as a cadaver laid out for the amusement of tourists. She would leave. If an old city like Paris could tear down its past and renew itself, so could she.

For years she had wondered what had happened to her father. She knew that his name was Duval and he had been born in Bordeaux. His last letter from New Orleans suggested that he was going to start a cattle business out in one of the new western states. That was twenty-five years ago. He had been in his twenties when he abandoned his family and the plantation, so he might still be alive. Maybe he had become a wealthy rancher with thousands of head of cattle. Fortunes were being made out west, the papers in Paris reported. Whatever he had done, she was sure he would have kept his name. Duval was not an uncommon name in France, but it would be unusual in the new territories of the western United States, where he would be easy to find. That surely was *her* manifest destiny.

A familiar question returned. Why had she taken so long to cast off the shackles that bound her to Paris? Why, why, had she stayed with him? Who was it who said that there were many rivers in the human heart but never a sea? Love was the impossible ideal—wasn't that what he wrote about? Well, everything had become possible now.

That strange publisher had tried to bribe her to go back to him. It was a nice lunch in a famous restaurant. She well knew the impression she had made as she sauntered to the door, trailing malice and lust among the lunchers. But the publisher's proposition had been absurd. Baudelaire's mother had made the equally ridiculous offer of a reasonable sum to leave him forever. As Duval looked around her at the chaos that had gripped Paris, the decision came easily. She would take the money and leave Baudelaire, Paris, France— everything.

It began to rain. Clouds the color of gunmetal slumped over the city roofs. She took shelter under the pillared façade of the Comédie-Française. Older generations still called the theater the Maison de Molière and it was here she had tried to audition when she first arrived in Paris. She smiled at her naïveté. She had actually thought that with her looks she might get a small part in one of the great plays, perhaps a

walk-on role in *Tartuffe*. But it was the same story as with
the wagoner who had brought her to Paris all those years
ago. A very junior member of the theater staff had hinted at
a promising future for her if she cared to disrobe so that he
might better assess her acting ability. She sometimes wondered if men thought of anything else.

She glanced at the clock above the Comédie-Française. It
was almost four o'clock. Simone would be finishing work
soon. Perhaps they would take tea together. She would be able
to pay this time. She had the offer of two thousand francs
from Caroline Aupick in her purse. She would write back
and accept. A bank draft would be sent and she would have
the cash in her pocket at the end of the following week. Then
she would do what she should have done years ago. And she
would tell nobody—except Simone.

Ever since his trial two years previously Baudelaire had
abandoned the rakish clothing of the man-about-town and
dressed only in black. The bright waistcoats, silk-lined jackets, and resplendent cravats had all been handed to street beggars. After he had shaved off his beard and mustache, his
pallid face and somber clothing made him look like an under-
taker's clerk; at least that was the joke among the bohemians
in the Café Momus. His face was deeply lined and his reced-
ing hair brushed forward in a ragged fringe. His friends noticed, however, that the black suit, cape, and boots had all
been handmade at considerable expense. As Le Vavasseur
said, Baudelaire may have been mourning his lost poems or
his departed muse, or both, but he was doing so in his

customary style. His friend had returned from service in North Africa, but Baudelaire had little to say to him or any of his old circle of friends.

He haunted the Momus, always sitting at a table in the corner scribbling furiously in a notebook. A table beside him was piled with books. Those who tried to talk to him were waved away. When strangers came into the café and asked for Charles Baudelaire, intimating they had urgent business with the poet, they were told he was staying with his mother in Honfleur.

At lunchtime a waiter would bring him soup, bread, and some fruit; dates and apples were his favorites. A small carafe of red wine would be placed on his table with a glass of water. Baudelaire would drink half the glass and then refill it with wine from the carafe. The bohemians watched this daily ritual without surprise and noted that the bill for lunch was never rendered—it was always added to the growing debt in the poet's name behind the bar.

One day in the late morning, Baudelaire noticed Théo Gautier and Poulet-Malassis drinking coffee at a table outside the café. They were, he reflected, two of his few remaining close friends. He left his corner of the café and joined them. They greeted him warmly, pulled up a chair, and poured him some coffee. He sipped the drink and nibbled a pastry, staring vacantly at the street. The two men knew better than to try to engage the poet in conversation. He sat there listening as they exchanged the latest gossip about the emperor and his wife and discussed the commercial success of the great department stores that had risen along the new boulevards.

"They are no more than brothels," said Baudelaire suddenly. His friends looked at him inquiringly. "They awaken desires in women to spend money they don't have—just as bordellos tempt men to do the same."

"You sound like a socialist," said Gautier.

"Nonsense. I am just making the point that women treat these stores like churches in some new religion."

"You should write about that," said Poulet-Malassis.

Baudelaire sat up a little and sipped his coffee. Yes, he could write a pamphlet damning the new commercialism that had placed such temptation in the way of women with even a little money to spend. Since the beginning of time it was men who had always surrendered to temptation and ruin; now it was women who were the profligates, lured by the siren call of cheaper household goods, personal toiletries, and clothing.

"I'll think about it," he said.

He stared once again into his coffee cup. A shadow fell on the table as a woman walked up and stood there blocking the sun. Poulet-Malassis and Gautier looked up while Baudelaire remained buried in his thoughts. Simone Clairmont shifted her weight nervously from foot to foot and clutched her purse tightly to her chest.

She had never met any of these men, but Baudelaire had become a familiar figure to most people in Paris since his trial. The newspapers and literary journals had carried a series of images, mostly sketches but also some early photographs of the man deemed to have scandalized society with his obscene poems. She looked at him, trying to attract his attention, but Baudelaire seemed unaware of her presence.

"Can we help you?" said Poulet-Malassis.

Simone stared at Baudelaire. "She's leaving tonight," she said.

"Who are you?" said Poulet-Malassis, rising from his chair.

"I am talking to *him,*" said Simone, motioning to Baude-laire.

Baudelaire looked up as if he had woken from a dream. He frowned, seeing the stranger at the table.

"On the train to Le Havre—Gare du Nord," said Sim-one.

She turned and walked away as Baudelaire stood up, spilling his coffee. He watched her go and then, without a word to the others, walked back into the café.

"What was all that about?" said Gautier.

"I think I know," said Poulet-Malassis.

28

Jeanne Duval sat on the lid of an old leather trunk, bouncing gently up and down to try to close it. Only a man could have designed such an utterly inefficient piece of equipment, she thought. She gave up the battle, opened the trunk fully, and delved into its depths, bringing out several dresses. She threw them onto the bed. The room in a cheap hotel near the Gare du Nord was small, filthy, and smelled of sweat and stale garlic. But it was close to the station, to the point of departure, to the end of her life in France. She could put up with anything now. She had spent her last night in Paris. She had a ticket to Le Havre and a passage booked on the steamer *Péréire* to New York. She sat down on the bed and bent double as the cough started, a deep spasm that shook her whole body and seemed to come from somewhere deep in her lungs.

There was a gentle knocking at the door and the sound of a key in the lock. Simone peered round the door.

"Can I come in?" she said.

Duval nodded, still coughing. Simone went to a basin in the corner, poured water into a chipped mug, and handed it to her. Duval took it and drank.

"Where have you been?" she said.

"I went to get some fresh air. This place is worse than a prison cell."

"I'll be gone in a couple of hours. Here, sit on that."

She pointed to the trunk and watched as Simone sat on the lid and closed it. There was her hatbox as well, containing the blue hat she had worn to lunch with Poulet-Malassis. She knew it had impressed him; indeed the whole restaurant had been impressed. Women did not wear such hats; it was not the fashion. She had had it specially made to her own design and it was coming to America with her.

Duval lay back on the bed.

"You have the time?" she said.

"It's almost seven," said Simone.

"And you've told nobody?"

"Of course not."

Duval raised herself on her elbows and looked at her friend. The look turned into a stare. Simone had argued fiercely against this departure to the New World, this leap into the unknown, as she put it. Irritatingly, she was right. Her friend had received half of the two thousand francs promised by Caroline Aupick. Duval now had enough money to see a doctor and get some treatment for the weight loss, the continuing coughs and colds from which she had been suffering for months. That would have been the sensible course. But the windfall had also presented her with an exciting, irrational alternative.

She accepted that the plan to travel to the United States

in a shared third-class cabin across the Atlantic to New York
and then take a train to the West was simply madness. But
she was going to do it. The idea that her father might be out
there, in the far-flung wilderness of America, had originally
been the imagining of a wishful mind, a passing fancy, an
entertaining daydream. But at night the fantasy became a
conviction. She went to sleep thinking about her father,
dreamed about him all night long, or so it seemed, and awoke
feeling certain that she would one day meet him again. She
knew he had fled to New Orleans—that was where all the
French in Haiti went after the uprising. And from what little
she had learned about her father, she knew him to be a man
of action and an adventurer but also a person of integrity.

Her mother had said he treated her better than most field
slaves taken into the big house for the plantation manager's
pleasure. He had not thrown her back in the fields after a few
nights' rutting. She had been transferred to the kitchen staff
and he had seen she was taken care of during childbirth. She
forgave him the fact that he had fled shortly after her baby
arrived. Black gangs from Port-au-Prince were hunting down
whites of any wealth and status, especially those on the plantations. All the French had fled by boat to America. The only
whites who remained were too poor to pay the extortionate
prices for a passage to safety.

At night she endlessly replayed the story of her father's
journey to the new states of the West. He had been a coffee
plantation manager, a man of business, and he would have
seen the opportunities in importing cattle from France and
building up breeding herds in the West. That was where he
said he was going in his last letter. That was surely where he
would have gone.

She had looked up details of the new states in the library of the American embassy in Paris. She knew all their names and she knew the railroad was pushing ever farther out west, making it easier to reach the expanding frontier.

The West was the American destiny, and that was exactly how she felt. She was fated to find her father in the new territories beyond the Missouri River. And if, as was possible, she didn't find him? Well, at least she would be rid of her old life, giving comfort and satisfaction to a man who sucked the lifeblood out of her, a man who treated her with contempt, a man whose feverish imaginings depended on daily doses of opium and alcohol, and whose poetry was the product of a diseased mind.

But therein lay the problem. He had told her she was the ghost who haunted his work, the melancholic, savage, seductive spirit that inspired him. He had said that over and over again. Maybe it was true, but it was equally true that the poems haunted her just as much as she was supposed to haunt them. She could recite whole verses of "Le Léthé," "Tristesses de la lune," "Harmonie du soir," "Parfum exotique." She could see herself in those poems. She was his "cruel tigress," his "licentious vampire," his "ebony-thighed witch," his "daughter of the shadows." Best of all, he called her an oasis where he could dream and drink the sweet wine of memory.

And what memories they shared! When he had moved her into those luxurious rooms in the Hôtel de Lauzun, there was a party almost every night. His friends at first tried to ignore her, then flirted with her, and then sent her secret notes proposing a tryst at some apartment or hotel. They thought she was a whore, but she didn't care. Only Le Vavasseur realized the depth of their relationship. Le Vavasseur understood his childhood friend better than most, although like the others he often despaired of Baudelaire.

What she loved about Baudelaire then was that he would suddenly vanish from the party and reappear in a few minutes with complete strangers he had met on the street, all well-dressed good bourgeois citizens, mostly men but often accompanied by their women friends, lovers, or wives. No one ever understood how Baudelaire managed to entice these strangers into the hotel, except perhaps that the Lauzun was famous and he was beginning to acquire a certain notoriety as a poet and art critic.

He would introduce them to his guests, pour the wine, and beg them to tell him their story—any story, really—he just wanted to hear about their lives. Surprisingly, after some wine, and occasionally a little hashish, those strangers talked, usually of the restaurants and shops they liked, the plays or operas they had seen, or the books they were reading. Baudelaire would listen, fascinated, gently asking questions.

His friends would be bored and start easing their way to the door, and then their host would leap to his feet and command everyone to gather in the hotel lobby for a musical entertainment. Every night except Sunday, the Lauzun produced a show for its guests—a little operetta, a solo violinist, or a pianist. Baudelaire and his friends would walk down the hotel's magnificent central staircase and order more wine and take their seats with other guests for the music.

The strangers who had been gathered from the streets would soon make their excuses and leave, as would the bohemian crowd, who preferred the raucous and bawdy conversation in the Momus or Procope to elegantly played contemporary music. By the end of the little concert, often only she and he would remain, and without a hint of fatigue he would suggest a walk. Wandering through Paris by night was his favorite pastime, and reluctantly, for it was always late and she would prefer to be in bed, she would join him.

They would walk across the river, sometimes up the Champs-Élysées, where Baudelaire would decry the wasted genius of the greatest Frenchman of any century. She would remind him that it was Napoléon who had reimposed slavery after the Revolution had abolished the practice in all French territories in 1794. At other times they would walk to Notre-Dame. He always chose a route through the dark, stinking back alleys of the slums. That was the real Paris, he would say; we must always remind ourselves that behind the grand boulevards and the expensive hotels and restaurants lay starvation, disease, and early death.

He never understood how much she did not wish to be reminded of that. She had had enough poverty. She wanted to enjoy the life of the mistress of a poet about town, a man who was prepared to spend whatever money he had on the best couturiers, restaurants, and theaters. But she never said that.

It was on these walks that he showed signs of real tenderness to her. He would slip his arm in hers and draw her to him in the darker streets. He would whisper silly things into her ear, tell her how much he needed her, how they would live together in a grand house on the Right Bank. Then somewhere deep in the slums—and it was always in the slums—he would lean back against a wall, they would kiss, and he would slide his hands through her hair.

In those days it was long, with flowing curls that dropped to her shoulders. The kisses would go on for a long time in the darkness, with mud underfoot, the smell of sewage, and the occasional growling comment from a passing drunk. That was what excited Baudelaire: darkness, the stench, danger, and the chance of discovery or, worse, robbery—all heightened his desire. Once she had unbuttoned him, it was easy to give him the satisfaction he found so hard to achieve in any other circumstance, except perhaps in a brothel.

But those days came to an end when the money ran out and the Lauzun reclaimed their suite of rooms. That was when they began their lives as debtors, hounded from one apartment to another. He begged her to stay with him and help him. Sometimes there were occasional flashes of what they had once shared, moments of laughter and affection, but always when he had been drinking or had taken opium.

Now all that was finally over. She was forty-eight years old. She had arranged her escape. She looked across at Simone and saw her pale, anxious face. Simone looked away.

"You're not lying to me, are you?" said Duval.

"Why would I?" said Simone. "The wolves are after you. You think I want them snapping at my heels as well?"

Duval bent over in the grip of another coughing fit. She muffled the rasping sound with a handkerchief and waved Simone away as she tried to put an arm around her. She looked at her handkerchief: blood and phlegm. She needed the sea air of an ocean voyage and the long hot summers out west in America. She would recover and find a new life— and her father.

The two women arrived at the Gare du Nord to find that the mania for destruction and construction that Baron Haussmann had inflicted on central Paris also applied to the city's new railroad terminals. The station had been completed only a few years previously, to link the north of the country to the capital, yet now the elegant façade was being pulled down and the huge engine shed was being rendered roofless as workmen removed the glass panels. A printed notice announced in red capital lettering that, owing to rising rail traffic, a new Gare du Nord was being built, but travelers were advised that the wondrous sculptures that graced the old station would be retained in the new terminal.

There they were, placed on temporary pedestals at one side of the station: twenty-three small busts of women, tastefully draped in classical togas, named after every major city one could reach by rail from Paris: London, Brussels, Geneva, Vienna, Rome, Lisbon, Madrid, Moscow, Warsaw, Copenhagen, Berlin, Prague, and Budapest. The architects had clearly commissioned rather more statues than destinations, because added to the list of European capitals were some of the great cities of the New World: New York, Buenos Aires, Montreal, and Cape Town. The statues had been individually carved from stone and each woman carried a different expression.

Holding her hatbox, Jeanne Duval walked through the milling crowds of passengers, their relatives, friends, and porters, and examined the statue representing New York. The woman was young and seemed to be looking hopefully at the far horizon. Duval took this as a good sign. She imagined the woman to be the daughter of Saint Christopher, the patron saint of travelers.

Baudelaire had delighted in telling her the story of how Christopher had been a clumsy giant outcast from his village in the Dark Ages because he kept breaking everything he touched. One day he had saved a small girl from a pack of

wolves by walking into a raging river and then helping her
across. He had taken the girl home, but the villagers, although
grateful, still would not let him return. They gave him wine, a
cooked chicken, and bread as a reward and sent him back to
the forest. That night he drank and ate so well that he did
not hear the encircling wolves until it was too late. They fell
on him in revenge and devoured him.

That was typical, she thought. The story had nothing to do
with the myth of Saint Christopher; it was characteristic of the
way Baudelaire would twist an innocent fairy tale to suit his
taste for the macabre and the grotesque. These days he looked
the part too, dressed like a scarecrow in those black clothes, a
salesman for an afterlife in Hell, a prophet of doom and damnation, an endless dabbler in the dark side of men's souls.

She shivered and looked around for Simone. Even without a roof, the building echoed with whistles, shouts, and the
hiss of steam as the engines gathered power for their jour-
neys. She saw her friend talking to a young porter who was
loading her trunk onto a barrow. Simone saw her, waved,
and turned to follow the porter to the ticket barrier.

Duval pushed into the crowd, using her elbows to carve a
way through the crush. She looked at the four-faced station
clock that hung from a girder, like a spider surveying the
chaos below. It was seven o'clock. She must hurry. Her ticket
was inspected and returned. Simone showed her visitor's
ticket and was told she must leave the platform the moment
the train left. They walked up the line of passenger cars
until they came to the third-class compartments at the end
of the platform right behind the engine. This was the fast
train to Le Havre, the port for the Atlantic steamers, and as
usual it would be packed.

The porter examined her tickets, took the trunk, and backed into the train, dragging the luggage behind him. Duval followed, carrying her purse and hatbox. The train was filling up and most compartments were occupied. The six seats in hers already had four other passengers. The porter pushed the trunk ahead of him, causing much shifting of legs and disapproving glares. He took one look at the luggage already stowed in the overhead rack and manhandled the trunk back into the corridor. He was breathing hard and sweating.

"Can you leave it at the end of the corridor?" she said, and stepped into the compartment.

He nodded and dragged the trunk away. Through the window Duval could see Simone looking more anxious than ever. She would miss her, the only true friend she had ever really had. The four other passengers were buried in newspapers and magazines, quietly hoping the new arrival would be the last and that she would sit down quickly and restore calm to the compartment.

She placed her hat on the corner seat. At the door, the porter had returned and was hovering for a tip. She opened her purse, frowned, and closed it. Stepping carefully over the legs, she went up to him and kissed him quickly on the cheek.

"Thank you," she said.

All four heads in the compartment looked up. The porter looked astonished, then irritated when he realized that was to be the only reward for his hard work.

She followed him back to the platform, feeling the beginnings of a coughing spasm somewhere deep inside her. Simone was waiting for her and hugged her, holding her close, two women clinging to each other as if in some lovers' last embrace. Duval was surprised and a little embarrassed at her friend's emotional farewell. She knew Simone was about to cry, which would only attract further attention on a platform that was rapidly emptying of passengers.

Duval broke away, doubling up to release a wrenching cough and holding a handkerchief to her mouth. Simone stood by her, rubbing her back. Late arrivals for the train glanced at the curious sight and hurried past. She began to cry. Uniformed guards were closing the doors to the train in what sounded like a succession of small explosions, while throughout the station the high-pitched whistles added to the air of slight panic that attended the departure of a train.

"Send me a letter—promise?" said Simone.

Duval straightened up, patting her chest as the coughing subsided.

"I will, I promise. And you write to me—I will send you the address when I find somewhere to live."

"But you don't know anyone in New York!" wailed Simone, repeating one of the many arguments she had mustered to change her friend's mind.

"I didn't know anyone here either when I arrived. I'll be all right."

Duval opened her arms and they hugged again. Simone was sobbing quietly and Duval was about to pull away, fearing that tears would ruin her makeup, when she felt Simone stiffen suddenly. Duval held her away. Simone was looking over her shoulder with wide-eyed wonder.

Duval turned. Charles Baudelaire was standing there, an expressionless, cadaverous figure a few feet away on the platform, wearing black and carrying his silver-knobbed cane. The guards were shouting something incomprehensible in the din of closing doors and whistles. Duval gave Simone a withering look that she hoped her friend would remember for a long time: the look Jesus must have given Judas. Duval watched as Simone turned and walked down the platform, her shoulders heaving with sobs.

Duval turned back to face Baudelaire.

"So you thought you could leave just like that . . . after all these years—no good-bye, nothing!" he said.

"We've said our good-byes. You threw me out—remember?"

"That doesn't give you the right to walk out of my life without a word."

"It gives me the right to do what I want. Now I have to get this train, so good-bye. Not au revoir—good-bye."

She turned to walk to the open train door beside which a porter was patiently waiting for the last passengers. She had one foot on the step when he shouted at her.

"Don't be ridiculous—you think the Americans are going to let an aging whore like you into the country?"

She took three quick steps back across the platform. He leaned back and raised his sword stick in defense. She slapped him hard in the face, twice. The few remaining people on the platform stared briefly and turned away. Faces peered from train windows made misty by the steam that was beginning to billow down the platform.

She wanted to hit him again. She wanted to knock him down, kick him, let him know once and for all that there was a price to pay for the pain he had inflicted on her, even if it was only in a few bruises and battered pride when he saw the next day's papers.

"Your aging whore is going to find a new life far away from you and this cesspit of a city!" she shouted, and ran back to the train. She had placed one foot on the step when he was at her side, grabbing her by the arm and swinging her around.

"Don't go. We need each other."

She had never heard that tone of voice before. He was pleading. She began coughing again.

"You may need me for those sick fantasies you call poetry, but I most certainly don't need you. Let me go!"

She shook herself loose and stepped onto the train. A guard walked past blowing his whistle. The porter began closing the door, but Baudelaire flung it open again and stepped into the car, taking Duval's arm, trying to pull her back. She shook him off as fiercely as she could as the last passengers pushed past while those bidding them farewell struggled to get off.

"This is madness!" he shouted, thrusting his face into hers.

She turned her head from the fetid breath and felt warm spittle on her cheek. Behind him she could see the porter signaling to the guard up the platform. There was a long whistle. She pushed Baudelaire back toward the door as hard as she could and seized the sword stick, pressing the release button. The handle of the blade popped up and in one motion she drew it, described an arc, and placed the point against Baudelaire's chest.

"Get off my train!" she hissed.

For a moment she thought he was going to lunge forward onto the blade, a suicidal act of revenge that would send her to the guillotine. Instead, looking bewildered and lost, he stepped back onto the platform. Duval threw the blade and cane after him and slammed the door shut. There was another long whistle and the train began to move.

• • •

She took her seat in the corner facing the rear as the train pulled slowly away. People on the platform were waving their good-byes. Then she saw the look of alarm on some of their faces as he came running alongside, hurtling through the onlookers, knocking them aside. He was running fast and gaining on the train. His face appeared briefly in the compartment window, then dropped away. The sight of that desperate face straining with effort made her heart beat fast. She felt faint.

The platform was now fast disappearing. The grimy back walls and windows of North Paris began to slide past. The other passengers settled into their seats, carefully sliding their legs out to get maximum room without touching anyone else.

The men opened their papers again while the two women closed their eyes. She placed her purse on the empty seat next to her. She felt the sadness of wasted years weigh upon her. She was suddenly fearful of the future, a middle-aged woman who spoke no English arriving alone and friendless in a foreign country. Tears coursed down her face. She bent forward, putting an open hand to her forehead to shield herself from view. Her shoulders shook. She could not stop crying. Without looking, she felt in her purse for a handkerchief. The other passengers ignored her. Finally, one of the men emerged from his newspaper, took a handkerchief from his breast pocket, and offered it to her.

"Please . . . ," he said.

She noticed the smile on a kind face. He had been a good-looking man when young but must be in his fifties now. His clothes were well made but worn. What was he doing in a

third-class compartment on the boat train to Le Havre? she
wondered. The well-clipped mustache and polished shoes
suggested a military background. Perhaps he was taking his
small army pension to America to try his luck: a final roll of
the dice, a chance to make some money, find someone to love,
above all to leave an old, spent life behind—just like her, really. She would talk to him on the ship; perhaps they would
become friends. She took the handkerchief with a grateful
smile and wiped away the tears. One or two of the other passengers slid curious looks at her. She offered the handkerchief back, but the man shook his head.

"Please keep it," he said.

Duval stowed the handkerchief in her purse and settled
back, closing her eyes. She was exhausted. She would sleep
on the two-hour journey to Le Havre. The ship would leave
at midnight. In spite of the discomfort of a bunk in a shared
cabin, she would sleep all the way to New York. Two whole
weeks of sleep. That was what she needed. Hunger and storms
would not wake her. When she opened her eyes it would be
as a new woman in the New World.

The compartment door opened and the other passengers
looked up.

"Tickets, please!" said a voice.

She opened her eyes, sighed, and reached for her purse.
Then she noticed the looks of surprise and alarm around
her. She looked up. He was standing in the doorway, dishev-
eled, wild-eyed, and still holding the sword stick. His hand
was outstretched toward her.

"Your ticket, please," he said again.

She turned to look out of the window, trying to make
sense of a jumble of thoughts in her head. How had he got

on the train? Could she call the guard and have him thrown off? Was he going to turn violent with that sword of his? Should she scream?

The man who had offered her the handkerchief rose to his feet.

"Who are you?" he said.

Baudelaire stepped roughly past him, forcing the man to sit heavily back into his seat, and before anyone could think to stop him he placed his hand on the emergency stop chain that ran over the window through every compartment. He pulled hard.

Jeanne Duval would remember the shriek of those train brakes for the rest of her life. It was the sound of a banshee wailing, a high-pitched, grinding scream that foretold death. The three forward-facing passengers were flung violently on top of those opposite them. She found herself flattened under the man with the kind face and gentle smile. Somehow in the tangle of limbs his hand reached hers.

"Are you all right?" he said.

29

The lid of her carefully packed trunk sprang open as it hit the platform. A chill night wind began to tug at a dress that had half spilled out. Her hatbox followed and rolled away, coming to rest against the wooden fencing around the small suburban station outside Paris. The guard stood in the train doorway, writing quickly on a pad attached to a large clipboard. Charles Baudelaire stood on the platform in front of him, arms folded, trying to look contemptuous of the machinations of officialdom. The engine was panting, billowing steam, anxious to be on the move again. In every window faces peered out at the two figures on the platform. She saw the kind man from her own compartment looking at her. He smiled and she nodded in return.

She wanted to tell the stranger she had known for all of fifteen minutes that she was all right, that she would survive, and that she would like to meet him when she finally got to America. Because she was still going to America. The madman was not going to stop her. And she was not going to cry, she told herself. She was going to survive.

The guard stepped down from the train. With a flourish, he presented the pad and a pen to Baudelaire, who scrawled a signature. The guard ripped off the top page, handed it to him, drew a whistle from the pocket, and blew a long blast. He turned his back on the platform, remounted the train, and slammed the door. With a long wail from its horn the train moved off, trailing clouds of steam that briefly drifted over the platform and then vanished.

"I want to know why," she said. "If you have any feeling for me, if you care for me at all, or even if you don't give a damn but can remember a time when you had some slight affection for me, then tell me why. Why did you do it?"

She was back where she had started. She was sitting on a bed in a cheap hotel that he had found in the middle of the night somewhere north of the city, exhausted but calm. She wanted him to explain himself, to confront the savage insanity of what he had done, to acknowledge the truth at last: that she had left him and her old life.

He sat down and tried to put his arm around her, but she shrugged him off and stood up. She cupped her hand beneath his chin, forcing him to look at her. He had not met her eye since they left the platform and found a nearby farmer to rent them a horse and cart.

"Are you going to say something?" she demanded.

She would have vented her fury on him at that moment, thrown restraint to the winds and made him face the reality of the demented bastard lunatic he had become. But the coughing started again, gripping her and forcing her to bend double. She fell onto the bed and buried her face in the pillow, trying to stifle the choking spasms.

He got up, went to the washstand, and poured a glass of water. Taking a small brown bottle from his coat, he shook several drops into it. He sat on the bed beside her and tried to show her the proffered glass. She flailed out with an arm and knocked the glass to the floor. He stood up and paced the room.

"You know they would never have let you into America," he said. "You've got consumption. Look!"

He bent over her and raised her shoulders gently. She wriggled free, but they both saw the dark-red spots on the pillow. She dabbed her finger at one: fresh blood.

"They have medical examinations for all immigrants in New York. You can get in with most things but not tuberculosis. They would have put you back on the boat. And when you got back, you would have been arrested for your debts. They would have sent you to prison. And you would have died there."

The coughing had stopped. She rolled over and looked at the ceiling, the same green flaking paint.

"The boat would have left tomorrow morning. I was going to be free from all this."

"You need a doctor," he said.

She waved an arm at the peeling walls, the bare floorboards whose varnish had long faded, the cracked mirror over the washstand, the unwashed sheets exuding the rank odor of every unfortunate who had slept here—her whole life in a single room, a life she thought she had left behind.

"I would have been in America in two weeks. I would

have found a job as a singer—they say out west there's plenty of opportunities, even for an old hag like me. My father is out there somewhere; he would have helped."

She began coughing again. Baudelaire picked up the glass from the floor and refilled it at the washstand, adding a stronger dose of laudanum. She sat up, took the glass, and drained it. Her coughing eased.

"I've got the money for a doctor. Our appeal is being heard tomorrow. And in any case there's a new edition of *Fleurs du Mal* coming out. And the Poe translations are bringing in money. I can get us a small apartment somewhere. I'll look after you."

"No you won't. You haven't got any money, and if you had, your mother would grab it the moment she heard I was back. You're mad, Charles. You've ruined us both. You didn't just stop the train—you stopped my whole life."

He walked to the window and pushed open the shutters. It was near midnight and in the distance the lights of Paris cast a white glow over the sky. Life flowed through those streets, gutters, bars, clubs, restaurants, and bedrooms like a river to the sea. In a few hours it would be dawn and the paradox would repeat itself: a sleepless city would awake. And he would be there with all the rest of them, struggling to stay afloat, to stay alive. He could no more break free from the embrace of that city than he could from this woman. He pushed away from the window to face her.

"You would never have had a life in America. Face it. You would have been taken straight from the dockside and put on the next ship back to France. The whole thing was a fantasy—like the idea of finding your father, a wonderful day-dream."

Duval sighed and lay back on the bed and closed her eyes. Baudelaire sat and gave her the doctored wine. He began to unlace her boots.

"Leave them on," she said.

30

The clerk walked down a long pillared corridor of marbled floors and mullioned windows beneath high whitewashed ceilings. He carried a leather-bound book tied with a ribbon. Since this was a message from the minister of justice, the clerk moved as quickly as the dignity of his office allowed. On each side of the corridor, on hard wooden high-backed chairs, sat rows of petitioners, notaries, lawyers, appellants, and in some cases ladies and gentlemen of class and distinction. Some of the petitioners had been here for months and some appointments with the minister were still awaiting the approval of his diary clerks after a year.

In this particular case the minister had moved with celerity, although it was still two years since the appeal had been lodged.

Achille Frenais was a man of seventy who had been born in the same month and year that the Bastille was stormed, July 1789. Left in the custody of a guardian when his wealthy parents fled to Russia, he found himself free to roam the streets as he grew up during the years of revolution in Paris. His guardian cared little for his whereabouts providing he returned to the same house they shared in the suburb of Vincennes. He had grown up with history unfolding before him and learned early on that political power was no guarantor of survival in the turbulent floodtide of revolution, counterrevolution, and the savage but uplifting years of Napoléon's mastery of Europe. Napoléon had implanted in the governance of conquered Europe the principle that the ruling power should act within the law, brutally if necessary but always legally. "I need soldiers to triumph on the battlefield but lawyers to secure the peace," the emperor would say. Accordingly, Frenais trained as a lawyer, and with the attributes of discretion and attention to detail that are a mark of success in that profession he rose silently through various government departments until he emerged to general surprise as the minister of state for justice under the old emperor's nephew Louis-Napoléon.

While the minister recognized the political imperative behind the prosecution, he confided to his diaries that it was a waste of public money and the prosecutor's time. He had found no difficulty in reaching a decision about the alleged obscenity of six poems in Baudelaire's *Les Fleurs du Mal.* The idea that such verse could corrupt public morals was clearly ludicrous. Under the Second Empire, Paris had become known as the capital of Europe, famed for a brutally but brilliantly remodeled city center, for the excellence of a new lighter, more creative cuisine, and for its licentious public entertainments.

The minister had personally seen several arousing and extravagant displays of the female form at cabaret shows frequented by society ladies and gentlemen. He also knew for a fact that every wellborn gentleman kept a mistress in a none-too-discreet apartment and that those who could not afford such necessities entertained many of the courtesans available to the wealthy at very high prices.

In this situation he found it difficult to see how passing mention of breasts, buttocks, and thighs in poetry that was unlikely to be read beyond the literary circles of Paris could possibly be judged a danger to public morality. As for blasphemy, there was certainly a prima facie case for such a charge, but the court had dismissed it.

Finally, although the police had never pursued the allegation that the public prosecutor had enjoyed and paid for the company of underage virgins from North Africa, Pinard's sexual tastes were well known among his colleagues.

In this situation, it would normally have been easy to uphold the appeal and strike a blow against the puritans who seemed to command such influence with the prime minister.

The problem was political. The emperor was weak and fearful. In a country that still banned the singing of that anthem of revolution "The Marseillaise," it was easy to see how sensitive authority was to republicanism. And that was the issue: Charles Baudelaire was openly hostile to the Second Empire. He had actually boasted that he had returned to the barricades in 1851, when Napoléon had seized power from parliament, to later declare himself emperor. Baudelaire had told anyone who cared to listen that musket balls had singed his beard and parted his hair.

He was not just a poet; he was an art critic, essayist, and man of pronounced opinions. He could have all the bosoms and bottoms he wanted in his poems if only he kept his mouth shut. But he would not do so. He and that gang of bohemians in the Left Bank were forever railing against authority, urging the return of a democratically elected parliament.

That was why the appeal had to be turned down and the poems had to remain banned. It would send a strong signal to the rebellious minded everywhere. However, the minister would allow the remainder of the volume to be published. In that way, the government could show it was still on the side of intellectuals, artists, and the sexually liberated ethos that had made Paris such an admired city in Europe.

The clerk turned off the pillared corridor and entered an anteroom that was crowded with more petitioners. He knocked at a door on the far side of the room, listened briefly to the command from within, and pushed the door open. The petitioners surged toward the door, but the clerk slipped in and closed it firmly behind him.

Baudelaire and Poulet-Malassis were seated at a desk in front of an elderly official, who appeared to be asleep. His head rested sideways against the back of his chair, his mouth was open, and he was breathing with difficulty. An inkwell, pen, blotting pad, hourglass, and open snuffbox were the only objects on the desk.

The clerk coughed twice to no effect and then let the volume drop onto the desk with a loud thump. He reached into his pocket and placed a letter beside it. The official woke up, took a large piece of snuff, sneezed violently, and opened the letter. He then looked at his two visitors and read the letter again. He undid the ribbon binding the volume, opened it, and flicked through the pages of a bound manuscript. He returned to the letter as if unable to understand or accept the instructions it contained. Finally, he raised himself to his feet and held out the volume. Poulet-Malassis and Baudelaire stood up. The clerk stationed himself by the door.

"Your appeal has not been granted," said the high official. "The offending poems will remain banned sine die.
However, the minister has seen fit in his infinite wisdom to
give you permission to publish the remainder."

Baudelaire and Poulet-Malassis walked behind the clerk
down the long pillared corridor. The publisher looked triumphant while his author thumbed rapidly through the manuscript. They had not won the appeal, but they had not lost
either. *Les Fleurs du Mal* would be published, if not in full,
then at least with the majority of poems. The clerk bowed
slightly as they reached the steps leading to the street and
left them.

Baudelaire snapped the volume shut and flung it to the
ground. "Bastards—they've torn the heart out of it."

Poulet-Malassis bent down and picked up the manuscript.
"Actually, it's not a bad result. We were never going to get
those six poems unbanned. But we have ninety-four poems
left—not bad. And we can publish."

"It's not the same—they were the best."

"Nonsense. If they'd condemned six other poems as obscene, you would have said they were the best. Let's get this
book out before they change their mind."

"What about the fine? I can't pay it."

There were times when Poulet-Malassis wanted to throttle the poet genius he had had the misfortune to meet all
those years ago. The man whined like a child, saw the dark

side of every moon, the thorn rather than the rose, and the glass always half-empty. He seemed actively to create the chaos of an indebted, drug-ridden existence in order to bask in the warm glow of self-pity.

He was incapable of understanding the basic economics of publishing and went out of his way to offend—no, enrage— the one person who loved and would care for him: his poor, benighted mother. God only knew what Caroline Aupick had done to deserve that child of hers. She at least had the excuse that her relationship was involuntary. He, Poulet-Malassis, had of his own free will placed in jeopardy a printing and publishing business that had been in his family for three generations, for the sake of a friendship and a business arrangement that had almost bankrupted him.

Why? Because Charles Baudelaire was a feckless, reckless genius whose singular gift had already given France imperishable poetry and ennobling ideals: that beauty could never be compromised, that the struggle between good and evil would rage in men's hearts beyond eternity, and that hypocrisy was the greatest human weakness.

Above all, the publisher admired Baudelaire's view that the supreme achievement of the Devil was to persuade a gullible, secular world that he did not exist. The glory of *Les Fleurs du Mal* was the statement that resonated from every line of the poems: Lucifer was alive and comfortably quartered in the soul of mankind. The great English poet Milton said the Devil knew it was better to reign in Hell than serve in Heaven, and Baudelaire's genius was to remind all humanity of those words.

"Neither you nor I can pay the fine," said Poulet-Malassis.

"The difference is that you have nothing to lose. I have a business that employs a staff who put bread in their children's mouths with the wages I pay them. So I repeat—shall we get to work?"

31

Jeanne Duval had never been naked in the presence of a stranger before. She never minded baring herself before her lovers of course, but this was different. For a start she was sober. She was embarrassed by the experience, surprisingly so for someone who had for years flaunted herself onstage wearing dresses a great deal more revealing than the law allowed. He had told her in the casual way of doctors, for whom the unclothed human form is only of interest in terms of its functional frailty, to get undressed. She was now sitting on an examination table in a chilly curtained cubicle, wearing only cotton camiknickers and with her arms folded over her chest to preserve at least the semblance of modesty.

She frowned at the reflection in the mirror on the wall. She had lost weight; her face was thinner, her figure shrunken. She had already answered, or more accurately lied in response to, personal and highly intrusive questions: Did she have regular sexual relations? Did she take opium in any form? Was her urine ever cloudy and discolored? The first question was unanswerable, because trying to describe the complex carnal appetites of her former lover was hopeless; the second question was laughable, because opium in its various forms was a daily staple of every Parisian who could afford the drug; and as for her urine, well, frankly, she never looked.

Her unease increased when the doctor appeared with an alarming piece of equipment—a long rubber tube with large pincers at one end and a small, shiny disc at the other.

"Do you know what this is?" he said, holding up the device. She shook her head.

"A great invention—the stethoscope, created by a great Frenchman, René Laënnec."

"What does it do?" she said nervously.

"I'll show you," he said. "If you'll let me."

The stethoscope felt cold and hard when he pressed it to her chest. The doctor listened and asked her to turn round. He tapped her back in several places and then listened with the stethoscope again. He looked in her mouth, peered into her ears, and asked her to stick out her tongue. Finally, he told her to lie faceup on the examination table. His hands pressed into her abdomen, on first one side, then the other. It was when he pushed deep into her lower stomach that she felt the pain, as if someone had plunged a knife into her side. She stifled a scream and rolled to one side. Just before she fell off the table, he caught her and held her while her body shook with a spasm of coughing.

"I'm sorry," he said, and stepped back. He closed the curtains, invited her to dress, and walked back to his desk.

The doctor was a middle-aged man who wore his weariness much as he did the long gray apron that hung loosely about him from neck to knee. The garment was stained and frayed. He held a chair out for her at his desk.

"René Laënnec was a great doctor," he said as he picked up the stethoscope. "This invention and the research that cost him his life have greatly helped our understanding of tuberculosis. He showed it was a contagious disease, an infection of the lungs that we think can spread to other organs in the body. We may one day find a cure."

She tried to look him in the eye, to understand what he was saying, but he gazed over her head at a wall chart of the human anatomy. Is this how doctors break bad news? she thought. A medical lecture on the latest research into a disease that is going to kill you, and then the useless assurance that science may provide a future generation with medicines to fight and survive the infection?

"What are you trying to tell me, Doctor?"

Now he looked at her with watery eyes, dimmed and bloodshot from the nightly brandy bottle.

"I am afraid that you are suffering from an advanced stage of that disease."

Tuberculosis. Consumption. The white plague. Everyone in Paris knew those names, just as they knew that the disease was responsible for almost a third of all deaths in Europe. At least that's what the newspapers said. So Baudelaire had been right.

"Am I going to die?" she said, knowing it was a silly question but asking all the same, because it was one that had pushed ahead of all the others crowding into her head.

"We're all going to die," he said. "But in your case I have

to tell you that you will probably not have more than a year to live, maybe less. You should go to a sanatorium somewhere in the mountains, in the Alps maybe."

"That's not possible. What about the treatment?"

"That is the treatment. Rest, mountain air, a good diet, fresh fish and meat, plenty of fruit."

"There must be something else I can do—surely?"

"I wish there were, but your condition has a complicating factor."

"What, more complicating than death?"

The doctor ignored the jibe. On the whole she was being remarkably calm. Some of his patients fell to the floor in a faint or screamed abuse at him when he delivered such news.

"Normally tuberculosis takes its time. People can live for several years with the disease and there is no pain, in fact the reverse: many patients talk of a heightened awareness of the world around them . . . but . . ."

He paused. She said nothing. The *but* hung silently between them, a spider on an invisible thread, twisting slowly in the still air.

"I am afraid I have detected a growth in your abdomen."

"A growth?"

"A tumor. I suspect it's malign. I don't think a surgeon would dare operate."

"Why not?"

"It's large and embedded in the wall of your stomach. I could feel it very clearly."

"So could I." She stood up, feeling faint and nauseous. "What does it mean—the growth?"

"It means you probably have a malignant cancer in your stomach. It is impossible to tell how far advanced it is, but, as

I said, an operation would be impossible, in my opinion. A surgeon may differ, but I doubt it."

He had said enough, indeed too much. She wanted to leave.

"Is there anything else?"

"You don't have long. Be selfish. Do what you want. Enjoy yourself."

The doctor stood up. The examination was over, the diagnosis was clear, and the case was closed. He went to the door and opened it for her.

One last question, she thought.

"How does one die—from tuberculosis?"

The doctor had never been asked that before. He frowned and thought for a few seconds.

"The infection intensifies as the immune system weakens. The blood becomes more poisoned and the heart slows down. Finally it stops beating. It is not a painful death."

"Like going to sleep?"

"Yes."

He opened the door a little wider, indicating that her visit was over. Other patients were waiting. She thanked him and walked into the street.

32

The six presses shook the ground-floor room, battering their ears with a continuous roar of machinery and throwing out the reek of printer's ink. Charles Baudelaire, Poulet-Malassis, and Gautier watched as the printed sheets spun off the presses into metal trays, where they were picked up by a printer to be hung on a line to dry.

Baudelaire was hopping from foot to foot with excitement. The long, thin-lipped mouth had stretched into a smile. He tried to pluck one of the sheets from the line but was restrained by Poulet-Malassis.

"Wait."

The publisher gestured to one of the workers, who brought over a sheet from the press and held it up for inspection.

LES
FLEURS DU MAL
PAR
CHARLES BAUDELAIRE

PARIS
POULET-MALASSIS ET DE BROISE
4, RUE DE BUCI
1857

Baudelaire reached for the sheet, but again Poulet-Malassis held him back. He beckoned to the other two and walked from the press room into an adjoining room. Two bottles of champagne were cooling in ice buckets on a table beside several fluted glasses. A large slice of foie gras lay on a dish beside a loaf of bread. A serving girl dressed in a checked pinafore stood behind the table. Poulet-Malassis nodded to her and she opened the champagne.

"The full edition will be here in a minute, unstitched and unbound, of course, but this is it—so let's raise a glass to our friend and *Les Fleurs du Mal*," he said.

Baudelaire was dressed in his habitual black and looked more than ever like an old crow who had flapped in from the fields, Poulet-Malassis thought. The poet hopped and skipped around the table, his hands fluttering down to take a glass of champagne. He threw it back, and then circled the table again to take another glass.

The serving girl pressed her back to the wall in amazement. Gautier observed his old friend with great pleasure. This was Baudelaire's moment, his triumph, and if he wanted to dress like a pox doctor's clerk and hop around the room like a frog in a sock, then so be it. Suddenly Baudelaire flung himself across the table, cut a large slice off the pâté, and put it straight into his mouth.

"For God's sake," said Gautier, a man known for both his appetite and his epicurean tastes. "When did you last eat?"

"I don't know and I don't care."

"Calm down, Charles, and raise your glass—we are drinking to your book."

Baudelaire stopped, raised his glass, and smiled at the serving girl. She blushed and looked down. She must be all of seventeen years old, plump, pretty—and probably from Brittany, he thought, where Poulet-Malassis hired all his staff. He poured a glass of champagne and handed it to her. She looked nervously at Poulet-Malassis, who nodded. Baudelaire raised his glass and clinked it against hers. He put his arm around her.

"Here we have innocence and beauty," he said. "What is your name, dear?"

"Marie-Haude," she said.

"A fine Breton name. Well, Marie-Haude, instead of drinking to my pestilential, perverted poems, let us toast you and your virginal beauty—you are a virgin, I trust, or have you succumbed to the fleshly pleasures of this city?"

"Leave her be, Charles," said Poulet-Malassis.

The door opened and a printer came in, followed by a wall of noise.

He was holding 130 pages of the first edition fresh from the presses. Everyone in the room knew this was not the edition they had hoped to publish. The titles of the six banned poems had been printed above blank pages. But as Poulet-Malassis kept telling his author, it was a great deal better than no edition at all. A black ribbon had been stitched through the margin to hold the cut pages together. The printer gave it to Poulet-Malassis, who in turn handed the copy to Baudelaire. The clattering of the presses subsided as the printer closed the door.

Baudelaire held the edition in both hands, then lightly ran his fingers over the type on the frontispiece. The ink was dry. The three of them watched as he placed the copy on the table and bent over it, turning the pages: the crow feasting on a fresh field kill. Without raising his head, Baudelaire reached across the table for his glass of champagne and drew it to him. He straightened, picked up the edition, and turned to Marie-Haude.

"This is for you. Take it home and ask your parents to keep it safe. I am sorry if I got a little carried away just now."

Marie-Haude took the pages and dropped a curtsey to him.

He turned to his friends and raised his glass.

"A toast to thank you for your forbearance, for your loyalty, and for putting up with what you must both believe to be a madman—and perhaps you are right."

The three men drank the champagne and held out their glasses to allow Marie-Haude to refill them.

"Now, let me ask you a question," said Baudelaire. "Are we going to make some money out of this? It should sell, shouldn't it? Everyone in Paris will want to read it after the trial, won't they?"

"Everyone in Paris will want to know whether you can pay your debts," said Poulet-Malassis. "Just how much do you owe around town?"

"What does that matter?"

"It matters if they find you," said Gautier.

"I've a new little apartment. It's in her name. They won't find us."

"One creditor is certainly going to find you. You owe your publisher five hundred francs for the advance . . . remember?

That will be subtracted from any royalties I owe you," said Poulet-Malassis.

"Damn. Couldn't we—?"

"No, we couldn't. And have you thought what happens if your mother ever finds out—?"

"Finds out what? That I've published my poems?"

"No, that you're back with her."

"She won't. Who's going to tell her?"

"Just one question," said Gautier. "Do you . . . ?"

Baudelaire put a finger to his lips.

"Do I love her? No. Do I lust after her? Sometimes. Do I need her? Yes. And if you want to know why—she's holding the answer."

He pointed to Marie-Haude, who blushed and bobbed another curtsey.

Jeanne Duval had rented a small apartment in the area of Paris she knew best, the Latin Quarter. The area had acquired a new and different character with the creation of the boulevard Saint-Germain, which had been driven in a long arc from the pont de la Concorde through to the pont de Sully at the east end of the île Saint-Louis.

The boulevard was the centerpiece of the new plan for Paris, and at two and a half miles it was by far the longest of the new thoroughfares. It was also the broadest, so that a four-horse coach could turn in a single circular movement. It was obvious to the students who populated the quarter that the real purpose of such width was not to facilitate coach travel but to enable the authorities to suppress riotous assembly.

The loss of a large amount of cheap housing had raised rents and property prices in the Latin Quarter. Duval was forced to pay a much higher monthly rent for a one-bedroom apartment than she had planned. It was on the top floor, up flights of rickety wooden stairs. The windows gave a fine view north over the city, but the slate roof leaked in really wet weather and she had to use a chamber pot to catch the drips.

The landlord had promised repairs, but that would have required scaffolding, and since she was the only tenant to suffer such leaks he did not think it was worth it. She had worked out that the money she had received from Caroline Aupick would cover no more than a year's rent and basic foodstuffs— and that was if she was on her own. But she had taken him back—more out of pity, she told herself, than for any other reason.

He had been right. Her tuberculosis had ended any chance of a new life in America. She had been to the embassy. They would have turned her back when the ship docked and sent her home to France. She hated him for being right, she hated him for dragging her off the train, and she hated him because here he was again in her life and in her bed. She had not told him about the doctor and his discovery of the tumor. He would probably have tried to borrow more money and send her to some sanatorium.

That was why she hated him most of all: for the single fact that had lodged in her life like the tumor in her stomach, the fact that she could neither deny nor alter—the fact that she still loved him. In his chaotic way, he was now trying to make up for the disappointment of America. He took her discreetly to restaurants where they would not be seen and told her of the new poems he would write for her and about her.

"I have only two responsibilities in my life—to my art and my Black Venus," he told her.

She didn't like the term because she wasn't black. If anyone had to describe her skin color, it should be likened to a dark olive oil made from sun-ripened fruit on a French Mediterranean hillside. She liked to think she was more white than black, more Mediterranean than Caribbean, more French than Haitian.

Her color did not matter. What mattered was that she was now his again, or he was hers—it made no difference. She was caught up again in the coils of a relationship that had almost destroyed her.

She had taken him back, or rather he had begged and wheedled and pleaded and she had agreed. Apart from anything else, he had nowhere else to live. His book was in the stores and he needed somewhere to lay his head at night after an arduous day traveling the bookshops to ensure that the slim volume was at least in the window.

Jeanne Duval always thought of her mother in moments of crisis. "When you have a problem, when you face danger, disease, or even death, then sit down and talk to yourself. Tell yourself your problems. Look to the future and do not be afraid of the past. Above all, do not be afraid." That was her philosophy and the advice she had repeated again and again to her young daughter: just have that conversation and tell yourself the truth, because if you don't, no one else will. And so she had sat down in her new apartment one night, with candles burning and a large glass of wine.

I am Jeanne Duval. I am forty-eight years old and I am dying. Whether by tumor or tuberculosis, the doctor said I will be dead in a year. He could be wrong, of course; the bastards often are. Worse than the prospect of death, my dream has died. The dream of traveling to America, going out west, and finding my father. He must be old now, almost seventy-five, but I am sure he is there. He will have married and had children, maybe even grandchildren.

So I have cousins in America—cowboys, ranchers, horsemen. I would gladly face whatever death God has in store for me if I could see them—just once.

Then I would truly understand the meaning of my life and end the wonder of why I was put on this world. Was it just to suffer? Was that the divine plan? Because if so, dear Lord, I have truly suffered. You have given me a man who is sometimes a monster, sometimes a devil, and sometimes, just sometimes, an angelic, brilliant child. But then, as every woman from Eve onwards has known, all men are children. They never grow up—they just grow old.

That helped. She liked talking to herself. She made a plan. She would earn some money, leave Paris, and go south, where the olive trees grew. It would be warmer there and maybe she would take a boat from Marseille to Morocco, find a little pension in Tangier. She would leave the child behind. With his book and his friends and his cheap whores, he could fend for himself. If I have a year to live, I will live it in my own way. When my life ends, my death will be my own. My death belongs to me and to no one else.

33

Baudelaire slung his black cloak around his shoulders and looked out of the window. Hard rain and low cloud made it difficult to see anything across the river. Even the towers of Notre-Dame had disappeared into the haze. Water poured from roofs into leaf-choked gutters and cascaded into the streets. Fall in Paris, he thought: the slum alleys awash with sewage; soaked horses slipping and falling in the shafts; beggars huddled in doorways; waiters flicking serving cloths at empty tables; large measures of anis, brandy, and gin being poured in small backstreet bars to help men get through the day. And the cheap china pot in the center of the room was almost full. The water from the ceiling fell in large, steady drips, each splashing up a small fountain that fell back and rippled to the lip.

"I thought I asked you to empty it," she said.

She was buttoning up her cloak by the door. He wanted to go with her, but she had refused, just as she had refused to listen to him. He would try once more.

"Can I say something?"

"No. Don't argue with me. Just empty the pot."

"You're too old. You'll make a fool of yourself."

"I'll make more money than you'll ever make out of that book."

"So what are you going to wear?"

She opened her black cloak with the silver lining to reveal a dark, shapeless dress that dropped well below the knee.

"They'll love that," he said, and slumped into a chair. He reached for a wine bottle. She walked across the room and took the bottle from him.

"First empty that pot."

It was seventeen years since Jeanne Duval had first sung at Le Rêve, and when she walked into the club it was if nothing had changed. The scar-faced doorman was still there, as were the two women behind the bar. She half-expected to find Céleste in the dressing room along with the flies, the smeared mirror, and the dead flowers. But the mirror was clean, the walls whitewashed, the flies had vanished, and there were fresh flowers in a vase. There were now also two chairs rather than one. But Céleste had long gone, the manager said.

He was a small, skinny man of about forty who smelled strongly of rancid butter; at least that was the only way she could describe it. A straggly mustache looked more like the remains of brown soup. One eye was dead, a lifeless orb in its socket, while the other darted around, looking her up and down and lingering too long on her chest.

He stood rather too close to her when they talked on the empty stage, so that she found herself stepping back to create a reasonable distance between them. He simply stepped forward, bringing with him the dense odor of sour milk. When they reached the backdrop, she felt like putting her hands on his chest and pushing him away. Thankfully, the conversation was brief. She would be paid twenty francs a week for a two-week season as the main cabaret act.

"No offense, but we don't normally book singers your age," he said. "The audience these days likes them young and pretty and with plenty to show, if you get me."

She did get him. The club wanted young strippers who could hold a tune. And she knew why she had been booked.

"You've got a reputation," he said. "The men will come because of the trial—you know, obscene poems and all that. We should have a full house for the run. We're selling you as a sort of Jezebel, if you get me."

She got him again, but to make sure, he showed her a promotional poster with the word "JEZEBEL" printed in red capitals. Beneath was a crude sketch of her that emphasized her breasts, much as Baudelaire had done in his drawing. The manager dropped the heavy hint that the municipal authorities were taking a more relaxed view about licentious behavior onstage, and that he hoped she would not disappoint her audience.

She listened to this without comment. The pay for the two weeks had been good, with an immediate deposit of half the money. He had agreed that she should be able to choose her own songs and wardrobe.

The first-night audience began drifting in soon after the offices closed. By seven o'clock the club was almost full and much as she remembered it. The same pipe-smoking, pale-faced men sitting in dense haze, drinking cheap wine and dipping bread into bowls of thin soup. The menu at Le Rêve was strictly limited: soup or thickly sliced salami. The serving girls were young, underdressed, and moved quickly between tables, brushing off stray hands.

The serious drinkers were at the bar, sipping brandy, absinthe, and anis and talking loudly. The serving girls shouted orders to two old ladies, who banged bottles and glasses onto metal trays, which were then carried precariously over the heads of the crowd. The din, the smoke, the cheap suits, the girls with the short black and white pinafores, the old crones behind the bar, and the hard-faced drinkers they served from fast-emptying bottles created a familiar tableau. Manet should paint this, Duval thought, peering out from the back curtain: the lower classes of Paris at play after work. Her casual lover and friend had become famous after his painting of the absinthe drinker. Portraits of beggars, gypsies, and Parisian street life followed. Manet had never known poverty, but he understood the reality of life for the city's poor.

The musicians appeared from the back of the hall and threaded their way toward the stage. She had met them for the first time that lunchtime for a brief rehearsal. The old trio she used to work with had vanished along with Céleste and the flies. These were workingmen who could spare only a half hour at midday. They had read through her lyrics, shrugged, muttered among themselves, and arranged a tune. They played it through twice and it seemed to work.

The arrangement was simple enough for piano, cello, and bass. She still had a good voice, the strong soprano that had taken her across the Atlantic on the *Hirondelle*. Her illness had weakened her and the fits of coughing had made her voice deeper and more throaty. But audiences seemed to like the effect, and a large brandy with a little liquid opium on the side helped her through performances.

The musicians raised eyebrows at the lyrics and looked incredulous when she told them she had written the song herself. It was her song, the best thing she had ever written. Had she checked it with the manager? the pianist asked. No need, she said, and amid more shrugging and muttering they left to return to the tedium of the clerk's desk.

She was wearing only a chemise when she smelled rancid butter and heard the knock on her door. He stood in the doorway, his one shifty eye looking approvingly at her state of undress. He probably thinks I am going on like this, she thought.

"Yes?" she snapped. She was due onstage in ten minutes.

"Full house tonight," he said, stepping into the room. She stepped back. "Very good for a Tuesday. Some of them out there remember your old act."

"I doubt that," she said.

He had backed her up against the wall. He had just come in for a quick look, a cheap thrill. She was thinner and older, but her figure was still a voyeur's delight.

"Don't look round," she said.

He turned immediately, his single eye scanning the room. "What?" he said.

"The door. You left it open. Please close it."

He turned back to her. A smile appeared beneath the soup stain.

"As you leave," she said.

• • •

Apart from her dressing room, the one improvement to Le Rêve was the stage lighting. The two old gas lamps had been replaced with four more modern gas-fired appliances, which threw out a stronger light. In the old club the musicians had played in the shadows; now they were well lit and in full view of the audience.

The trio was playing a medley of popular tunes before she was due on, but the audience paid little attention and the music went unheard amid the din. The noise in the club had become such that even the regulars at the bar had difficulty making their orders understood. When the manager went onstage it took him some time to quiet the crowd sufficiently to make himself heard.

As he had predicted, the club was packed, with late arrivals forced to stand at the back. There were two hundred people in the club that night. If he could keep that up, there would be a handsome profit at the end of the run. As long as the poet's whore did her stuff, he would be in the money. And surely she knew that's what she was here for. She was a bit thin, but the Caribbean melons were in good shape— pity he hadn't seen more of them. She had a nice ass on her too, from what little he'd seen—and he was going to see a lot more of her before the run was over. He'd never had a half-caste girl before, but he'd heard they were as dirty as they come. If she did as she was told, he might book her again.

As Duval feared, the introduction he gave her made much of the wicked woman who had inspired the obscene poems banned by the state, a Jezebel who had seduced the infamous poet Charles Baudelaire, a woman who was here tonight to entertain them with her own songs all the way from the lusty shores of the Caribbean—the club's very own JEZEBEL!

She walked onstage, blinking in the light, and nodded to the musicians. The manager saw the long front-buttoned dark dress and frowned. Maybe there was something more showy underneath; this was probably a bit of a tease.

She bowed and faced her audience, who had now fallen quiet.

"Someone I love dearly is dying and I have written this song for them and for anyone who has lost the one they love. It's called 'Dying for Love.'"

The musicians struck up and she sang:

"When the sun grows cold
And the night comes down,
You're alone in the dark
With the awful fear
That you've seen your last dawn
And lived your last day."

The slow tempo of the song did not suit the audience any more than the sight of a well-dressed woman onstage who seemed to be showing no more than a shapely ankle. The crowd began to mutter as she moved into the second verse.

"That the past is dead
And the end lies ahead
And those lights in the night
Are the flames of Hell,
So don't say good-bye,
But take me tonight,

Because the sun will never rise
On our love again."

She had turned to the musicians, signaling a change in tempo for the third verse, when a voice bellowed, "Get off! This isn't a funeral parlor!"

A piece of bread arced over the brightly lit stage and struck the pianist. He picked it up and threw it back.

"Get on with it! And this time show us your tits!"

It was the same voice. She could see him at a table halfway up the hall: a florid, wine-soaked face perched on a large belly that began below the chin and billowed down to his knees. A thick leather belt strained to prevent it from falling farther. Thin strands of hair were slicked down over a bald pate. The man rose and threw a piece of what looked like half-chewed salami at the stage.

A chorus of slow hand clapping began at the back, mingled with booing. From the wings the manager surveyed the scene with one eye heroically darting between the stage and the crowd. At this rate he wouldn't make any money at all that night. What on earth was the girl doing coming on dressed like that?

Jeanne Duval stood, hands on hips, staring at the fat man. The slice of salami sailed back into the audience, bringing a volley of bread, salami, and olives in return. The musicians got to their feet. The manager moved out of the wings and onto the stage, raising his hands.

She walked down from the stage and slowly threaded her way through the crowd toward the fat man's table. The booing died away as people turned in their chairs to watch. No one tried to hinder her as she pushed past the tables. She kept her eyes fastened on the fat man as she twisted and turned to negotiate the tightly packed tables.

He stared back defiantly, seated now, with a large hairy hand clamped around a pewter mug of wine. The group around him nudged one another and laughed as she approached. The crowd in the club had fallen silent. Onstage the pianist had quietly taken the manager to one side. The fat man sat up and pushed out his chest and chin as she reached the table. She stopped and locked her eyes on his. Slowly she began to unbutton the front of her dress.

"Is this what you want to see?" she said loudly, so that everyone in the room could hear.

"Give it to him!" shouted a voice from the crowd.

The man raised his mug, slurped some wine, and leaned forward, nodding. The men with him shuffled around the table trying to gain the best vantage point as she undid one button after another. The fat man and his friends merged into a large drunken blob of craning heads, foul breath, and cheap, sweat-stained clothes as they pushed forward over the table.

Duval undid the buttons to the waist of the dress. She paused, and looked at the hydra-headed creature before her. It was licking its various lips and showing black pointed teeth on smiles that sliced through flaring red faces.

Behind her on the stage, the manager once again raised his hands and tried to speak. The crowd noisily shushed him. She pulled open the dress and bent forward, her hands cupping her breasts and pushing them up against a low-cut black chemise.

"Is this what you like?"

The creature pushed closer to her, all eyes on her chest. It was breathing heavily and its arms began to snake across the table.

"You want to see some more?"

She bent farther toward them, her hands gripping the top of her chemise, preparing to rip it open. The fat man and his friends were now all on their feet, their bellies on the table, pushing into one another.

She straightened up, jerked the table toward her, and tipped it up in a single movement. The hydra-headed creature separated into five bodies falling backwards amid a cascade of glasses, bottles, and candles. There was a roar across the room as the crowd jumped to their feet and leaped onto chairs and tables to get a better view.

Duval buttoned up her dress. She turned to the stage and waved to the three musicians. The manager was once again raising his hands to try to speak. The roar from the crowd had become applause, clapping, shouts of approval. A single rose fluttered in her direction. The serving girls pulled back chairs to let her pass as she headed toward the door. The scar-faced doorman had her cloak ready. He placed it around her shoulders and she turned with a swirl, showing a flash of the silver lining as she left.

34

Paris was a news-hungry city. Rumors crowded the streets, thronged the theaters, and burst into restaurants, cafés, and taverns at every hour of the day and night. The speed with which malice, imagination, and intrigue could transform the mundane into news of national importance was pure black magic. A rumor merely had to turn a street corner or spend a few minutes in a bar before it became a fact. Truth was left limping behind, a lonely face pressed against the window. And such facts were the stuff of gossip that lubricated every conversation in the capital. It was the means by which those seeking power sought to destroy their rivals and those in power thwarted usurpers. It was the common currency of every conversation.

As the French chef Adolphe Duglére said, the most important item on the menu for his guests was not the food or the wine but the gossip. Without gossip he would have no business. Gossip was the piquant sauce that transformed even a simple meal into a feast.

There was plenty to gossip about in Paris under Emperor Louis-Napoléon. Everyone knew, or professed to know, that the Empress Eugénie had withdrawn from the marital bed, having delivered the male heir necessary to perpetuate the Napoleonic line. It was also said that the emperor's ferocious sexual appetite required the provision of successive mistresses. The court chamberlain Count Bacciochi was kept busy arranging such liaisons and the identity of these ladies was of bottomless interest to café society. The rumor mill regularly ground out the names and even supplied some of the exotic practices they were required to perform. The scandalous rumor that placed the English music hall star Cora Pearl in the emperor's bed created a frenzy of gossip that preoccupied Paris for months, not least because she was supposed to have been paid far more than any of his French mistresses.

Royal gossip was not the exclusive preserve of high society, but the poorer quarters of the city preferred their rumors to be political. The latest unrest in the army, reports that the government had suppressed news of cholera outbreaks in the suburbs, the vast sums being made by a new generation of corrupt railroad magnates, and efforts by the state to tax prostitution—such were the staple rumors among the working population. But the rumors that united Parisians in feverish speculation and exaggeration were sexual. The city was known throughout Europe as the international capital of decadence. If the Second Empire had a political philosophy, it was that you could have what you paid for, and that applied to women as much as any other commodity. Sex was for sale at every level of society and in every form, and who was doing what to whom was the subject of endless salacious, but very satisfying, gossip.

So it was that a minor incident in a working-class club became a lunchtime sensation across Paris the next day. Apparently, Jeanne Duval, the scarlet woman who had ruined a great poet by inspiring his obscene poetry, had stripped naked and bared all to a group of drunken lawyers in Le Rêve. She had danced shamelessly in front of them without a stitch on her generously proportioned body; when they tried to take advantage she had seized a wine bottle and broken it over their heads. The reason the club had chosen to employ such a controversial woman, who was, frankly, well into middle age, was because of her affair with the manager. But since he was a well-known homosexual, it must be evident that she too had peculiar sexual tastes, including, so it was said, a predilection for orgies with both men and women.

That was the talk of the town on a cold November morning in 1859. The manager of the club had placed the story with a number of journalists and was surprised at the speed with which he acquired a mistress and became a homosexual. But he was a happy man. The club would be booked out for months.

Baudelaire heard the story at lunchtime in the Momus and immediately left for the small apartment he shared with Duval. She was not there and he went next to the perfumery on the rue de Rivoli where Simone worked.

Simone had indeed seen Jeanne Duval that morning but said nothing to Baudelaire. Duval had been kind and forgiving about the betrayal of her plans to cross the Atlantic and start a new life in America. As she would not have been admitted to the country, her friend had probably done her a favor. They had arranged to meet that night for supper. Duval had also said something to her that kept repeating itself in her head: "I am closing my accounts. I need to talk to you. I need your help. Tell no one of our meeting."

Then she had left.

Baudelaire began to walk the streets. He did not believe that the woman who was his mistress, in name if not in fact, had been dancing naked on a table at Le Rêve, but clearly something dramatic had happened at the club the previous night. Whatever it was, he had to find her. But at every bar and café he visited he found that journalists from the evening papers and the more sensational magazines had been there before him. Everyone was looking for Jeanne Duval. The latest rumors were that the police were seeking to arrest her for assault and that a prominent politician was offering to pay the bail for her release. The story took flight, with the added twist that evening that the emperor had shown interest in the Black Venus of M. Baudelaire's poems. He had asked the justice minister for a copy of the unexpurgated edition of *Les Fleurs du Mal* and was that very night closely studying the banned poems. His current mistress, a singer named Hortense Schneider, had apparently been so incensed by the emperor's interest in a book of tawdry poems that she had left and planned to take the night train back to Berlin. Although no one could be sure of this latest twist in the story, rumor quickly established the emperor's involvement in the scandal as fact. His valet had been discreetly asked to find the whereabouts of Jeanne Duval. That was a fact, because the valet's sister worked at the reception desk of the Hôtel de Lyon close to the royal palace and had repeated the story to her own lover, the editor of *Figaro* himself. As it happened, the emperor quickly lost interest in *Les Fleurs du Mal*. The departure of his mistress had created a vacancy that was swiftly filled by one of the many English beauties who conducted highly profitable affairs in Paris at the time.

It was the flash of silver from the silk lining of her sealskin cloak that gave her away. She was walking slowly down the rue du Bac carrying a large bag that seemed to weigh heavily on her. Her bonneted head was lowered against a chill wind as she turned into a side street. The cloak flapped open briefly and Baudelaire spotted it from the main street. He stepped into the road, dodging the evening jam of hansom cabs, and ran after her. Hearing footsteps and perhaps guessing their origin, Duval quickened her pace. Baudelaire took her arm as he caught up.

"Why are you running away from me?"

"I'm not. Let go of my arm."

He stepped back and bumped into a passerby, who muttered angrily. Beneath Duval's bonnet Baudelaire saw a tired, strained face. He realized he should have been taking better care of her. She looked older and thinner. She should never have gone back to Le Rêve. It was madness. She had done it for the money.

He felt sudden sadness, an aching remorse that this woman had grown old and he had not noticed. She had been forced back onstage at a sleazy club and he had not cared. She had been caught up in the latest scandal and he had not been able to defend her. After all, she had defended him, indeed saved his life, by the Seine. She had also stood up for him at his trial and paid the price. Whatever she had done to him, she had not deserved all this. Was he not the one to blame for her plight?

She turned and began to walk away. He caught up with her again.

"All Paris is talking about you. You know that?"

She spoke with her head down, quickening her pace.

"Of course I know. Don't patronize me."

"Why didn't you tell me about that awful club? I would have come!"

"I did tell you. But you chose not to come. I am not talking here on the street. Go home. I will be in later."

"But where are you going?"

"Never mind. Leave me alone. Just leave me. Go home."

She had stopped and faced him now. The two of them stood swaying as people pushed roughly past them. She let him guide her to a shop doorway.

"You don't understand. I love what you did last night. Everyone in Paris thinks you're a heroine. You stood up to that sleazy mob! I wish I had been there. I *should* have been there."

He put a hand to her cheek, but she brushed it away.

"It was a mistake. I'm too old for that nonsense. I'm just too old. It's over. Don't you see? It's all over."

She suddenly kissed him, her arms around his neck pulling him onto her. He felt her body pressed against him and for a moment it was as if they were one. The tide of people on the sidewalk swirled past, heads turning at the couple in the doorway. He felt the warmth of her kiss, a deep embrace that took him back to the lavender-scented rooms in the Hôtel

de Lauzun, the endless days and nights when they would kiss
like this, and take laudanum in their wine until dawn, and
then order champagne and pastries for breakfast.

Her lips left his and she took off her bonnet. Her hair fell
to the shoulders of the sealskin cloak. She slid a hand around
his neck, pushing fingers through his hair.

"I'll see you tomorrow night at La Chandelle," she said.
"Seven o'clock."

"La Chandelle? Why?"

"Why not? I was there last week. It reminded me of you.
We used to go, remember, in the old days?"

"No, I mean why meet out when we can go home? I want
to talk to you."

"I'm not going home. I'll see you tomorrow night."

"But—"

She silenced him with another kiss and hugged him.
Baudelaire buried his head in her hair, smelling the rich sandalwood perfume she always wore. She wasn't going home?
He didn't understand. She began to cry as he held her. He
could feel her shaking.

He held her away, his arms on her shoulders, and looked
at the teary face.

"Don't worry," she said. "It'll be all right. Trust me."

"No, no, this isn't right," he said, beginning to panic, unable to understand her, to find any meaning in what was going on.

She wiped tears from her cheeks and touched his lips
with wet fingers.

"Until tomorrow. Don't follow me, please."

She picked up her bag, put on her pink bonnet, and
walked away. Baudelaire started after her, but she turned and

smiled and shook her head. She was smiling and shaking her head at him just like his mother had at the little house in Neuilly. He stood buffeted by the crowd but unable to move. She turned again and vanished into the throng. He craned his neck, looking after her, watching the pink bonnet floating along in the stream of people. Then it disappeared.

35

Jeanne Duval met Simone Clairmont at Chez Michel, the well-known fish restaurant off the rue Berger. The restaurant's signature dishes included monkfish lightly curried with Goanese spices, a crayfish bordelaise, and larks stuffed with cherries, but it was the owner's passion for horticulture that attracted most diners. With large windows and a long skylight over the main dining room, Chez Michel looked more like a greenhouse than a restaurant.

An array of ferns, evergreens, and bamboo plants had been grown over an arched trellis inside the main door, creating a leafy tunnel, so that those entering had no view of other diners until they had reached the reception desk. Once reservations had been confirmed and coats taken, the extent of the floral enhancement of the main dining room became apparent. White orchids and red flowering amaryllis plants had been placed on every available surface. Tables sheltered in alcoves fringed with broad-leafed plants.

The centerpiece of the restaurant was a round oak table on which the red trumpet-shaped flowers of the amaryllis rose with the white orchids in tiered rows. The long stems of the amaryllis lifted their extravagant red blooms well above the frail white-petaled orchids, creating the effect of red waves cascading over a white waterfall.

Restaurant customers emerging from the tunneled entrance usually stopped and looked around in wonder. The more cautious also wondered just how much of the cost of such lavish arrangements was added to the bill. But there was no point coming to Chez Michel if you worried about how much it was going to cost.

The owner made no secret of the high prices charged for his fine dishes. He knew that his customers were happy to pay for the magnificence of the flower arrangements, because they provided a considerable degree of discretion. The array of flowers and plants shielded diners from general view. Equally long-stemmed fronds and bamboos had been placed around the windows so that no one from the street could make out what was happening inside.

Most important in the owner's view, the profusion of plants and flowers made it difficult to hear what was said at a neighboring table. In Chez Michel intimate conversations could be conducted without fear of being overheard. Thus the restaurant became a favorite meeting place for lovers, lawyers, and politicians intent on making assignments, trading secrets, and negotiating the next step up the greasy ladder of power.

Jeanne Duval arrived a little late just after eight o'clock. Through the restaurant plant life she could just see her friend seated close to the floral castle. Simone looked pale and tired. Duval followed a waiter, glancing at tables as she passed. The restaurant was packed. Food, wine, and gossip were in full flow. She saw no one she recognized. Simone waved when she saw her and then quickly placed her hands beneath the table as if to conceal the gesture. Duval smiled. Her friend was obviously expecting a journalist to jump out from behind the potted plants. Simone was still a country girl. She had never really settled in Paris and disliked the filth, confusion, and high prices in the capital. Simone was lonely; it was as simple and as sad as that. Duval kissed her warmly on both cheeks and sat down.

Simone began to whisper urgently, "Are you all right? You know that Paris is talking—"

Duval cut in and took Simone's hand. "Simone, please. Be calm. Look around you. Don't you love this place?"

"Yes, but it's so expensive. How can we afford it?"

Duval squeezed her hand. "Don't worry. Let's sit back and enjoy ourselves. A glass of champagne, perhaps?"

Simone raised her eyebrows and nodded. A waiter appeared, as if he had been listening to the conversation. He moved two silver salt and pepper pots, shaped as a lion and a unicorn, to one side of the table, handed out menus, and placed water and bread rolls on the table. Duval ordered champagne and the waiter disappeared back into the leafy fronds. Duval picked up one of the silver figures, turned it upside down over her hand, and shook it, sending a shower of salt onto her palm. She brushed her hands together and picked up the menu.

"They say the monkfish is very good."

Simone's fingers rattled off a drumbeat of irritation on the table.

"Jeanne, all Paris is talking about you, journalists are looking for you, and you want to discuss monkfish?"

"Why not? It's served in a Goanese sauce. A very light curried flavor with a strong hint of pineapple. But perhaps not a curry tonight. As for Paris, let them talk. It's chitter-chatter, just another scandal, distraction for bored people who are weary of their boring lives. Tomorrow there will be another story and they will have forgotten me."

"But they say the emperor wants to see you!"

Duval laughed and put her hand over her mouth. She had an unladylike laugh, but it was good to let it go sometimes, although maybe not in this place.

"That's just another rumor, Simone; you've been in Paris long enough to know that. You think the emperor is going to summon an old bag like me?"

"They say he has strange tastes."

"Oh, thank you—"

"No, I didn't mean that."

Duval laughed again. The champagne arrived and they ordered, each choosing the sole. They raised their glasses to each other.

"Come on, I want to know. Did you really dance naked in front of those men?"

Jeanne Duval told her the story from the very beginning— how she had taken a small apartment with the money left over from Mme Aupick's settlement and how Baudelaire had moved in with her. In spite of all that had happened, she couldn't say no; he was old, ill, and had no money.

"We are two of a kind," she told Simone. "Neither of us will live long, so why not help each other out?"

Simone was shocked. She did not know what upset her more—news of the tuberculosis or the fact that her friend had taken that monster back into her life.

"We're not lovers," said Duval. "You must understand that. I am just helping him."

"It's your choice," said Simone.

Duval explained how she needed to raise money, not for treatment in an Alpine sanatorium, it was too late for that, but to fund a final adventure, a journey that would give her huge pleasure. So she had turned to the only job she really knew and had gone back to Le Rêve. She was determined to sing a song she had written by herself, without any help, because it was how she felt about her life at that moment. She knew they wouldn't like it, but she had hardly thought a table of drunks would start throwing things at the stage. And so she had reacted and given the bastards a taste of their own brutish manners.

She paused. Simone had listened quietly, sipping her champagne, thinking how odd it was that somebody she thought she knew so well could suddenly become a stranger. Maybe despite all those years of gossip and laughter in cheap cafés she had never really known her friend. There was something within Jeanne Duval she would neither share nor explain, the memory of a brutal, frightening childhood perhaps.

"Two things," Simone said. "What is this journey? And I would love to hear the song—you know, the one that started all the trouble."

She promised to sing her the song but said nothing about

the journey. They drank their champagne and ate sole meunière with black butter sauce, girolles, and new potatoes. Around them the restaurant rustled with whispered conversations. Duval ordered a second bottle of champagne. It could have been the glow of good wine or the private arbor in which they were lunching, but Simone suddenly felt happy for herself and her friend. Jeanne seemed content, a woman who had indeed settled her accounts and was prepared to meet whatever the future had in store. For the first time Simone saw Duval as a woman with an inner peace. She was in control of herself; she laughed and brushed off all questions about her illness.

"The point is, I don't fear death, I really don't," she said. "The beauty of tuberculosis is that it takes you to the other side without pain or suffering. Don't forget we all share the same destination, don't we? But that's grim; let's not talk about it. Here's to our new life—and especially yours."

They drank and ordered a tarte made of oranges and cream.

Simone looked sad. "Why especially my life?"

"Why not? You have a wonderful future."

"I'm a shopgirl who sells overpriced perfume to ladies who should know better and to gentlemen who do know better but still think it's the way to a woman's bedroom. Some future!"

Duval picked up the unicorn salt cellar and held it up to Simone.

"Supposing I said I could change it for you with a wave of this mythical creature and put you on a magic carpet?"

"I would say you had drunk too much champagne."

"You would be right! Now, have another glass and listen to me."

She had worked out just what to say. Simone was not young, being in her forties, but she could still have a good life before her. She came from one of the most depressed rural regions of France. She would never go back home, but in Paris she could not go forward. She was stuck as a shop assistant in a perfumery. She could sell herself to some of the wealthy men who came to the shop, of course—many young girls did that in the smart new department stores. The lucky ones were set up in a small apartment and given an allowance as a kept woman.

But that was not for Simone. Her Catholic faith may have lapsed in that she never went to church, but she was a woman of integrity. In any case, she had neither the figure nor the face to make a mistress. But she did have the energy, the honesty, and the talent to start a new life in a new world, a life where she could find a husband, adopt children, do everything that she, Jeanne Duval, had thrown away, everything she had been cheated of.

"I want you to go to America," said Duval.

Simone would always remember that she had just sliced her fork into the orange tart when she heard those words. She looked up.

"You've definitely had too much to drink," she said.

Jeanne Duval talked in a fast, tumbling stream of words that fizzed forth like champagne bubbles.

She had reclaimed the cost of her canceled ticket. She had enough money to pay Simone's passage to New York. America was looking for new emigrants from the Old World, young people with the courage to make a new life for themselves. This was especially true in the new frontier states of the West, where great cities were springing up. From Wyoming to Texas they were building hotels, shops, restaurants, and schools. That was where Simone would find her new life; that was where she could create a future she would never find in Paris.

Simone broke in, "You want me to find your father; is that it?"

Duval reached for her glass. A telling thrust from a knowing heart, and it went right to the point. Why was she doing this? She reflected for a few seconds. No, it wasn't her father; that dream had died and so in all probability had he.

Duval reached across the table and took Simone's hand.

"You're looking at someone who loves you; you're my friend. This isn't about finding someone I have never even met. It's about you. Think what life holds for you here. You will grow old in that job, and then the shop will fire you and hire someone younger, and you will be an old maid in Paris selling flowers on rainy nights outside the Opéra. Some well-oiled old gent will come up one night and offer you fifty sous for a quick one in an alley around the back. It happens all the time, but I don't want it to happen to you."

Duval stopped. There was a silence. Simone's tarte lay barely touched.

"I don't know what to say; I really don't. I mean, we are best friends and you want me to go away?"

"I wanted to get out of this place, Simone. I desperately wanted to escape. Paris is a prison to me. But I can't. You can, and I can give you that chance."

"The chance to live the life you can no longer have?"

Duval turned and parted the greenery, looking for the

waiter. She needed more champagne. She caught his eye and he nodded.

Those two women were going to get drunk, he thought. His shift ended soon, but he might just have a chance with the older one if he hung around until they left.

Duval turned back to Simone and smiled. "Yes," she said.

"It's a lovely dream and I thank you for sharing it with me. But think about it. I have family here, I don't speak English, and what on earth would I do over there?"

The pop of a champagne cork signaled the appearance of the waiter, who set the bottle on the table. He smiled at Duval. Why does a young man's smile always seem like a leer? she thought. She began talking again, a fast, irrepressible flow of words, leaving Simone an island in a stream of argument. She had to persuade her friend to do what she knew would bring happiness to them both.

"I cannot promise you success in America; you may be miserable, lonely, homesick," she told her. "But don't you see, if you don't take the chance, you will never know. You can always come back if you hate it. English? So what? It's easy. Baudelaire even taught me some. Once you make friends there you will speak it in no time. Your family? Well, think about it, Simone. You don't see them from one end of the year to the other. And, frankly, they will probably be happiest thinking of you in a new country with a new life."

"But I don't know anyone there," said Simone plaintively.

"You didn't know anyone in Paris when you arrived. You're an attractive, good-looking woman."

"I'm over forty—they'll think I'm an old maid in America."

"You're chic, French, glamorous. They'll love you in America, especially in the West. It's new territory; they won't have seen anything like you out there."

"You mean, I'll be the only woman among a whole bunch of cowboys . . . ?"

"Maybe. So what? It's life. It will be exciting, different, even dangerous, but you will be alive instead of stuck in a shop with bread and soup for lunch and old men's eyes scuttling over you like crabs."

"Ugh," said Simone, and shivered. "What a thought."

An arm pushed aside the leaves, refilled their glasses, and withdrew itself. The waiter remained on the far side of the greenery, continuing to eavesdrop on this weird conversation. Maybe they were lesbians, he thought.

Simone cast around for another line of reasoning to stem the tide that was overwhelming her. Can you change your whole life and tear up a predictable but utterly sad future in one drunken lunch? It was beginning to look like it.

"Are you sure this isn't about your father?" she said.

Duval threw her napkin on the table in frustration. "I've told you. It's about you."

"About me living *your* dream."

"Why not? It would give me great happiness to think of you settled there in America, meeting a nice man, maybe a wealthy rancher, and adopting a family—yes, that was my dream. What's wrong with wanting you to have it?"

"Nothing," said Simone hastily. "But are you sure you can afford it? Won't you need the money?"

"Yes I can and no I won't."

"And you really want me to do this?"

"I do, I do, I really, really do."

When he saw the two women embracing by the reception desk while their coats were being fetched, the waiter realized he had been right. They were hugging each other and both were crying. Definitely ladies of the sapphic tendency. Typical of his luck. Still, they'd left him a decent tip.

36

The sales of the expurgated edition of *Les Fleurs du Mal* had not met the publisher's hopes of a rich return for the risk he had taken. It sold slowly because word had spread that the remaining poems in the book lacked the sexual candor of those that had been banned. However, the critical reviews were more positive and several writers noted with interest the promise of a full second edition with added poems. Baudelaire suspected that this change of heart was due to guilt within the literary establishment that no eminent artist or writer had stood up to defend him from the obscenity charges.

Poulet-Malassis was an eternal optimist, however, a state of mind that was essential, he told himself, when dealing with authors such as Charles Baudelaire. The poet had found some commercial success with his translation of several books by the American master of the macabre, Edgar Allan Poe, but there were signs that literary fashions were changing. French readers were beginning to weary of gothic tales of horror and were turning again to lighter romances.

There was no chance of persuading his famous author to meet this new trend. Instead, the poet finally delivered more poems for a second edition of *Les Fleurs du Mal.* Unusually, Baudelaire appeared in a benign mood, almost happy, as he entered the publisher's office to hand over the manuscripts. He was still garbed in black, but there was color in his face and a sparkle to the way he twirled his cane at the boy who was still fast asleep in the outer room. When he failed to respond, Baudelaire prodded him gently with the silver knob. Albert woke up with a start and rubbed his eyes. It was that madman again. He would be wanting his glass of wine. Albert shambled over to a cupboard, leaving Baudelaire to enter the office and greet his publisher.

Scarcely had the two men shaken hands when Baudelaire explained that he had completed the first draft of a new book. It was called *Les Paradis artificiels* and was a personal account of his experiences as an opium addict and a hashish smoker. It was bound to be popular, because the French of a certain class took opium as the English milords and ladies took tea—was that not right?

Even Poulet-Malassis's sunny charm wilted when he heard the news.

"Could you not for once write about something other than death, damnation, drugs, and disease?" he said.

"What else is there?" said Baudelaire. "I have written about love, and look where that got us."

Albert entered the office with two glasses of red wine. He placed them on the table, glanced meaningfully at the clock, which showed the time as eleven o'clock, and left. He was tired, he needed to rest, and he did not need idiot poets poking him with canes.

Poulet-Malassis raised his glass. "Here's to your second edition. And to *Les Paradis artificels.* And to some very surprising news."

Baudelaire sat down. "Good news?"

"Excellent news. You will be surprised."

"So?"

"The Ministry of Education has decided to give us a grant of one thousand francs as a contribution to the costs of the new edition. They regard it as a work that should be distributed to university libraries and taught in the senior classes of the lycées."

"So I go from being an obscene poet to a teacher of young students?"

"Exactly. It's politics, of course. The minister wants to make a point to the emperor, but that doesn't matter. We have the money."

"We?"

"Well, I do. There is still the fine to pay and we have the first-edition costs."

Baudelaire rose and held up an empty glass.

Poulet-Malassis left the office, tiptoed past his sleeping assistant, and retrieved the bottle from the cupboard.

"You spoil that boy," said Baudelaire.

"He's an orphan. He lives with some drunk of an uncle. One has to help the less fortunate a little if one can."

"In which case, perhaps you can help me."

The publisher had not once conducted business with his

author without being asked for money. He was surprised that Baudelaire had taken so long to raise the subject this time.

"How much?"

"I am feeling better. I am writing a big poem called 'The Voyage' and—"

"And you are back with that woman!"

"How did you know?"

"Never mind. Tell me about the poem."

They finished the bottle and then another. By lunchtime both men were in agreement. A loan would be made as an advance against sales of the second edition. Baudelaire promised to work on further poems.

As for Jeanne Duval, Poulet-Malassis shrugged. "It's your life," he said.

"It's different now; we have found each other. You know what she did the other night at Le Rêve?"

"I did hear," said Poulet-Malassis, who tried to reconcile the elegant lady he had taken to lunch with reports of her public striptease in a seedy club.

"Well, that shows she's turned a corner. The old Duval would have joined the mob for a drink. We're celebrating at La Chandelle tonight. She's booked it. Drop in for a drink."

"La Chandelle?"

"Yes. She suggested it. Cheap and good."

"Charles, La Chandelle closed two months ago. The owner committed suicide. Drank a bottle of cognac and jumped into the Seine. Something to do with one of his kitchen boys."

"I think you're mistaken. It must have reopened."

Poulet-Malassis wondered if he had another bottle of wine in the cupboard.

"It has reopened, Charles. It's a gun shop—the latest rifles from America, I am told."

"But she said she went there last week!"

This time he knew he wouldn't find her. There was no sign of her at the usual cafés and bars. Her friend Simone had left her job in the perfumery shop without giving an address. She had also left her apartment in Neuilly.

Back in their top-floor apartment in the Latin Quarter, all of Duval's possessions had gone: clothes, shoes, toiletries, luggage—everything. There was just a note. It said: "Farewell from the albatross."

Faint traces of sandalwood and cedarwood lingered on the bedsheets, the fragrance of loss, the perfume of the departed. He did not wander the streets searching for her as before. He knew he wouldn't find her, knew that she had gone. His Black Venus had finally left him. She would not be coming back.

After a few days he wrote to his mother. He would go to Honfleur and stay there until the summer.

My dearest mother,

Forgive this rather emotional letter. I wish to tell you that Jeanne Duval has left me forever. She never said good-bye. I think she thought that would hurt both of us too much. She left me with a promise she never kept. Her whole life was a promise to me she never kept. I should be relieved—you are, no doubt—but I cannot be. She is ill. She needs help. She needs me. Perhaps I need her, who knows?

But what I do know now is that I will never see her again. And that, dearest Mama, makes me feel more wretched than I can describe. I pray I will see you soon.
Your loving son
Charles

37

"I just don't feel I can leave you. Who's going to look after you when I have left?"

Simone held Duval in her arms as she whispered the words, rocking gently back and forth. They were lying on the bed in Duval's new lodgings. In a corner Simone's trunk was packed, everything she owned in the world carefully stowed inside. Her friend appeared asleep but stirred herself and sat up drowsily.

"You're not well; you have to go back to the doctor."

Duval gave a catlike yawn, rubbed her eyes, and smiled. "There's nothing he can do. The important thing is to get you on that ship and— I am coming to Le Havre with you!"

"You can't. You're not strong enough."

"Simone, for the first time in my life I am doing something I am really proud of, something worthwhile. You've no idea how happy that makes me. You are going to America. You will be in New York in twelve days. You will walk the streets of that amazing city and I will be there with you. Don't you understand? That's why it is so exciting—we're *both* going to America! You have the tickets?"

"You've asked me that five times already! Yes, I have the tickets."

"Good. Remind me: when is the train?"

"Gare du Nord, tomorrow night."

"Of course. And you're packed?"

Simone put her arms around her friend and hugged her. "Dearest Jeanne. I have the tickets, I am packed, and I am very excited. But what about you?"

"I have told you. I am going to be sitting here waiting for your letters—promise you will write?"

"Every day."

Duval swung her legs over the bed and doubled up, clutching her side. Simone moved to comfort her but was waved away. Duval straightened up, her face pale, the dark eyes lacking all luster.

"Some cognac and a little water, please."

When Jeanne Duval saw the long lines of passengers boarding the paddle steamer at Le Havre she felt a pang of jealousy. The boat train had arrived at the port at ten o'clock in the evening and the ship looked like a fairy castle, lit with hundreds of lanterns. The two funnels and the masts reared up from the dockside, making the passengers walking up the gangplank look like toiling elves entering a magic grotto.

The combination of steam-powered paddles and a single

screw had made the new generation of transatlantic ships faster, cutting the crossing to just twelve days. The ships had been hailed in the press as one of the technological marvels of the age, and the Paris journals had carried drawings and photographs of the *Washington*.

Yet nothing could have prepared Jeanne for the sight of the ship that night. This was her ship, her fairyland, and she had lost it. Simone would share a crowded and no doubt fetid cabin for the twelve-day voyage. She would be seasick on the crossing, and homesick and utterly alone when she arrived. But she would be in New York, a city that had captured the imagination of a Europe weary of poverty, repression, and the threat of war.

And she, Jeanne Duval, would be left behind to live out her old life alone in a city that offered her only a bitter end to everything she had once hoped for. She had sung her way across the Atlantic all those years ago to find freedom from terror in her homeland. She had escaped servitude, the lash, and the certainty of an early death in Haiti to find a future in a country that had promised her so much. Those hopes had turned to ashes. Disease had denied her the chance of re-demption in America.

The two women looked up at the ship in silence for a few moments.

"You never did sing me that song," said Simone.

Duval smiled, linked arms, and steered her friend toward a dockside tavern. The place was crowded with people say-ing farewell. Everybody seemed to be crying, wiping away tears, promising to write. The travelers, both sad and excited to be leaving, were anxious to board. Friends and relatives clung to their loved ones for a few last words, knowing they were unlikely to meet again.

Simone and Duval squeezed themselves up to a table and ordered some wine.

"How are you feeling?" Simone said.

"I am excited for you. To think of you on that extraordinary machine, being thrown around on the waves for almost two weeks—and then suddenly a new world, a new life!"

"I'm still worried about you."

"Stop it. We've talked about that—just make sure you write."

"I will, but let me take a little of that song with me, the one you have promised me."

Duval raised her glass, wiped away a tear and began to sing in a low, husky whisper:

"In the silver mirrors of my mind,
I see the girl I left behind.
I shed tears for her childish dreams,
Because life is never what it seems.

"But the hopes we shared and held so high
Were passing clouds in an empty sky.
Now I turn from the truth I find
In the silver mirrors of my mind."

Around them people had stopped to listen. Duval felt embarrassed. She got up.

"We must go," she said. "And you must board your ship."

They said their good-byes briefly on the dock. Simone

hugged her and began to cry. Duval felt the tears on her cheek. She gently broke away from the embrace, turned, and walked away. Don't look back, she told herself. It will hurt too much.

38

Charles Baudelaire settled into his mother's house in January 1860. To his surprise, he slipped easily into a daily routine, rising at eight and beginning work a half hour later with a large pot of coffee at the window desk of a room overlooking the sea.

The house was well situated on an avenue running from the old port along the coast, and its slightly elevated position offered a good view of the tides that bubbled in over the sand and mudflats twice a day. He found comfort in the rhythm of the tides, the wheeling flocks of gulls, the shifting patterns of silky clouds, and the daily beach theater: young girls with kites, children making elaborate sand castles, old ladies with little dogs, bearded men wrapped in scarves puffing pipes, lovers hanging on to each other as if the wind might blow them away.

The ordered world of the seafront gave him solace. Mariette, now a middle-aged woman, had remained in his mother's service, and she too was a reassuring presence in what seemed to be an orderly world that had removed him from the misery and misfortunes that attended life in Paris.

Lunch was served to him in the small sitting room where he worked. Mariette brought fresh fish from the market—plaice, sole, or hake—and usually fried them in butter and garlic and served them with potatoes and carrots. In the afternoon, on the instructions of his mother, he took a walk along the beach, breathing in the sea air and holding lungfuls deep in his chest for as long as possible before expelling the air in cloudy vapors.

On his return, Mariette served English tea from a pretty bone china teapot and then he would work until a bell tinkled somewhere downstairs at 6:30. That was his mother's signal to descend and take a glass of sherry with her. It would be the first time in the day they had seen each other, and mother and son would sit facing each other in armchairs by the fire. A bottle of dry sherry from Spain would be placed on a table with two crystal glasses. Mariette would open the bottle, pour the drinks, and then leave the room. Above the fire General Aupick would look down sternly on them in full military uniform.

Mme Aupick always raised a glass to her late husband and Baudelaire dutifully followed suit, but the general's name was not otherwise mentioned. Her friends in Honfleur did not join them for evening drinks. They did not approve of Baudelaire, regarding him as the personification of metropolitan debauchery. Caroline Aupick forfeited her place in local society, relinquishing the gossipy afternoon teas, the bridge evenings, and the occasional luncheon in order to concentrate on her son.

They talked a lot about his health ("I feel so much better

here by the sea, Mother") and his writing ("The poem is a long one, but it is coming on well"), while both carefully avoided the taboo subjects of money and Jeanne Duval.

If the weather was bad and a Channel storm was rattling rain against the windows, Caroline Aupick would serve small glasses of the local spirit, Calvados, a fiery drink that left an aftertaste of burned apples. He had never tried Calvados before and after a few stormy days he came to appreciate the warm afterglow and sense of well-being imparted by a few glasses. He decided it was the poor man's cognac and began to watch the barometer in the hall, waiting for the needle to swing round to *rain* or *stormy*. Yet he never asked for Calvados and in the house drank only the sherry that his mother offered and a glass or two of wine at dinner. He felt such restraint was in keeping with the peace and routine of the household. The regularity and relative sobriety of his life at Honfleur made him believe that finally he might recover his health.

He had known for years that he had been infected with a strain of venereal disease as a young man. He had admitted that only to a few close friends and fellow sufferers but never to Jeanne Duval. Manet suffered from a similar complaint as well, and the two friends would discuss the various horrifying treatments advised by doctors. Since the most common of these involved the injection of hot mercury into the male member Manet and Baudelaire persuaded themselves, as did every other young man in Paris, that their cases were mild and would disappear in time. The guilt that tormented him over this dishonest denial now seemed to ease, as did anxiety about the question of his debts.

Somehow the domestic tranquility of his mother's house

and the provincial calm of the port city seemed to place all his problems in a benign perspective. He would get better; there was talk of a new treatment for his infection that required the injection of mercury into the scrotum. That sounded impossibly painful. But in his penitent mood he welcomed the prospect of such an excruciating procedure as a means of redemption.

He also persuaded himself that as his evening fireside talks with his mother grew more loving, so she might finally be persuaded to release all his remaining funds. Then he could pay off his debtors and resume his rightful place in literary society without being hounded from one lodging to the next. The second edition of *Les Fleurs du Mal* would achieve deserved success, thus providing him with a small income.

Baudelaire became a familiar figure in the seaside town, striding along the beach every afternoon with his black cape and silver-knobbed cane, or strolling through the cobbled streets by the harbor, pausing to examine paintings by local artists in the many small galleries.

After a few months he had become something of a local celebrity. People would point to him in the street: "There goes Mme Aupick's son, the poet pornographer from Paris." He knew of his reputation and wondered what on earth the local worthies would make of his next book, *Les Paradis artificiels.* After years of addiction he had turned his back on the pleasures of hashish and opium. Smoking hashish had been a constant habit since his senior school days, but he had ended use of the drug after Jeanne Duval had introduced him to the dangerous delights of opium. She had provided it in the liquid form of laudanum and seemed to have an endless supply. She made him pay of course, but he didn't care and neither did he inquire about her source. He told himself that opium was an inspiration for his poetry and a palliative for his various illnesses. It was Manet, another opium addict, who changed Baudelaire's mind. The painter told him that for days after taking laudanum he could not lift a brush in his studio. Opium was destroying his art rather than inspiring it, he said. Baudelaire not only agreed but went further. In letters, magazine articles, but above all his favourite cafés he warned of the spiritual degradation and loss of willpower caused by drug taking.

This sudden conversion was no surprise to his friends, who had long grown accustomed to the ebb and flow of Baudelaire's passions. This was a man who could loftily condemn both the monarchy and the mob intent on its overthrow, a critic who would heap contempt on modern music and yet hail the young Wagner as a genius, a poet who publicly despised the material world and yet dressed like a dandy and borrowed money to dine in good restaurants. Little wonder, then, that he had turned against a drug habit in which he had indulged since an early age.

Les Paradis artificiels was much more than an attack on drug use. The book condemned the false promise of such drugs as opium and went on to question man's right to happiness. Why believe such an ideal when the truth is obvious that we are not placed on this earth to be happy but to endure suffering? Hallucinatory drugs, wine, tobacco, and the material comforts of a prosperous society merely rob us of the truth we all have to face: that only through suffering can we find any meaning in the pitifully short time we exist on earth.

He knew the book was going to be a disaster. It had

already been published as two long magazine articles under a different title and received a hostile reception from the critics. They were no kinder when the book appeared with the new title. Flaubert had written to him and after a few polite comments had told him how much he disliked the moralizing tone. "You are a supreme romantic," he had said. "Go back to your poetry. I want more such poems as in *Les Fleurs du Mal*."

Where do I find poetry in the pretty town of Honfleur? he wondered. It's like a desert mirage seen from a distance: beautiful buildings, pretty painted boats in the harbor, families on the beach, clouds creating their own works of art in the sky, and when you look closer . . . there's nothing there. Even the one place in which one might expect to find an inkling of man's spiritual existence, the church, has been closed, its doors locked.

He wondered what his Black Venus would make of Honfleur. She would wrap herself in that silver-lined cloak and sit by the harbor drinking absinthe from a flask and talking to the sailors. She would allow them to take her to a bar for more absinthe or wine. They would crowd around her on a floodtide of excitement, lust. How much to offer this exotic, half-caste creature? Where to go to enjoy a woman like that? She would laugh with them and at them, and when they found out who she was—the former mistress of the poet pornographer, the woman who had destroyed the prosecutor at the obscenity trial—the tide would ebb and one by one they would return to their boats.

Where was she now? Had she become one of the daily procession of corpses on view at the mortuary? Or perhaps she had become the mistress of an old man with a top-floor apartment on boulevard Haussmann overlooking the city. Would he ever know?

Flaubert had been right. He started work again on "The Voyage," a poem that would take him on a journey to discover the truth about a woman who had never loved him, had wronged him, and now had left him. And he had forgiven her. Why? Because he could not forget her.

Occasionally friends would come from Paris, especially Gustave Courbet, who delighted in Honfleur and began a series of paintings of the port, with its fishing boats, cafés, and quaysides. He and Courbet would dine in one of the harbor restaurants, which provided relief from the nightly small talk with his mother. Not that he didn't enjoy the first real conversation he had had with her since he was a young man. But after a glass or two of wine, she always talked to him in a tone of irritated disappointment, as if his troubles were somehow of his own making.

It was at dinner one night that he and Courbet solved a mystery that had puzzled the parishioners of Honfleur for weeks. St. Catherine's church was the largest in the city and a magnificent example of wooden architecture from medieval days. Baudelaire and Courbet had intended to visit the church but discovered that it had been closed on the orders of the Bishop of Rouen. A sign had been placed on the great double doors stating the closure would be indefinite but giving no reason. At the same time, the parish priest who had drunk so much of his mother's sherry had left his grace-and-favor house, equally without explanation.

It was Courbet who discovered the scandalous truth. The serving girl behind the bar at the Hôtel Maritime, where he was lodging, knew the story. But it was and must remain a secret, she said. Her mother worked as a cleaner in the church and had sworn her to secrecy. He tried offering her money, but she had laughed and shaken her pretty head. She wanted much more than money. Finally, she extracted the promise that he would include her as a small figure in one of his paintings of the harbor. He immediately made a sketch and obligingly drew her in with a few pencil strokes.

He took the news she imparted to dinner with the poet that night. They met in one of the busiest restaurants on the harbor front. Baudelaire was incredulous when he heard the story. He was slightly drunk, having taken Calvados with his mother that evening, and immediately ordered a further large measure.

"You mean to say that the mayor's wife was caught in the confessional box fucking her lover?" he said in a deliberately loud voice.

"Shh!" said Courbet as diners paused to consider the news that had boomed around the restaurant.

"And apparently the priest turned a blind eye, knowing what was going on," whispered Courbet. "They met every Sunday after the evening service when the church was still warm."

This story of provincial lechery in a holy place delighted Baudelaire. It was a marvelous parable of human frailty and authoritarian officialdom, a sign that even in a remote town in Normandy, Satan was still tempting the unwary.

It also exposed the hypocrisy of a society in which his mother's friends played such a prominent role. They had effectively banished her from their social circle while he was in Honfleur. He knew that this had deeply upset her.

"They close a church and punish an entire congregation because the mayor's fat-assed wife was being pleasured in a place of God?" said Baudelaire without lowering his voice.

It was the end of Baudelaire's stay in Honfleur. The local dignitaries could tolerate the scandal in their midst only if it remained a private affair. But they could not accept the shame of public disclosure. Everyone knew the mayor and his wife. They were some of the oldest and most respected residents in the town. It was widely known that the mayor was a little dull and his wife rather flighty. They were not a well-matched couple. Her rumored transgression was disgraceful and the church had rightly been closed to allow the confessional box to be torn down and rebuilt. While the affair made for delightful private gossip and was the source of much satisfactory condemnation, it most certainly was not for a wider audience. The view was that Caroline Aupick's renegade son had deliberately set out to shame the town. He would have to leave.

Baudelaire was happy to return to Paris. By now, the daily routine, the sea air, and Mariette's cooking had made him feel better than he had for years. He had almost completed the new poem, the longest he had ever written, and it was time to show the work to Poulet-Malassis. He had nowhere to live in Paris and little money for lodgings. But he had to leave Honfleur.

Apart from anything else, he knew that his mother wished to resume the social life she had enjoyed before he came to stay. And the fact was that Honfleur bored him. The hypocrisy of the bourgeois elders of the town had been entertaining for a while, but now he was being blamed for revealing the secret of the closed church. They were probably all at it, he thought. It is hardly likely that the mayor's wife was the only woman who sought some relief from the boredom of the marital bed.

In Paris he found a single room in the Hôtel Dieppe in the Latin Quarter. He had no money, but once again Poulet-Malassis paid the one month's rent demanded by the manager. The payment was another advance on the second edition of *Les Fleurs du Mal,* which contained thirty-five new poems as well as many revisions to the original poems. He had little expectation of success. The reviews of *Les Paradis Artificiels* had been bad and sales negligible.

He went back to the Momus, where he found that Le Vavasseur had returned from a second assignment of military duties in Algeria. This time he had changed. He was deeply sunburned and much thinner. Baudelaire noticed that his friend's hands shook as they raised a glass to each other. Le Vavasseur would not talk of what he had seen and done, but he said that even at the risk of a court-martial he would refuse further service in North Africa. They drank and talked deep into the night, until the last of the barmen insisted they leave. They heard a nearby church clock strike three.

39

The stamp featured a bewigged George Washington set against a blue background. The date had been franked over and the envelope was grubby, as if it had been passed through many hands. This was the letter she had been waiting for. Six weeks had passed since Simone's ship had sailed and every day Jeanne Duval had left her room in Neuilly to take the horse-drawn omnibus to the office of *Figaro* in the city center. There she waited her turn to read one of the two copies of that day's edition that were held in wooden spines and secured to a reading desk with a light chain. She turned to first the shipping news in the business pages and then the weather reports at the back of the paper. The arrival of the *Washington* in New York had been reported on the twelfth of the previous month, almost four weeks ago. It was February 1861 and she noticed news reports that America had a new president-in-waiting, someone called Abraham Lincoln. He was to be inaugurated the following month.

Dearest Jeanne,

I hardly know where to begin! We had a good cross-ing, although everyone was seasick, but they said that was normal. I didn't eat much on the whole voyage— just didn't feel like it. So I have lost a lot of weight! But I did really try to learn as much English as I could with that book you gave me, and by the time we landed I could really have quite a good conversation.

But you don't want to know about that, do you? What can I say? New York is amazing but frightening, full of crowds rushing in every direction. If you think the streets of Paris are crowded, you should see this city! I am staying in a hostel for single women close to Broad-way and hope to get a job in one of the big department stores. There are so many of them.

Everyone is talking about the coming war with the Southern states. They have formed a confederacy and peo-ple are waiting to see what the new president will do. It's all about slavery and there are a lot of black people in New York here who have escaped from the South. All very exciting, but I don't really understand it.

Now, my plans, my darling Jeanne! I am going to get that job, save a little money, and then travel out west. I heard on the boat that the new state of Texas has great opportunities. It's almost the size of France, with wonder-ful weather. But now everyone tells me the new states in the West are the place to go, places I have never heard of, beyond Missouri, wherever that is.

I can't wait! Forgive a very short letter, but I am writ-ing by candlelight and the wick is almost burned out.

But finally, my dear friend, I know how much you wished to be here instead of me. But you are here with me; I feel your presence everywhere.

With love,

Simone

Duval lay on the bed and read the letter over and over again. There was a civil war coming in America; that much had been obvious from the reports in *Figaro*. But it would all be in the South, wouldn't it? Anyway, it was all about slavery and it would soon be over. Simone would be safe in New York. She was in the most exciting country in the world. She would soon get a job. Duval could imagine her behind the counter in a big store enchanting everyone with her French-accented English. She would make enough money to travel and then go out west, maybe to Texas. She would meet a nice man, marry, have children, live on a ranch with lots of cattle. And she would write to her all the time.

She closed her eyes and placed her hands on her stomach. She pressed and gave a slight cry. She could feel the lump inside her now, down there on the left side. The doctor had said it would get bigger. And she was coughing all the time. She would go back to the doctor. She had very little money left, but he was a good man. He would help her. She fell asleep dreaming of Simone in New York, Simone getting on the train to Texas—could you get a train to Texas from New York? Probably not. It would be quite a journey, maybe in those stagecoaches she had read about. Then there were all those Indians—and that trouble in the South. It was going to be a very big adventure for her friend.

. . .

Two years later, in 1863, Charles Baudelaire wrote a letter to his mother from the Hôtel Dieppe. He told her that he intended to join Poulet-Malassis in Belgium, a new French-speaking country that was both more liberal in its attitude to artists and a great deal cheaper than Paris. His publisher had fled there to escape his debts. So they were both bankrupt and virtually ruined. Baudelaire's health was bad; he was suffering from seizures and fits. Sometimes he woke and could not see anything for an hour. He ended the letter:

This may not interest you, but you should know that I heard that Jeanne Duval has died, apparently in some home for the terminally ill run by the Catholic nuns in the 16th. It is just a rumor, of course, and I have been unable to find the place. I have been to the mortuary on the île de la Cité, but they have no records of names. I looked at those pitiful bodies, some of them found dead on the street and some dragged from the river, and I just pray that my Black Venus did not finish like that. Whatever anyone thought of her, she deserved better.

I know you never cared for her, Mama, and no one else gave a damn for her either. And none of you understood why I cared so much.

But now I am coming to the end of my life—and it won't be long now, my kindly doctors assure me—I realize I have only ever had two sacred obligations on this earth. The first was to my poetry and the second was to my Black Venus. I failed them both. But I have never given up looking for her. It's been years now and I haven't

*written a word worth anything to anyone. I feel the
wings of death hovering over me.*

> *Your loving son*
> *Charles Baudelaire*
> *PS: It would be a great kindness if you could send me
> some money—maybe 200 francs for my doctors' bills.*

Baudelaire never received the money from his mother.
Instead, she sent a letter admonishing him once again for his
spendthrift ways and urging him to come and live with her
in Honfleur instead. In a long and loving letter he declined
the offer. In Belgium, he told her, he would make enough
money to repay his debts and fund the medical treatment
denied him in Paris. Brussels, he said, was the most bourgeois and boring city on earth, which was exactly why a man
of his artistic talent and temperament would triumph there.

Neither his mother nor Baudelaire himself was fooled by
such delusions. In the real world of poverty, artistic failure,
and illness, he began to talk with increasing urgency about
suicide.

"I think my life was damned from the start and damned
forever," he told Apollonie Sabatier at a lunch to which she
had invited him. Without money and with few real friends
left, he had accepted the invitation with pleasure but insisted
on paying. Sabatier foiled the offer by arranging for the restaurant manager to make a fuss over his famous customer and
refuse payment for the meal. She would then discreetly pay
the manager later.

On that basis, the former lovers met in the Café de Suède
on the boulevard Montmartre, where such fine dishes as
goose stuffed with chestnuts were served in private cubicles.

The cuisine was less important than the discretion afforded within the restaurant. Mme Sabatier had become the mistress of Alfred Mosselman, a Belgian millionaire who was famously jealous and who was known to employ private detectives.

Baudelaire rose to his feet when she arrived at the table, struck by the beauty of a woman who had just turned forty. Her fair hair was coiled into a bun, revealing a slender neck set off by long arrow-shaped emerald earrings. She wore a modest, long-sleeved white lace dress. Her complexion was that of a woman half her age, with a milk-and-roses coloring that gave her the air of innocence so admired by a succession of much older lovers. She greeted him with a shy smile and sat down.

He remained standing, lost in the thought that here was a woman who seemingly defied the creeping decay of time. She was, he told her, as beautiful as when they had met for the first time at the wedding ball all those years ago. She smiled, thanked him, and begged him to be seated.

Their talk that lunch began as a river does at its source, flowing quietly through a familiar landscape. He assured her his mother was in good health and greatly enjoying her life at Honfleur. She told him of the disappointment she felt when Courbet's portrait of her had been refused a hanging by the French Academy. He told her of his despair that the second edition of *Les Fleurs du Mal* had not proved a success. They talked of his poetry but not of the woman who had inspired the sensual poems that had led to the trial. He in turn avoided the subject of Théo Gautier, whose letters to her were widely said to have been pornographic but whose whereabouts remained a mystery. In fact, she had showed them to a few friends and then placed them in the hands of a lawyer with instructions that they be returned to Gautier's estate after his death. The letters were the talk of Paris for years.

Baudelaire ate little but drank glass after glass of wine as they talked. She drank only water. He was, he said, very grateful that she had wished to meet the wretched ghost of a man she had once admired and loved.

"Maybe I still have such feelings," she said. "Maybe I recognize the genius in your work—maybe I always have—but that is not the reason I am here. I am worried about you. People say you talk of killing yourself."

Somewhere in his mind a dam broke and the river became a flood. His words became a torrent of despair and self-loathing. He was desperate, he told her; he thought of death all the time, night and day, even in his dreams. It would be an easy escape from the torment of poverty, debt, and illness—and above all from the crucifixion of artistic failure.

"I have never lacked courage," he said. "I have always faced and fought my enemies. I have always told the truth. But now I fear to face the death I so desire. Why should I live? What for? My work is finished. Nothing I have ever written can be found in the bookshops. My publisher is bankrupt. My mother would be well rid of me. I am afflicted by disgusting diseases. And . . . and . . ."

"And she is dead," said Mme Sabatier.

Baudelaire drained his glass and refilled his own when she declined.

"Yes, she is dead."

"And you still love her?"

"How can you ask me that?" he said, his face now flushed

with wine and sudden anger. "Do I have to be reminded of a woman with whom I wasted so much of my life, a woman who squandered my money and humiliated me with my friends?"

"No one has to remind you of her," she said. "Your Black Venus is alive and living in your own words—in *Les Fleurs du Mal*."

"I wrote many beautiful poems for you as well, poems of passion, love, and joy," he said.

Apollonie Sabatier drank the remaining water in her glass, reached for the bottle of wine, and poured a measure. She raised her glass to him.

"I don't think you would ever have written a word about me without that woman. That's the truth, isn't it?"

Baudelaire slumped back on the banquette, drank more wine, and said nothing.

"Maybe we should all be grateful to her," she said. "Shall we drink to that?"

There was a pause. "No," he said. "Let us drink to getting drunk."

He pulled his watch from a coat pocket and dangled it in front of her.

"Drink is the answer to this! If I can't kill myself, I shall drink to ease the burden of living in this hell."

He was drunk, his voice had risen, and the occupants of other cubicles were peering over the partitions. Apollonie Sabatier rose to leave. Baudelaire got to his feet unsteadily. He took her hand and bent to kiss it. She looked down at the thinning gray-white hair that fell in greasy strands over the back of a cheap broadcloth suit. His lips brushed the back of her hand and he straightened up. She moved around the table and kissed him on the cheek, a gesture so surprising that he fell back onto the banquette.

"'Poetry is the endless adventure of self-discovery,'" she said. "'Man has but to find his unconquerable soul to prevail.'"

"Who said that?" he asked.

"You did. In your last letter. Good-bye."

It was raining hard and horses and carriages were fighting for space along the rutted avenue of the Champs-Élysées.

Baudelaire sat slumped at the back of a carriage looking old and frail. His one small suitcase was lashed to the top of the cab behind the driver. He was on his way to Gare du Nord to take the train to Brussels, and as usual he was late. This might be the last time he saw Paris, he reflected. The cab stopped in the traffic and faces appeared at the rain-spotted window, peering inside and mouthing obscene propositions. He banged angrily on the window with his sword stick. Had it always been like this in Paris? Maybe he was just too old; maybe in the old days he would have swung open the door and some young girl would have scrambled in to pleasure him briefly and take her two francs back into the rain. Maybe.

A violent crash propelled him from his seat into the leather upholstery. The cab swayed and almost overturned. His driver, unseen on the outside seat, began shouting and cursing. Baudelaire grabbed his stick and opened the door.

An overturned carriage lay alongside his vehicle, with the horse on its side rearing and kicking between the shafts. The carriage driver was sitting on his overturned vehicle with blood pouring from a head wound. A well-dressed man, presumably the passenger in the overturned cab, was shouting at his driver. He too was bleeding from a face wound. A crowd had gathered to contribute to the volley of insults and threats that were being exchanged. The pouring rain added to the chaos.

Baudelaire tapped his driver on the shoulder with his sword stick. "What happened?" he shouted above the din.

The driver pointed at the upturned cab. "Asshole came straight out of the rue de Berri without looking or stopping. Happens all the time these days; country boys come in, get a job as a groom, then get a cab license and before you know it . . ."

Baudelaire was not listening. He was staring down the rue de Berri, as if mesmerized. He leaped into the throng, barged his way through, and started running across the mud and potholes.

Ahead of him a cloaked figure using a crutch walked slowly up the sidewalk. It was clearly a woman, but her face was hidden by the hood of her cloak. There was a flash of silver from the lining. Baudelaire pushed people out of his path, leaping into the road to avoid the press of pedestrians and jumping back again to escape the scything carriage wheels.

"JEANNE!" he shouted.

Duval stopped and turned. Her face was now visible under the hood. An older face, thin and deeply lined, the pallid skin like faded parchment. She smiled and hobbled into a side street.

Baudelaire reached the corner, panting, and rested against a wall. He looked along the street and saw her at the far end walking with difficulty on her crutch. She stopped and looked back.

For a moment they gazed at each other along the rain-drenched street. Every moment of their years together came to life in that look. He saw her as she had been—young, with lustrous black hair and that bewitching smile beneath black, smoldering eyes. She was standing there, tall, straight, willing him to join her.

She smiled at him—a deep, warm smile from within the cowl of her hooded cloak. With a swirl of sealskin and another flash of silver lining, she turned on her crutch and disappeared.

Baudelaire started running again and reached the corner where he had last seen her. He paused, breathless. He looked at the street beyond but saw nothing but people with umbrellas, raincoats, and cloaks.

He stumbled along the sidewalk. A carriage splashed him with mud. A passerby barged into him roughly. He staggered against a wall and slid down. Rain and tears washed over his face. He sat in the mud with his back to the wall, head raised skywards, eyes closed. Was that a hallucination, a ghostly image summoned by a fevered mind? No. After all these years, she was alive. But it would not be long now. At least he had seen her for the last time as she once was, and not as she had become.

Epilogue

Jeanne Duval had not been surprised to hear her name called on the street that rainy morning. She had known she would see him one more time. And she was glad. He looked like a starving scarecrow in his black garb—gray faced, gaunt, and his hair now snow-white. He clearly did not have long to live. Not that she was long for this earth either, but at least, and at last, she had made sure her final resting place would not be as a public spectacle on the grooved marble slabs of the Paris mortuary.

Édouard Manet, now famous, wealthy, and well married, had not forgotten her. When she asked him for help in her final days, he responded with characteristic generosity. He told her that her formal portrait was now hanging in a gallery in Budapest. "And what about the painting of me in the nude?" she asked. He laughed and told her it was in his private collection. Paris was not yet ready for the splendor of an unclothed Jeanne Duval.

She told him she wanted to spend her last weeks, months,

or whatever God had given her high up in the mountains where the air tasted like champagne and the vista stretched to eternity. Manet arranged lodgings for her in the village of Ferney-Voltaire in the mountains close to Geneva. He also provided sufficient money to cover her upkeep.

She accepted Manet's generosity on condition that he did not reveal the arrangement to anyone, especially Charles Baudelaire. She had been on her way to meet Manet and receive the necessary letters of introduction and the bank drafts when Baudelaire had seen her.

Six months after landing in New York, Simone gave up her job at the department store and bought a ticket on the Union Pacific Railroad to the West. She wanted to get as far away from the city as possible. It was September, the summer heat had passed, and the trees were still in leaf. New York looked its best, but the country was at war with itself and the city was trying to absorb a wave of refugees from the South.

There was relief throughout the Northern states that the poisonous issue of slavery had finally been confronted. The newspapers had total confidence in a quick victory under Abraham Lincoln. But Simone found no gaiety in a sullen, resentful New York. The new president had declared that all freed slaves would be given jobs in the city. The Irish emigrant population was alarmed and angered by the growing number of black refugees from the South. There were signs that the Irish protests would turn violent. The police, mostly Irish themselves, did nothing to stop the street fights between the rival Irish and black gangs. The Irish always won, because of their greater numbers. Having escaped from the slave plantations of the South, young blacks would all too often find themselves cornered by an Irish mob in the backstreets of Brooklyn. Occasionally the police fished the blacks' badly beaten bodies out of the Hudson River.

Simone did not mention the city's rancorous mood in her letters to Jeanne. It would have broken her heart. But Simone had decided to leave for the West and booked a thirdclass ticket from New York to Chicago. Despite the outbreak of the war, the papers had been full of the fortunes to be made from the cattle boom in the West. Cowboys were driving tens of thousands of long-horned cattle from the great plains to the railheads in western Missouri. From there the steers were packed into freight cars and sent to the slaughterhouses of Chicago. The profits flowed back to the cowboys, farmers, and ranchers on the Great Plains, pushing the railroad farther west and building cities along its line.

Simone decided that Kansas City in Missouri would be her first destination. It was the gateway to the new territories that had arisen on the Great Plains: Nebraska, Dakota, Montana, Colorado, and Wyoming; she matched the names to the rattle of the wheels as the train panted and puffed to Chicago: Nebraska–Dakota–Montana–Colorado–Wyoming. She fell asleep dreaming of cowboys riding on a sea of buffalo grass, of elegant cities rising from the plains, and of a certain man, older than her, wiser than her, who was carving a fortune for himself in the new territories, perhaps in mining, ranching, or business, who would see her and woo her, somewhere in Nebraska–Dakota–Montana–Colorado–Wyoming.

• • •

Publication of the second, expurgated edition of *Les Fleurs du Mal* bankrupted Poulet-Malassis. As with all of his books, the paper was of the highest quality, the binding the work of craftsmen. But such attention to detail was expensive. The book did not sell well, in spite of the scandal. By 1862 he still had not paid the court fine from the obscenity case, nor was he able to pay his creditors. He was imprisoned for two years, after first transferring his publishing business to his brother-in-law. On his release he fled to Belgium, where he was joined by Baudelaire. There, in spite of the disasters they had inflicted on each other, the two old friends gathered around them a group of similar refugees from creditors and critical disdain in Paris.

The last year of Baudelaire's life was one of illness, hardship, and despair. His long-standing application for membership in the French Academy had finally been turned down without explanation. It was the ultimate humiliation for a man who had always scorned honors and derided the establishment that gifted them. Yet he had felt that such an honor might at least persuade his creditors to give him more time. As it was, he could not pay for the cheap hotel in Brussels and had barely enough money to eat. He gave poorly paid lectures on art to scant audiences.

Obsessed as ever with the march of time, Baudelaire chronicled the exact positions of all the public clocks in Brussels, just as he had once done in Paris. He never gave up what he called life's struggle. As he said in his last letter to his mother: "As long as I have no conclusive proof that I am vanquished in the battle with time, I will struggle on."

Paris was his paradise lost and he dreamed of the boulevards, the cafés, the bright lights, the gardens, and the company of old friends. He found Brussels boring. The Belgians
did not know what a decent café was, he told friends. As illness closed in, he hardly had the energy to leave his hotel
room. What he had long dismissed as a mild venereal disease had now become tertiary syphilis, which led to increasingly frequent seizures and paralysis, although the doctors
in Brussels did not make the connection between the two.

Poulet-Malassis, the last and most loyal of his friends,
stood by him. When Baudelaire was well enough they would
lunch in the cheaper cafés or restaurants. Continually the
poet returned to the subject of Jeanne Duval. The publisher
found himself forced to repeat again and again the account
of their meeting in the Café Anglais and how she had attracted the attention of every man in the room as she left.
Baudelaire would listen to the story, ask for exact details of
what she had been wearing, what they had eaten and drunk,
and sit back, eyes closed, with a smile on his face.

Four months after she arrived at the lodging house on the
edge of Ferney-Voltaire, in the spring of 1866, Jeanne Duval
died peacefully in her sleep. Beside her on the bedside table
were three letters from Simone Clairmont tied together with
a ribbon. Duval asked to be cremated with her letters and the
ashes scattered on the mountain. Her final wish, expressed to
the landlady of her lodgings, was that any further letters from
America should be burned unopened.

Simone's letters continued to arrive in Ferney-Voltaire for
months after Duval's death. They were thrown straight onto

the fire. Finally Simone stopped writing. Jeanne Duval's weekly letters chronicling the indignities of her illness and begging for information about America had ceased. Simone guessed her friend was dead. She only hoped that Duval had learned of her own happiness. She had not found the rancher of her dreams, nor had anyone heard of a Frenchman, or anyone else, called Duval. But she had found the new life in the West that her friend had promised her.

The assistant manager of the Wells Fargo office in Wichita, Emmanuel Cadwaller, known to all as MC, had seen Simone through the window of a store in Kansas City. He had gone inside, pretending to take an interest in drapery. Life in the American West was a fast-moving, rough-and-tumble affair in those days, and within a fortnight he had proposed. Despite her Catholic upbringing, Simone happily consented to a Baptist wedding in a pretty wooden church in Wichita. It was in that frontier city in the cattle-boom years after the Civil War that she raised her family, became an American citizen, and lived out her life.

In her last and greatest act of loyalty and love, Caroline Aupick, by now elderly and herself unwell, traveled to Brussels with Mariette to rescue her dying son in the early summer of 1867. They returned together to Paris, planning to move back to Honfleur.

The appearance of a white-haired, shriveled old man partially paralyzed and unable to speak shocked Baudelaire's friends. He was moved to a clinic in the rue du Dôme in the center of Paris. Manet sent two of his paintings, one of which was his copy of Goya's portrait of the Duchess of Alba, to be hung in Baudelaire's room. His mother sat at his bedside, stroking his hair and crooning to him, just as she had when he was a little boy. He died on August 31, 1867, holding her hand and smiling.

Baudelaire's funeral took place on September 2 at the Saint-Honoré church in the Paris suburb of Passy. Neither Théo Gautier nor Sainte-Beuve, with whom Baudelaire had been reconciled, was among the small gathering of mourners. The poet was buried at the nearby Montparnasse cemetery, where a thunderstorm broke as the coffin was lowered into the grave. Heavy rain soaked the few remaining mourners, most of whom scattered before the graveside speeches had ended.

Historical Note

It was not until May 1949 that the appeal court in Paris officially set aside the ban imposed in 1857 on the six poems deemed obscene in *Les Fleurs du Mal*. By then Charles Baudelaire had achieved the success denied him in his lifetime. His reputation today is that of the greatest poet in the French language and the first modern poet in any language. T. S. Eliot said in a BBC broadcast in 1946 that without Baudelaire his own poetry would not have been possible. More than any other poet of his time Baudelaire was aware of what mattered most: the struggle between good and evil, he said.

History has not been so kind to Jeanne Duval. In almost every biography of Baudelaire she has been damned as little more than an illiterate drug addict who wrecked the life of a great poet. But Charles Baudelaire's greatest biographer in English, the late Dr. Enid Starkie, gave a different and more sympathetic view in her biography of the poet published in 1958.

She wrote:

Many harsh things have been said about Jeanne Duval,
yet no one is justified in judging her, since Baudelaire
was able to understand and to forgive her. It is best to
think of her in the days of her flaming youth, at the Hôtel
de Lauzun, when she kindled in him the passion that
is responsible for the magnificent cycle of sensual love
poems.

Author's Note

This is a work of fiction, but I have grounded the story and its main characters in fact as much as possible. A great deal is known about Baudelaire's life and times, and apart from my own research I have on the whole stayed true to the work that has gone into numerous biographies. Thus it is true that the poet was seen on the barricades in 1848, brandishing a looted musket and loudly declaring his intention to shoot his stepfather. It is also known that Baudelaire first saw Jeanne Duval perform at a small theater in the Latin Quarter around the time of his twenty-first birthday in 1842.

The account of the obscenity trial in 1857 is drawn from contemporary reports, and although Jeanne Duval was not a witness, she was thought to have been in the public gallery for the hearing. Her own origins remain a mystery, as is the date of her birth. She was certainly of mixed race and literary historians mostly conclude that she did come from Haiti. Her background matters less than the fact that for twenty years she was the dominant figure in the life of Charles

Baudelaire. Édouard Manet's portrait of Jeanne Duval hangs today in the Budapest National Gallery.

Baudelaire described her throughout his life in contradictory terms: as his sole joy and only companion, a woman of extraordinary beauty and sensuality; and at other times as his tormentor and someone he damned for continually humiliating him. In these moments she became the vampire of some of his poems. But through good times and bad she remained his Black Venus, a name he bestowed on her at the outset of their relationship. It is beyond dispute that without his Black Venus, Charles Baudelaire would never have written *Les Fleurs du Mal*.

Charles Baudelaire in Translation

There have been many translations of *Les Fleurs du Mal* over the years, and I have drawn on several of them to make my own freestanding translation of the poem "Les Bijoux" in this book. I list those I have consulted here:

Aggeler, William. *The Flowers of Evil*. Fresno, CA: Academy Library Guild, 1954.

Campbell, Roy. *Poems of Baudelaire*. New York: Pantheon Books, 1952.

Howard, Richard. *Les Fleurs du Mal*. Boston: David R. Godine, 1982.

MacIntyre, C. F. *One Hundred Poems from Les Fleurs du Mal*. Berkeley: University of California Press, 1947.

Martin, Walter. *The Complete Poems of Baudelaire*. Manchester: Carcanet Press, 1997.

Scarfe, Francis. *Baudelaire: Selected Verse*. Middlesex: Penguin, 1961.

James MacManus is the managing director of *The Times Literary Supplement*. After studying at St Andrews University, he began his career in journalism at the *Daily Express* in Manchester. Joining the *Guardian* in 1972, he later became Paris and then Africa and Middle East correspondent. His debut novel, *On the Broken Shore*, was published in 2010, and his acclaimed book, *Ocean Devil*, about the life of the adventurer George Hogg, was made into a film starring Jonathan Rhys Meyers. He lives in London.